JACK SAVAGE—A burnt-out adventurer, a deep-sea diver with a corrosive fear of the depths . . .

DIMITRI ALEKO—A multimillionaire with a gladiator's strength and a paralyzing weakness . . .

LADY SARA HAMILTON—A British aristocrat of heart-stopping beauty and mysterious reserves . . .

Bound together by a web of intrigue spanning the Aegean, they headed inexorably toward . . .

Night Judgement at Sinos

Night Judgement
at Sinos

Jack Higgins

A DELL BOOK

Published by
Dell Publishing Co., Inc.
1 Dag Hammarskjold Plaza
New York, New York 10017

Dell ® TM 681510, Dell Publishing Co., Inc.

ISBN: 0-440-16263-7

Reprinted by arrangement with
Doubleday & Company, Inc.

Printed in the United States of America

First Dell printing—October 1982

For my sister-in-law,
Shelagh Hewitt
who thinks it's about time . . .

CHAPTER I

IN A LONELY PLACE

I found him in about ten fathoms of smoky green water a couple of hundred yards beyond the Point. It was the parachute that first caught my eye. Somehow he'd managed to release it, a reflex action, I suppose, even as he drowned. It hovered above the weeds like some strange white flower, pale in the green light.

He lay six feet below in a patch of open sand, still strapped into his ejection seat from what I could see. I swam on and saw the plane almost at once, crouched on its belly in the weeds like some weird sea beast. I don't know why, but it made me feel vaguely uneasy. It was almost as if the damned thing was alive.

It took all the guts I had, which wasn't much at that time, to move in close. I looked inside the cockpit at the multiplicity of controls and instruments, dials phosphorescent in the dim light. The control column stirred gently in the water, moved by an invisible hand. It was enough. I went up fast, found the anchor chain and followed it in a cloud of champagne bubbles. Suddenly the water was green glass saturated with sunlight, the *Gentle Jane*'s hull clear above me.

There was no need to decompress. I hadn't been down long enough, but I was cold which was my own fault for not wearing a wet-suit and when I surfaced beside the ladder, an east wind stirred the water briskly, sending a wave of greyness through me so that I shivered as I scrambled over the side.

Morgan gave me a hand, his face anxious, that worried look there again. I could smell the whiskey fresh on his breath.

"All right, Jack?" he said.

I managed a tired grin and unbuckled my aqualung. "I'm getting old, Morg, that's all. I'll have that drink now."

He passed me a half bottle of Jameson from the pocket of his old reefer and I took a long pull. It didn't exactly burn its way down, I'd been on the stuff too long for that, but it certainly hit some kind of spot, and deep inside, a warm glow started to spread outwards.

"You can taste the peat," I said and gave him the bottle back.

He handled it nervously for a moment. I nodded and he had a quick swallow, hesitated, took another, then screwed on the cap with some reluctance and put the bottle back in his pocket.

The Egyptian M.T.B. was tied up to our starboard rail and Hakim was standing with his back to us talking to the captain, a young naval lieutenant, and an army officer. Hakim turned and seeing me, stepped over the rail, a tall handsome, olive-skinned man, elegant in an off-white linen suit and old Harrovian tie.

More English than the bloody English. The Irish in me came to the surface rather easily at times or perhaps it was only the whiskey talking.

"Ah, Mr. Savage," he said. "Any luck?"

I nodded. "Just as you thought. Israeli. Mirage III."

"What kind of condition is she in?"

"Not a scratch on her. I don't think your anti-aircraft had a thing to do with it."

"That is absurd. I have a report from the officer commanding the battery concerned. The plane was definitely brought down by ack-ack fire."

The army officer had joined us. He was about thirty, a major in military intelligence with a face badly scarred by shrapnel and dark, mad eyes. The kind who'd had a bad time in Sinai, for whom there could only ever be one solution. The total obliteration of the State of Israel.

"Major Ibrahim has only recently been seconded from Cairo to assist me." Hakim took out an elegant gold case and offered me a cigarette. "When they fly in off the sea like this on these hit-and-run missions, Major, they come in low. Usually six hundred feet or less to get below our radar."

Which didn't leave much of a margin for error. The Mirage has a maximum level speed of 1,450 miles an hour and climbs ten thousand feet in a minute. Nudge the stick or even cough at six hundred feet and you were in trouble. The lad on his back down there beneath the parachute must have been playing at submarines before he knew what was happening.

The major opened his mouth to argue the point, then closed it again. The cigarette was Turkish, but not the kind you can buy in Burlington Arcade and the smoke bit at the back of my throat harshly.

I started to cough and Hakim said with some concern, "You are tired, my friend, this has been too much for one man."

"No one else available," I said. "I've got the main crew working off-shore at Abu-Kir on the Liberian cargo ship that went down in the shallows."

"And Guyon, the diver who usually works with you? What about him?"

It was Major Ibrahim who had spoken and there was something in his voice, something I didn't like. The same uneasy feeling I had felt down there with the Mirage stirred in me again.

"He's gone into Alex to see the doctor," I said. "He pulled a shoulder muscle yesterday."

Ibrahim was going to take it further, but Hakim put a hand on his shoulder and said smoothly, "To come back to the Mirage. You can salvage her?"

"A couple of days' work at the most. I'll have to bring the two work boats in from Alexandria and as many pontoons as I can lay hands on. Another thing, I've only got one floating crane. I'll need another."

"It will be provided." He looked pleased with himself which wasn't surprising. It isn't every day you pick up a highly sophisticated, supersonic jet complete with air-to-air missiles, for free, which was what it came down to.

"I think you will find my country not ungrateful for your co-operation, Mr. Savage," Hakim went on.

"A co-operation we should be able to count on without question." Ibrahim again. "You are privileged, Savage. We have allowed you to stay in Egypt, to develop a most valuable business undertaking. Few Europeans can say the same."

He delivered his little speech with some bitterness, but it was water off a duck's back to me.

"I'm more than grateful, Major," I said. "On the other hand I think I should point out that I'm a citizen of the Republic of Ireland, the most neutral nation on earth. We showed you all the way a long time ago. And politics bore me. We invented them."

"Those who are not for us are against us," he intoned, straight off page 53 of the manual.

"Not me, friend, I never take sides. You live longer that way."

I stood up and nodded to Morgan who was looking more anxious than ever. "I'll have the other aqualung. This one is almost empty. A single cylinder should do it."

"Hell, Jack, you've chanced your arm enough down there for one day on your own. You're on borrowed time now."

He was right, of course. Rule number one in any manual was never dive alone, but in this case I didn't really have a great deal of choice and he knew it because even as he argued, he was buckling on the aqualung.

"Is it necessary to go down again, Mr. Savage?" Hakim asked me.

"The pilot," I said.

"Ah, of course." He nodded in understanding.

"Let him rot," the major cut in, real anger in his voice.

He put a hand on my shoulder and he was shaking. God knows what had happened to him in the war, what mental anguish he had suffered since, but there was real pain in the dark eyes. More than that—hate.

"You go to hell," I said.

I turned to the rail. There had been at least twenty fishing boats scattered around us when I had first gone down. I saw now that they had been joined by a red and white speedboat that floated no more than a dozen yards away.

So close, in fact, that the occupants must have heard most of what we had been saying.

There were two of them. At an inch over six feet and with the poundage to go with it, I'd always thought of myself as being reasonably sizeable, but the man who sat at the wheel was a giant. He was stripped to the waist and built like a gladiator, a scarf knotted carelessly about his neck. He wore a yachting cap and dark glasses which made it difficult to make out much of his face, but for some reason he looked familiar.

But it was the girl who seized me by the throat from that very first moment and would not let go, standing there in the stern, hands on hips, staring straight at me in a black bikini that barely managed to cover what it was supposed to, and long hair hanging straight to the shoulders, so pale that it was almost white, glinting in the sunlight.

She could have stepped right off the cover of the summer edition of any top-flight fashion magazine if it hadn't been for the face. Now that was something special. Calm grey eyes that looked straight through you, high cheekbones, a wide mouth that lifted slightly at one side in perpetual scorn at the world and over all, the inbred arrogance of your natural aristocrat.

For some reason, I nodded. She called, "Can you manage?"

That beautifully clipped, upper-crust English voice just had to bring out the Irish in me. I thickened the brogue and replied cheerfully, "And why shouldn't I? A fine day to die in, thanks be to God, as my old grandma used to say."

That's all it took. She knew me then till the crack of doom right through to the backbone. The lip curled, but in laughter this time. I pulled on my face mask and went over the side. I paused to adjust my air supply and went straight down following the anchor chain for most of the way.

I'd made a mistake. I was tired—too tired for this kind of game and I could feel the cold seeping through my flesh. But there was more to it than that. As a diver descends, the deepening layers of water filter the sunlight,

absorbing all red and orange rays. At fifty feet, I entered a
neutral zone. Visibility was good, but colours were muted
and autumnal.

The parachute blossomed unexpectedly from the green
smoke. I went into it, the pale fronds enveloping me so
that for a moment, I had to struggle to break free. The
fear moved in my belly again. The same fear that had risen
like bile in my throat on that nightmare occasion the previous year when I had wallowed helplessly in the black mud
at the bottom of the outer harbour at Alexandria, waiting
to die as the ice-cold water rose to chin level inside my
helmet.

And then I was free and moving down towards the pilot,
knife ready. I sliced through the cords of the chute which
drifted away, giving me a look at him. His eyes were open
in stunned surprise, one arm floating upright as if reaching
out for help. The chain around his neck carried a tiny
gold Star of David.

Poor lad, he looked so young. I couldn't leave him down
there in the cold. I think it was then that the fear left me,
but I was tired—so damned tired.

I wrestled with the straps on the ejection seat for a minute or so and then he drifted free, legs straightening, one
arm sliding about my neck. It seemed the most natural
thing in the world to put an arm round his waist and we
went up together.

God, but it was slow. My brain seemed to have stopped
functioning and I was caught in an endless spiral that had
no ending. I broke through to the surface with something
of a surprise and found myself closer to the speedboat than
to the *Gentle Jane*.

I caught a quick glimpse of the girl staring down at me
and went under again. I surfaced minus the pilot and
found her companion in the water beside me holding him.
I struck out for the speedboat which seemed the obvious
thing to do, and the girl reached over and held my hand
in a way that said she hadn't the slightest intention of letting go again, even if it meant going down with me.

"Easy, big man," she said. "You've had it."

She hooked a ladder over the side with her free hand

and I summoned up everything I had and went up it. Behind me her friend seemed to be towing the body of the pilot across to the *Gentle Jane*.

I pulled off my face mask, aware of her hands busy with my aqualung straps. I was dizzy, lightning streaking my vision, the sun too bright and the scent of her filled my nostrils, my mind. It was like some strange, strange dream.

"What perfume are you wearing?" I gasped.

She chuckled and eased me out of the aqualung. "Intimacy."

"Now that's more than flesh and blood can stand," I said and opened my eyes.

The sun was behind her, the pale gold hair like white fire in a cloud about her and the eyes, those strange grey eyes turned me inside out.

"I wonder what it looks like spread across a pillow?" I said.

"Irish." She leaned over me. "I might have known. What's your name?"

"Savage—Jack Savage."

"Right, Jack Savage. Let's get you home."

She started the engine, took the boat round expertly, throttled back and laid her alongside the *Gentle Jane*. The gladiator came over the side, water dripping from the kind of body that wouldn't have disgraced a heavyweight wrestler.

He held out his hand. "Aleko—Dimitri Aleko. You are a brave man, Mr. Savage. To go down once on your own is bad enough, but twice . . . Now that, I respect."

And he meant it, every damned word of it. I heaved my aqualung up to Morgan. "I owe you a drink, both of you. I'll be in the bar at Saunder's tonight if you feel like collecting."

"You've got a date, my friend."

Greek he might be, but his voice was pure American. I scrambled over the rail and as I turned, he took the speedboat away fast. The girl didn't even wave. She sat in the stern and lit a cigarette and never looked back once.

"You were a fool, Jack, every kind of a fool." Morgan's voice was sick and angry. "I told you not to go."

I ignored him and said to Hakim, "Is that the shipping-line Aleko?"

"Amongst other things. His firm has only recently invested ten million dollars in a new oil installation complex in Alexandria. He is a good friend to Egypt. He arrived from Crete this morning in his yacht the *Firebird*. A short holiday, or so I understand."

"And the girl?"

"His sister-in-law, Lady Sara Hamilton. His wife was killed in a car crash at Antibes last year. She is English," he added rather unnecessarily.

"A harlot," Major Ibrahim said, his voice shaking. "A shameless harlot exposing her body to the eyes of men like that."

"So you fancy her, too?" I said.

For a moment, I thought he might take a punch at me which would have been unfortunate as I'd have almost certainly broken his jaw in reply which wouldn't have done me much good in the long run.

I don't know why, but something obviously made him think better of it, perhaps the knowledge that he was going to have his say later. In any case, he turned and went back over the rail to the M.T.B.

"I'm sorry," Hakim said in a low voice, "but don't treat him lightly. He has considerable power."

I shrugged it off and looked down at the pilot. A couple of sailors had lifted him on to a stretcher.

"He looks very young."

"He will receive a military funeral according to the rites of his religion, Mr. Savage," Hakim said as if in answer to some unspoken question of my own. "We are not savages."

We shook hands, he smiled gently and followed the stretcher bearers over the rail to the deck of the M.T.B. It moved away with a burst of speed and Morgan brought me a towel and produced that half-bottle of Irish again.

I took a swallow and he said, "I don't like it, Jack."

"What don't you like?"

"That guy Ibrahim and the way he was going on about Guyon. He means trouble."

"You worry too much." I gave him the bottle. "Have another drink and take us into harbour."

Perhaps if I'd listened to him, given it some thought, things might have turned out differently, but her perfume was heavy in my nostrils, the sound of the voice sharp and clear, the eyes grey as mist on an Irish morning. She had me by the throat and I could not, would not shake free of her.

CHAPTER II

THE MOST BEAUTIFUL WOMAN IN THE WORLD

Only the Egyptians, with their curious love-hate relationship where the English are concerned, could have allowed the continued existence, especially after Suez, of a hotel with a name like Saunder's.

But then the entire establishment was something of an anachronism. A throwback to the great days of Victorian Imperialism and it consistently refused to move with the times. No air conditioning for Saunder's. Enormous electric fans turned monotonously in each room except when there was a power failure which was often.

It was run by a man called Yanni Kytros, Greek by nationality, but with an Egyptian mother which was useful. He had another place on Kyros in the Aegean, north of Crete through the Kasos Strait, and seemed to split his time between the two.

He was the kind of man who had his fingers into everything. An operator in capital letters. Women, guns, cigarettes. You name it, he could supply it. The one thing he wouldn't touch was drugs. Something to do with a sister who'd got hooked on heroin years before and had died unpleasantly. He told me a little about her on one memorable night of women and drink when we were both three parts cut. He had never mentioned it since.

He was about fifty which I always understood was a pure estimate as he didn't seem to be able to lay his hands on a birth certificate. Bearded, genial, badly overweight and constantly smiling, one of the wittiest men I've ever known, and underneath it all, utterly unscrupulous and hard as nails.

Although I ran my main operation out of Alexandria, I liked Bir el Gafani so much that I'd been living there on a semipermanent basis for almost two years. I had a room on the ground floor at Saunder's with a terrace to the garden which suited me perfectly and a regular mooring for the *Gentle Jane* in the old harbour. Morgan usually slept on board when he wasn't sweating it off in the corner of some bar or other.

I couldn't remember actually getting into bed, but in it I was, or rather, on it and mother-naked. The room was a place of shadows, white muslin curtains billowing palely at the windows open to the terrace. It was evening and very quiet. It was several moments before I realised that the fan had stopped.

I pushed myself up on one elbow, reaching for a cigarette to the wickerwork table beside the bed, and there was a stirring in the shadows on the other side of the room, the chink of a bottle.

"You okay, Jack?"

Morgan got off the divan by the far window and moved out of the shadows, stowing the bottle furtively away in the pocket of his old reefer.

"Fine, Morg," I said. "What happened?"

"You passed out, Jack, fainted clean away, just like you done before. Remember?"

I nodded slowly. It wasn't something that happened often, but when it did, was complete enough to be alarming. I'd gone into the whole matter thoroughly with a specialist some years previously who had told me it was some kind of stress ailment, but chemical rather than psychological. It seemed I had unusual reserves of vitality, could keep going full-blast for longer periods than the average man, but when I reached a certain point I keeled straight over, burned out.

"When did all this happen?"

"Coming in through the garden. I left the Land-Rover at the side gate. You had an arm round my shoulder. Just as we reached the fountain you went down so hard you took me with you."

"How did you get me inside?"

He grinned wickedly. "The girl, Jack, the girl on the speedboat. That feller Aleko's sister-in-law or whatever. She was sitting on the terrace. She gave me a hand with you." He wiped sweat from his eyes with the back of one hand. "By God, Jack, there's a woman for you. Worth any ten I ever seed."

"And who undressed me?"

"Why, she did, Jack, who else? They had to come off. You were soaked. Shivering like a baby and that's a woman's work. They got the touch." He cackled. "Anyway, my hands was dirty."

What a woman indeed. I got up and went into the bathroom and turned on the shower, the Saunder's only concession to modern living. It was lukewarm, but refreshing. I started to live again.

Morgan leaned in the doorway and filled his old pipe. "Guyon came by to see you."

"How was he?"

"Fine. He said the doctor told him to lay off diving for a week. I was thinking that might be inconvenient." He hesitated. "Maybe I could help out."

I came out of the shower towelling myself briskly and shook my head. "Thanks, Morg, that's good of you, but we'll see how things work out."

It was a game we played, something to bolster up his self-esteem. He would never dive again. Once was all it would take and he was a dead man or insane for whatever span was left to him. He knew that and so did I, but the game kept him happy along with the drink.

"Guyon was real excited about the Mirage, Jack," he went on. "You could make a real killing there. Those Gypos should pay plenty for that baby. And I told him about that Ibrahim guy asking all those questions."

I pulled on a clean shirt and started to button it up. "What did he say?"

"Nothing much." Morgan scratched his unshaven chin. "Hell, Jack, you know how Guyon is. He's a funny guy to figure. He sure went off in a hurry, though."

I felt that coldness in my belly again and for the second time that day pushed it away, refused to acknowledge that something was wrong. The truth was that Sara Hamilton had filled my mind to the exclusion of all else, a disturbing sensation at my age. Not that I was against women. I was all for them in regular doses, but in their proper place which meant not intruding into the more important aspects of life.

"You going down to the bar now, Jack?" Morgan demanded eagerly.

"I owe the man a drink, remember?"

"And the girl."

He wiped a hand across his mouth, eyes bright, and I punched him in the shoulder gently. "All right, you old soak. You can come down."

He grinned like a schoolboy and scurried to get the door open for me. We went along the passage, still dark because of the power failure, and down a dozen broad marble steps into the hotel foyer.

Kytros was behind the reception desk talking to his clerk. He waved. "I hear you tried to commit suicide again today."

"It all depends on your point of view, Yanni," I said. "But I'm alive and well and living in Bir el Gafani. You can buy me a drink on the strength of it."

"In a little while," he said. "Business—always business."

The bar was a large square room with french windows to one side giving a view over the harbour. There was gaming in the next room, but not until later, and to one side the eighth wonder of the world, the famous Saunder's long bar, about a mile of Victorian mahogany presided over by three of the most immaculate barmen I have ever seen anywhere, eager and able to serve you with any drink known to man or woman, however esoteric.

It was early and the place was deserted except for Lady Sara Hamilton who sat at a beautiful old Schiedmayer square piano, another relic of Empire. It was Yanni's especial pride, mainly because it said in faded gold lettering inside *Specially made for the climate of India,* whatever that was supposed to mean.

She was working her way through *A Foggy Day in London Town* and she knew what she was doing. The phrasing was perfect and the chords echoed inside you.

"Hello, Savage," she said. "Any special favourites?"

"You're playing it right now. Rain through the trees, mist on the river, a hooter droning down there in the Pool of London. All we need is Big Ben and perhaps a siren or two. I'm burning up with nostalgia."

"That's going back some, even for you, isn't it?"

"A couple of hundred thousand Irishmen came across to fight for England during the last unpleasantness," I reminded her. "My turn came in July, 1943 on my sixteenth birthday. I added a couple of years and joined the Marines."

"For love of dear old England?"

"For love of eating, ma'am," I told her and gave her my best Abbey Theatre accent. "God save us, seven to feed on one cow and three goats. And then we have a tradition down south. We always fight England's wars for her."

The laughter bubbled out of her. "Give me a cigarette."

She leaned across for a light and I caught that perfume again and for some reason my hands trembled slightly. She held my wrist, her fingers cool to the touch, but made no comment.

"Care for a drink?" I asked.

"Why not? Long and cool and non-alcoholic. Iced tonic water for preference."

"You're sure?"

"You put away enough for both of us, don't you?"

I let that one ride and crossed to the bar. I had intended my usual large whiskey to start the evening right, but for some reason hesitated. She had me rattled, that was for certain. I finally settled for a cold beer.

She had left the piano and was standing by one of the open french windows looking out over the harbour. The sky was orange and flame, the land dark and very still and there was a new moon. She turned as I approached and stood, legs slightly apart, the right hip jutting out to one side, one arm across her stomach supporting the elbow of the other.

She was wearing the kind of deceptively simple little summer dress that had probably been created by Balmain. It was short even for that year and buttoned down the front, the bottom two being left undone, though whether by accident or design was uncertain. You could never be sure of anything where she was concerned, as I was to discover.

One thing I did know. She looked bloody marvellous and she excited me physically in a way no woman had in years. Certainly not since the departure of my dear wife.

I handed her the tall, frosted glass. The ice tinkled as she took a sip. "Sixteen in 1943? That makes you forty-two."

"And too old for you," I said. "Way, way over the hill. Isn't life hell?"

"Every day of the week if that's the way you see it. I wasn't even around in forty-three so I wouldn't know."

Which was direct enough and for some reason about as brutal as a boot in the side of the head. And she knew it and instantly regretted the fact.

"One thing you might as well get straight about me right from the start. I don't like having my mind made up for me. All right?"

She sat down on the window seat, crossing those magnificent legs of hers, and Morgan arrived. Poor devil, I'd forgotten all about him. He actually removed his cap and bobbed his head.

"Evening, miss, I mean Lady, Hamilton."

She smiled, really smiled, gold all the way through, reached up and brushed his chin with her knuckles. "It's Sara to you, Morgan. From now on it's Sara. We've been through a lot together."

He cackled and scratched his chin nervously. "Hell, you sure seemed to know what you was doing, I'll say that."

"I had three younger brothers," she told him. "It has its uses."

"What was wrong with the hired help?" I demanded sourly. "Or was the castle roof leaking?"

She glanced up at me sharply. "As I said, I had three younger brothers, so it isn't the first time I've seen what you've got."

She touched me on the raw there and I swung back. "I bet it isn't, angel. Did I come up to scratch?"

She shrugged. "I don't know whether 1943 was a good year."

I reeled back on the ropes from that one and turned to Morgan who was tugging at my sleeve.

"Okay," I said. "Tell Ali, the usual, then get into the back of the Land-Rover and sleep it off. I'll drop you at the jetty later."

He moved away eagerly, lurching slightly from side-to-side and went to the bar.

"What would the usual be?" Sara Hamilton enquired.

"A large Irish whiskey every ten minutes for an hour. Jameson if they have it which they usually do. They pride themselves on being able to provide every drink ever heard of here."

"He looks half drunk now," she commented and there was an edge to her voice as if she disapproved and somehow blamed me.

I shook my head. "It gets him like that sometimes. What divers call the staggers. How old would you say he is?"

"I don't know." She shrugged. "Sixty-five or so I suppose."

"He's forty-nine. Seven years older than me. That's what can happen to a man who goes down too deep and too often, fails to compress properly. A dead man walking." I said that last bit to myself.

"And you blame Jack Savage, don't you? Why?"

I turned, looked at her for a long moment, trying to see her face, but it was by this time too dark and in any case, the moment was lost for Aleko appeared on the terrace behind her. A second later, the lights went on and the fans started to revolve again.

"Ah, there you are." He smiled and held out his hand. "I've come to claim that drink you promised me. A China Clipper would do admirably. Let's see if we can catch Kytros out."

I could have called one of the barmen, but he turned, putting his hand on the girl's shoulder in a curiously intimate way that I definitely didn't like and I decided to leave them to it.

As I reached the bar, Kytros appeared from his office lighting a cigar. "One China Clipper," I called with a straight face.

He turned to Ali, the head barman and said calmly, "You'll need a Chinese golden lime. There are half-a-dozen in the stillroom put up in earthenware jars. And make it yellow dry gin. We must get the colour scheme right." He turned to me blandly. "Anything else?"

"I surrender," I said. "I'll have a large Jameson."

He snapped a finger at another barman. "You're looking very sharp tonight, Jack. Bogart in his prime. Yes, I like that. Could it be the young lady who has restored the bloom to your cheeks?"

Which was hitting low, even for him. "Do me a favour," I said, "I'm old enough to be . . ."

"Her father? Ah, Jack, the English have succeeded in putting their damnable brand on you. What a pity." He glanced across the room. "Nineteen is a beautiful age, but that one." He shook his head. "She was old the day she was born."

Perhaps he had a point, but I still didn't like it. However, he came round the bar and insisted on carrying the tray across himself.

"Your China Clipper, sir," he told Aleko.

Aleko took a sip and nodded gravely. "You never let me down, Kytros. Will you join us?"

"I'd be delighted."

Yanni nodded to Ali who came across on the double with his usual Bacardi. Aleko offered me a cigarette. "I've been doing a little checking up on you since this afternoon, Mr. Savage. I understand you've put quite a sizeable outfit together during the past seven or eight years."

"Not too difficult," I said. "There was plenty of salvage work going in Alex and Port Said after Suez and I did have the advantage that I knew the area."

"Yes, I heard about that also. You were a captain in the British Marine Commandos specialising in underwater work. I'm surprised the Egyptians allowed you to stay on."

"No trouble there. I'm Irish, not English. It's very useful. My passport gets me anywhere I want to go without a visa, even China."

"I wouldn't advise it."

"Perhaps not."

There were voices in the foyer and Hakim entered. He

glanced around quickly and seeing me, threaded his way between the tables. He looked really worried for the first time since I'd known him.

"It's important that I see you, Mr. Savage. Very important."

He got no further. Major Ibrahim marched in briskly flanked by a couple of military policemen. He ignored everyone, including Hakim, and concentrated on me.

"We are looking for the man Raoul Guyon, employed by you as a diver, Savage. Where is he?"

"I haven't the slightest idea." I turned to Hakim. "What's it all about?"

Before he could reply, Ibrahim cut in, "Raoul Guyon is a Jew, Savage, an Israeli agent. Of course you would know nothing about that, would you?"

In other circumstances a blow like that would have taken the wind out of me, but I couldn't afford it, not now. I was on dangerous ground. One step and I might be swallowed up.

"Major Ibrahim," I said evenly. "Just what kind of a fool do you take me for? I've got a salvage business in Alexandria worth just over two hundred thousand pounds in equipment, work in hand and money owing."

"Which my government will be fully entitled to confiscate in a situation like this."

"As far as I was concerned Guyon was a French citizen when I took him on." I appealed to Hakim. "Your own ministry confirmed his status."

"True enough." He turned to Ibrahim. "Mr. Savage cannot possibly have had any foreknowledge of this man and his activities."

"Which remains to be seen. We will examine your room now," Ibrahim told me curtly.

None of the others had said a word. For once, Kytros wasn't smiling. Aleko looked calm, relaxed, ready for anything. And Sara Hamilton?

She emptied her glass, turned casually to Morgan who crouched at his table, sweating with fear. "Be a sweetie and get me another, Morgan."

He took her glass, hand shaking and she looked up at

me coolly and smiled. "Hurry back. We didn't finish our talk."

The room was as empty as I had expected it to be, which didn't stop Ibrahim and his boys from turning the place upside down. He wanted me dead to rights, that was the trouble. Wanted an excuse to drag me off into the night to see what he could squeeze out of me the hard way.

After fifteen rough minutes, he gave up with every sign of reluctance and we returned to the others. They were still sitting in the same group by the open french windows except that Morgan was now with them, clutching a glass that was half-full of whiskey, too frightened to drink it for the first time in years.

"It will be necessary to leave guards around the hotel," Ibrahim said and made an effort to be diplomatic. "I regret this, Mr. Aleko, but I'm sure you will appreciate my position."

"Perfectly," Aleko told him.

At that moment the electricity was cut again, the fans stopped abruptly, the room was plunged into darkness. Outside, the only light was the merest trace of orange fire on the world's edge and a pale glimmer from the new moon.

Kytros called to the barmen and a second later, there was a violent rumbling explosion out there beyond the harbour. About twenty pounds of plastic gelignite going off from the sound of it, tearing several million dollars worth of Mirage into as many pieces.

I could have told them then where Raoul Guyon was.

CHAPTER III

IN HARM'S WAY

In the glare of the M.T.B.'s searchlight the fact of the matter was plain to all. The surface of the sea was strewn with wreckage, pieces of fuselage carpeting the water as far as the light extended. So extensive was the damage that I could only conclude that the air-to-air missiles the Mirage was carrying had also exploded.

Ibrahim grabbed my shoulder and swung me around. "And now will you tell us that you had nothing to do with this."

"I've been up at the hotel since the middle of the afternoon," I told him patiently. "Plenty of witnesses."

"He is right, Major," Hakim said. "You are pursuing the wrong line of investigation. Guyon is our man."

But Ibrahim wouldn't let go. He wanted me so badly he could taste it. "How do we know that he did not plant a charge when he went down this afternoon?"

But that was going too far, even for Hakim. "Now you are being stupid. Must I remind you that we were here, watching everything the man did?" He turned to the naval lieutenant who had been listening impassively. "You will take us back into harbour as quickly as possible then return and search the entire area thoroughly."

"I must protest." Ibrahim started again and Hakim gave him the blade right across the back of the neck.

"You seem big with words and little else, Major. Less talk and more action is what I require of you. I will give you till midnight to find Guyon. If you have not been successful, it will be necessary for me to inform your superiors of that regrettable fact and to request a replacement. You understand me?"

I think Ibrahim was close to tears as he turned and stamped away in utter frustration.

Hakim offered me a cigarette. As I took it, I said, "So, you *can* be rough when you want to be?"

"You are forgetting, Mr. Savage." He smiled gently. "I was a prefect in one of the better public schools. The English are past masters of all the arts, but excel more than most in being bastards when it is necessary."

He certainly had a point there.

He left me at the hotel with strict instructions not to leave without permission. On that he was polite, but definite and the two military policemen on the door were not just there for show.

The bar was empty except for Morgan who had obviously had more than his usual quota. He was slumped across the table, eyes wide, staring. I hauled him to his feet and gently slapped his face. He returned to life with a start.

"Go on, out to the Land-Rover. Sleep it off," I said.

He had difficulty in forming his words. "What about Guyon?"

"God knows, it's one hell of a bloody mess. I'll tell you about it later. Go on, get out of it."

I gave him a shove towards the foyer and turned to the bar. Kytros had come out of his office and his face was grave in the light of the oil lamp which had been placed on the counter.

"The Mirage?" he said.

I nodded. "Give me a whiskey. I need it."

The barmen were no longer in evidence so he got it himself and joined me, which was unusual. "Any sign of Guyon?"

"Not a trace. A guard on the jetty did some shooting into the water as we came back into harbour, but it looked like a false alarm. With the kind of charge he used, he's probably in as many pieces as the plane."

He shivered, obviously finding the idea rather unpleasant and poured himself another drink. "What's wrong?" I said. "Did someone just walk over your grave?"

He tried to smile, but there was more to it than that.

Much more. A kind of uncertainty and he refused to meet
my eyes.

"Good God," I whispered. "You knew. You knew what
he was all along, didn't you?"

"My dear Jack, don't be absurd."

He tried to shrug it off, but I wouldn't let him off the
hook. "Now I get it. All those trips to Kyros. You were
channelling stuff out for them. They must have been paying you a fortune."

He actually smiled at that. "One of my more lucrative
ventures, I must admit." I was unable to stifle my laughter.
"It takes a rogue to recognise one, Jack," he added calmly.

"Which doesn't help me. I've nothing against the Israelis,
even if one of their damned frogmen did blow me out of
the water back in Jaffa harbour in forty-seven, but I'm
damned if I want to take sides. What in the hell am I going to do?"

"Hang on," he said. "If things turn nasty, make a run
for it in the *Gentle Jane*. Wait for me in Kyros. Plenty of
work for you in the Aegean, I'll see to that."

"And leave a business worth two hundred thousand quid
to Ibrahim and his pals? Not on your life."

"So what will you do if Guyon comes to you for help?
Turn him in?"

Which was the one question I didn't want to hear, the
one I wanted to avoid at all costs. "I won't take sides," I
said. "I've done my share. Palestine, Malaya, Korea,
Cyprus. Other men's wars. To hell with that for a game
of soldiers."

I turned away, the Celt in me well in control, and found
Sara Hamilton seated at a nearby table taking it all in.

"And you can fry in hell, too," I said and stormed out
through the french window to the terrace and the garden
beyond.

The new moon was hooked into the branches of the
cypress tree by the far wall and on either side, palm trees
nodded gravely in the slight breeze. The garden was another of Yanni's special prides and the night was fresh and
alive and filled with its perfume.

I wandered aimlessly from one tiled path to another,

shoulders hunched, hands pushed into my pockets, a cigarette hanging from one corner of my mouth, unlit because I couldn't find a match. The fountain drew me as it always did, a piece of pure Victoriana. An impossibly virginal-looking lady spraying water from her mouth assisted by half-a-dozen cherubs of doubtful sex.

I stood with one foot on the raised rim of the pool and stared into the night. A hand appeared in front of my face holding a gold lighter. *That damned perfume again.* I touched my cigarette to the flame and turned to her.

"Is it really called Intimacy or were you kidding?"

She sat on the edge of the pool and made ripples in the water with one hand. "I like fountains, they relax me. We had one something like this at Hambray Court when I was a little girl. My earliest memory."

"A thousand years ago?"

"At the very least." When she looked up her face was quite different. For a moment, she was that little girl again in the secret garden, life held at bay by a mile of Elizabethan brick wall. "Sometimes I think it was just a dream. A story I read somewhere, or had told to me. Does that make any sense?"

"The only kind there is."

I don't know what happened exactly, but she changed gear again, assumed her usual role. Even the tone of voice altered, became harsher.

"So, Kytros sold you out?"

I glanced down at her sharply. "Shame on you, listening to other people's conversations."

For some reason she was angry. "Do you *have* to make a joke of everything?"

"Can you think of a better way of keeping your sanity in this loving world?"

"Several."

"Oh, sure. I'd forgotten you were a swinger," I said. "The *Kama Sutra* beside your bed and fifty-seven varieties with every third man you meet walking down the King's Road. Wasn't that last year's newest kick for the jet set?"

"It was marvellous," she said calmly. "Every golden moment."

I laughed out loud, unable to contain it. "They broke the mould when they made you."

"Seven hundred and twenty-three years of breeding," she said. "You can always tell."

"You were the nearest thing to kick."

"I know. Are things that bad?"

"Just about. Maybe they'll be satisfied if they lay hands on Guyon."

"And if not?"

"Eight years of sweat down the slot."

I moved a few paces away, ears strained as I heard an engine start up down in the harbour.

"Tell me about your wife," she said in a matter-of-fact voice.

"You've been talking to Morgan?"

"I truly believe he'd do anything for me."

Curiously enough I didn't feel annoyed. Was even prepared to speak the name itself for the first time in years, a thing I'd had a superstitious dread of doing.

"It's soon told. I met Grace just after the end of the Palestine troubles in 1948. I was a lieutenant then, commissioned from the ranks at the end of the war. Gallant record, decorated, lots of promise. On paper, anyway."

"What went wrong?"

"I made captain and that was it. Eight years later after Malaya, Korea, Cyprus, I was still the same rank."

"Any particular reason?"

"I wasn't at my best when dealing with my superiors and I'd hung on to my Irish passport. They didn't care for that. Grace and I only saw each other about twice a year anyway and there were no children which didn't help. She dropped me in fifty-seven and married again the following year. An American."

"Has it worked out?"

"As far as I know. He's got shares in Fort Knox."

"So you decided to prove yourself by becoming salvage king of the Mediterranean?"

"Something like that." I grinned. "All by accident, mind you. I resigned my commission and bought the *Gentle Jane*, which took about everything I had. I'd fancy ideas about making a living as a sponge diver in the Aegean and doing a bit of archaeological diving on the side. There can be real money in that if you know what you're doing. They have every kind of ship from the Bronze Age onwards at the bottom in those parts if you know where to look. I could take you to a reef off the Turkish coast near the Dodecanese where they've found traces of eleven different wrecks starting with the Bronze Age and ending with a Turkish transport of the Crimean War period."

"Did any of this work out?"

"Not really. There isn't the demand for real sponges that there used to be. Oh, there was a living, but a damned poor one and finding new Bronze Age wrecks turned out to be rather more difficult than I had imagined."

"What happened next?"

"Yanni Kytros," I said simply. "I started running American cigarettes into Italy for him. Amongst other things."

"Spare me the details. The salvage work came later?"

"It was what I wanted to do. I'd had a lot of experience at that kind of thing in the Marines. It's another world down there, you know. Something you can't really describe."

"I had a brother who felt the same way about flying."

"That's it exactly. There was just Morgan and myself back in fifty-nine when we started. I had a crew of Egyptian deckhands, but we did all the diving. Raised a Lebanese coaster that had gone down in fifteen fathoms and cleared twenty thousand pounds."

"And never looked back. Tell me something. Why did you dive on your own today? Isn't that considered dangerous?"

"Hakim was in a hurry and it pays to keep in with the Ministry crowd. And there was no one else available."

"What about Morgan?"

"But I told you," I said. "He's had it. Oh, there was a time when he was good. The best. He was a chief petty officer in the U. S. Coast Guard. Where diving is concerned, you name it, Morgan's done it, but that was a long time ago. He was going downhill even when he first came to me. And now . . ."

"A dead man walking." I frowned. "You said that yourself earlier," she explained.

"That about sums it up," I told her reluctantly.

"And you blame yourself? Why?"

She was right, of course. It boiled up inside me, all the anger, the frustration, the self-hate, the fear that had twisted in my guts down there with the Mirage.

"All right, you asked for it. The truth is that until last year, about eighteen months ago to be precise, I dived regularly myself, even when there was no need. Dived because I loved every single minute of it like that brother of yours loves flying. One day I got a call in the office at Alex. A barge had gone down in the outer harbour. The main crew were away on a job, but I went out with Morgan to size up the situation. He went down first in a regulation suit."

"You mean with an air hose and so on? I thought that was a thing of the past these days."

"In most circumstances, it is. I'd always use a self-contained rig under a hundred feet. Anything over, a regulation suit. Sure, you can dive three hundred feet in an aqualung. You can also bleed from the mouth, nose and ears. I've seen a lot of men do just that."

"All right," she said impatiently. "Point taken. But what happened to Morgan?"

"He found the barge in just over a hundred feet, half-buried in thick mud. When he came up, he advised me to wait till the full crew were available."

"And you didn't agree?"

"I thought I could tunnel through the mud and get a hawser under her. I wouldn't listen to him."

"What went wrong?"

"The tunnel caved in on me."

I shivered involuntarily, sick to my stomach at the memory of it. "I couldn't move an inch. Just lay there with water rising in my suit, no light, nothing. Only the darkness and the water getting higher and higher till it was inside the helmet, touching my chin."

She grabbed my arm and shook me back to the present. "And Morgan went down for you?"

"That's it. He came down and dug me out. Came down in an aqualung. My suit was so badly torn that he had to have me taken straight up. You see the length of time I'd

been down at that depth I needed to decompress for around
an hour and a half. Go up in stages."

"Then what happened?"

"We had a portable decompression chamber on board.
A Swiss thing, just big enough for one man. He had the
deckhands put me inside."

"And Morgan?" she whispered.

My mouth went dry at the thought of it. "There wasn't
any room for him, was there?" For some reason, I'd raised
my voice. "He could have gone back over the side and
taken his time about coming up, but there wasn't another
diver around to help and he collapsed anyway. By the
time they got the boat in and tied up it was too late."

"And he's been like that ever since?"

I nodded.

"And you don't like diving any more."

"Not really. Oh, I've tried—like today, for instance. I go
down through the sunlight and that isn't so bad and then
it gets deeper and the colours fade and the darkness moves
in, just like it did down there in the mud last year."

There was sweat on my face. She put a finger to my lips
and smiled. "You've punished yourself enough for one
night. All right? Now we'll take three nice deep breaths
and go and have a drink."

"I'll never make it to the bar." Which was the plain
truth for I felt as shaky as a kitten.

"Is that a fact? Where would you suggest?"

"My room. A step across the terrace, french windows
standing invitingly open to the night breezes. Soda, ice-
water and good Irish whiskey always to be had."

"Amongst other things."

"Now that entirely depends on the customer."

She slipped a hand through my arm and laughed, that
distinctive, harsh chuckle of hers. "You know, I've decided
I like you after all, Savage."

"Something I slipped into your drink at the bar."

"No," she said. "I like the way you don't surrender."

"The motto of entirely the wrong Irish political party,"
I said, without understanding what in the hell she was talking about.

We went up the steps and moved towards the open

french windows. They stood wide to the night air as I had said, and the curtains were drawn. Inside, it was as black as the hob of hell and very, very still.

"I'll get the light." I started across the room, forgetting about the power failure. I tripped and went over with a clatter, sending a chair flying.

"Are you all right?" she called.

I put out a hand and touched a face.

"Don't scream," I said. "I think we're in for a nasty surprise."

When I struck a match, there was blood all over the expensive Persian carpet and Raoul Guyon was lying in the middle of it.

CHAPTER IV

ONE KIND OF ANSWER

The guard on the jetty who had fired into the water as we returned in the M.T.B. had been closer than he knew. Guyon had been shot in the back three times, that much was evident from the ragged holes in the black Neoprene wet-suit. Things didn't look any better when I got it off him.

The two which had penetrated the upper part of the left shoulder were nasty, but hardly mortal, even if they did leave him partially crippled for life, which was the way it looked.

Number three was a different proposition. It had entered at a point six inches below the left shoulder blade and when I turned him over, there was no exit hole. Which meant it was still in there!

Sara Hamilton crouched beside me holding the oil lamp I had lit. It didn't waver, not even at the first sight of all that blood when I unzipped his wet-suit.

"How bad is it?" she whispered.

"Bad enough. He's stopped one in the left lung from the looks of it."

One thing I've always needed plenty of in my line of work was medical supplies. I told her where to look and she took the lamp and moved to the storage cupboard next to the bathroom.

I crouched there in the dark listening to her rummaging about. I could hardly hear Guyon's breathing which worried me. Lung wounds were funny things. You could never tell where you were with them. One minute alive, the next, dead. I'd seen it all before.

She returned with a large tin box painted grey with the insignia of the British Admiralty on the lid. It was the kind

of kit carried on most smaller naval craft that couldn't rate
their own doctor. I had several of them in stock bought
through war surplus channels.

There was sweat on his face now and he moaned a
couple of times. I poured sulphur powder on his wounds
after swabbing as much of the blood away as I could, then
I bandaged them quickly using several field dressings.

Sara held him upright for me, the lamp on the floor.
We managed to get my old bathrobe on him. Just as we
finished, he opened his eyes and stared at her, then turned
to me. There was recognition through the pain. He tried
to reach out to me, muttered a few words and fainted.

"What did he say?" she whispered. "I couldn't catch
it."

"He spoke in Hebrew. He said he was sorry."

There was a sudden fragile silence between us. I reached
out and touched her. "We could have used you in the
Commandos. You've done this sort of thing before."

"In a way. What happens now? He needs to go to
hospital surely?"

"I wouldn't give much for his chances if he does. I'd say
Major Ibrahim would get to work on him long before any
surgeon could and with less fortunate results. No, this is
one for Yanni Kytros. Time he came into the firing line,
too."

I moved to the door, opened it and peered outside. The
corridor was still in darkness, a little light seeping through
from the foyer at the end. She stood at my shoulder, so
close that to put an arm about her waist seemed the most
natural thing in the world.

"All right?" she said.

God knows why, but I felt alive in a way I had not
done for years, full of myself, my own ability to take on
the whole damned world and knock it flat on its back. My
hand moved up from the waist and cupped her left breast.
She glanced up, eyes widening, and I kissed her on the
mouth.

"We do have fun, don't we?"

"Go on, get out of it." She almost managed a smile,
which would have been remarkable under the circumstances, shoved me into the corridor and closed the door.

I moved cautiously towards the end and peered round the corner and down into the deserted foyer. Two oil lamps stood on the reception desk, but I could see no sign of the night clerk. Behind me, a door opened and Yanni Kytros appeared, an oil lamp in his hand. He wore a dressing gown and looked ready for an early night, at least by his standards.

"Jack?" He frowned. "What's all this?" And then he moved closer. "My God, there's blood on your coat."

I grabbed him by the lapels and jerked him forward. "And there will be a little on you, if you don't come up with something fast. Guyon's flat on his back in my room with three rather large holes in him. In his condition I wouldn't give him long with Ibrahim before the good major was extracting everything he needed to know about you. He'd hang you up by your big toes. Would you like that?"

His eyes widened, but not for a moment did he panic. "Not one little bit, I have other plans. How bad is Guyon?"

"I've patched him up as best I can, but he's stopped one in the lung. He needs surgery fast."

"There's a doctor in Alexandria, an Austrian named Schiller who runs a clinic for heroin addicts near the main harbour. Kanayis Street. He'll see to him. Tell him I sent you."

"And how the hell am I supposed to get him there? They'll have troops out on every road."

We didn't get a chance to take it further because several vehicles arrived outside in a hurry. A moment later, Major Ibrahim strode in followed by four military policemen. He went to the desk and rang for the clerk who appeared from the office yawning.

"Where is Kytros?" Ibrahim demanded.

"I am not sure, Major."

The clerk looked scared and I didn't blame him. "And the man Savage? Have you seen him?"

"I think he will be in his room, Major."

As Ibrahim turned I whispered in Yanni's ear, "If you want to live, stall him. Three minutes at least or we've all had it."

I gave him a shove down the steps and started back fast along the corridor. "Oh, Major, I wanted a word with you!"

I heard him call and then I had the door open and was into the bedroom.

Somehow she'd got Guyon on to the bed and was sitting beside him. I stripped off my bloodstained jacket, tossed it down on the floor beside the wet-suit and rolled the whole lot up inside the Persian carpet.

"You'd better get out of here fast," I told her. "Ibrahim's on his way."

I ran to the storage cupboard, kicked open the lid of my old cabin trunk and stuffed the whole lot inside. When I turned she was still there, standing beside the bed.

"For God's sake, be your age," I said. "How long do you think a girl like you would last in an Egyptian gaol? They'd be queuing up."

"According to you, I should enjoy that, shouldn't I?"

I picked Guyon up in my arms. "We certainly pick one hell of a time for this kind of conversation, don't we? You'd better pray that electricity doesn't come on yet."

I went out through the french windows and plunged into the darkness of the garden. She was hard on my heels. We just about made it into the safety of the bushes when the door of my room was flung open so violently that it re-bounded from the wall. There was the clatter of boots, confused voices, then a chair went over.

Ibrahim walked on to the terrace followed by Yanni Kytros and a military policeman holding a lantern. The major couldn't stop moving, anger and frustration churning inside him.

"But Savage was told to stay here," he said loudly.

Yanni spread his hands and managed to look bewildered. "Perhaps he is in the bar? He is there most nights."

Ibrahim paused, stared at him, presumably because the suggestion made sense. He told the military policeman to stay there on the terrace and went back into the room followed by Kytros.

"Right, let's get out of here," I whispered and moved cautiously away.

We fetched up against the far wall within a couple of minutes and I paused for a breather, aware of Guyon's weight. There was a wicker gate not too far away which gave access to the lane at the side of the garden where I usually parked the Land-Rover, mainly because it was the quickest route down to the harbour. If I could once get him safe on board the *Gentle Jane* there might be some sort of chance. To reach Alexandria by road would be impossible now, but by sea . . .

I told her briefly what I hoped to do and she put a hand on Guyon's forehead. "I don't think he can stand much more of this kind of thing. Anyway, I should have thought they would have put a guard on your boat."

"Perhaps, but I was supposed to be confined to the hotel remember. In any case, I'll only find out by taking a look. You can get that gate open for me then clear off out of it. No need for you to be involved any further."

She ignored me. Simply stood up and went and opened the wicker gate, holding it wide. I moved out, paused for a moment, then staggered towards the Land-Rover. She was there before me and had the flap open at the rear.

"Have you got a death-wish or something?" I demanded.

"Oh, shut up, Savage, you're wasting time."

There was a stirring inside and Morgan sat up. "What in the hell is going on out there?"

"It's me, Morg," I told him. "We're in bad trouble. I'm shoving Guyon in beside you. Cover him with a blanket and pray."

That sobered him and fast. I said to Sara, "All right, if you want to go down with the ship, so be it. Get behind the wheel and release the handbrake when I give you the word. It's downhill all the way so we'll keep it quiet."

She nodded briefly and went round to the other side. I gave her a moment to get set, then put my shoulder down and pushed. The Land-Rover started to roll, slowly at first, then faster. I ran alongside and scrambled into the passenger seat. As we gathered speed, plunging down into the darkness, every light in the hotel came on as if by magic. Too late for us.

She smiled in that habitually ironic way of hers and said, without looking at me, "You know, there are definitely times when I almost believe in God."

The M.T.B. used the inner harbour which was what the locals called the new harbour although it dated from the turn of the century. A lot of expensive yachts and motor cruisers were tied up there, mainly owned by weekend sailors from Alexandria.

I had the *Gentle Jane* at the end of the Admiralty pier in the old harbour where the mooring was free and used mainly by local fishermen. At this time of night it was as quiet as the grave. We managed to run about halfway along the pier before finally rolling to a halt.

"This will do," I said and she pulled on the brake. "I'll carry him from here."

I went round to the back and Morgan peered out at me, sweat shining on his face in spite of the cold.

"How is he?" I asked.

"Hasn't stirred." He scrambled out to join me. "What happens now?"

"We get him to the boat and make time for Alex," I told him. "You go on ahead and make ready to cast off and we'll use the silencers."

They had been an expensive innovation when I'd first had them fitted, but necessary at the time, considering the kind of work I'd been doing for Yanni Kytros. With any kind of luck, they'd get us in and out of harbour without being heard which was all that mattered.

Morgan stumbled away into the darkness and I pulled Guyon out as gently as I could and followed. He was dead weight, out cold, but that was all to the good in the circumstances.

Sara kept pace with me, a shadow in the darkness. I could smell the sea now, strong and salty in a light breeze that pushed the waves into harbour in long, straight lines, rocking the fishing boats below, filling the night with the uneasy groaning of the rigging.

I went down a flight of stone steps cautiously, telling her to be careful. Morgan was waiting at the bottom to help us over the side and there was plenty of light from the lamp on the end of the pier.

Morgan had the main saloon lights on, curtains drawn, when I went down the companionway. I laid Guyon down carefully on one of the bunks and sat on the edge beside him. His face was like marble and very cold, but he was still breathing.

"He doesn't look too good," Sara said in a low voice. I nodded. "All I can do is get him to Alex as quickly as possible and hope. An hour's run, that's all. He still has a chance."

I stood up and she moved close. "And afterwards? What will you say when Hakim and Ibrahim come looking for you?"

"I'll think of something. Once he's off my hands, they can't prove a thing. Now get out of here. Back to Aleko as fast as you can. Nobody need ever know you had a thing to do with this business."

"Is that what you want?"

"Be sensible. For once in your life be sensible."

She stood there staring up at me, then turned and moved out. I followed her up the companionway as the engine came to life with the faintest of rumblings.

She paused at the rail and turned, her face a pale blur in the darkness. "It won't work, Savage, you've had it. You know that, don't you?"

"What did you expect me to do, leave him to rot?"

She said slowly and after a long pause, "No, you wouldn't do that."

I surprised myself by laughing. "Funny, but some days life is just all hell. Now get moving."

She went over the rail. As she reached the first step I called softly, "It's been nice knowing you, Sara Hamilton. You're pure gold. Don't let anyone ever tell you different."

There was a kind of dry sob. Now that did surprise me, or did it? In any case, I didn't have time to consider the point because in that same moment, headlights cut through the darkness back there on the waterfront, and a Land-Rover came along the jetty fast.

Morgan was already casting off, but as always, just a little bit too late. Sara Hamilton was back over the rail before I could stop her, which was an added complication.

I stepped into the wheelhouse, reached under the chart table and pressed a neat and inconspicuous button. The flap which fell down held an Israeli Uzi submachine gun with a 25-round magazine in place, all ready to go. But the Walther automatic was handier in this kind of situation. I pulled it from its clip, shoved the flap back out of sight and switched on the deck lights. When I moved out, I was holding the Walther flat against my right thigh.

Hakim, Major Ibrahim and a single military policeman stood on the edge of the jetty peering down. Ibrahim looked like Satan himself straight out of some Islamic netherworld.

"Hello there!" I called cheerfully.

"Stay exactly where you are, Savage," Ibrahim replied rather unnecessarily. "We are coming on board."

He led the way, revolver in hand. I breathed in Sara Hamilton's ear. "Anything I do now gets you out of this thing with clean hands whatever happens, so do as you're told."

The military policeman had a Russian submachine gun hanging from one shoulder, so Ibrahim's revolver was the only thing I had to worry about. I waited until he started to scramble over the rail, judged my moment and kicked the gun out of his hand. It splashed into the water. I rammed the Walther into Sara's backbone, turned her to one side so that they all could see.

"I will if I have to, Hakim, I've nothing to lose, and I don't think Aleko would be very pleased. Think of all that lovely investment money going elsewhere."

"He wouldn't dare," Ibrahim said and turned on the M.P. "Shoot, damn you!"

The military policeman stood there looking worried, the Russian submachine gun still hanging from one shoulder. It was Hakim, as always, who had the last word.

"Mr. Savage, I would appear to have misjudged you. What happens now?"

"We go for a little ride," I told him. "If you all behave yourselves, I'll put you ashore at Canayis. Plenty of fishing boats work that area. You'll be all right."

"Colonel Hakim, do we have to . . . ?"

Ibrahim gave him his official rank for the first time in my hearing and Hakim chopped him off with a simple gesture of the hand.

"And Lady Hamilton?"

"Goes with you. I'm sorry she had to be involved. She

just happened to be on the terrace outside my room at the wrong time, that's all."

Hakim nodded gravely. "I accept your conditions. I give you my word we will make no trouble." He turned to Sara. "A terrible experience. Please accept my apologies."

"For what?" she said, speaking for the first time, then turned to me. "Is it all right if I go below and look at your friend?"

I nodded and she went down the companionway. I reached across and unhooked the submachine gun from the M.P.'s shoulder. Ibrahim didn't say a word. There was a storage hold in the stern deck and I lifted the hatch cover, keeping them covered.

"Right, gentlemen, down you go. There isn't much room, but it won't be for long."

The M.P. went first, then Hakim. Ibrahim, game to the last, made a grab for my ankle on his way down. I stamped on his hand and shoved him into the darkness on top of the other two.

Morgan was already casting off the stern line. As he moved off, his face looked yellow and old in the glare of the deck lights. Poor Morgan, adrift on the high seas again and I owed him more than that. Much more.

I went into the wheelhouse, gave the engines a little more power and took her out past the end of the jetty, nice and slowly, the silenced engines a whisper in the night.

The door banged and Morgan appeared. He opened a locker and found a bottle. I could smell the rum when he took out the cork. This time he didn't ask, he just swallowed.

He half-choked, leaned on the chart table, head down. "Why, Jack? Why?"

"Does it matter? It's done, isn't it? Go below and see what the situation is."

He went and I reached for the bottle and took a pull myself although rum was never one of my favourites. Now what happened, for God's sake? There was nothing for me in Alexandria, that was for certain.

We were well out to sea now, so I took her off the silencers and pushed up to full power. The Penta petrol engines had been specially modified and would give me thirty knots when needed, so I wasn't particularly worried about being chased for the *Gentle Jane* handled superbly.

The door opened softly, clicked shut. I spoke without looking round. "How's Guyon?"

"He died about five minutes ago," Sara Hamilton said quietly.

I got about fifty pounds of chain from the locker, then I carried Guyon up from the saloon and laid him out on an old canvas tarpaulin. I wrapped the chain around his ankles and Morgan started to sew him up. He was a good man with a sailmaker's needle, something he'd picked up as an apprentice on Finnish windjammers on the old grain run before the war.

Guyon might have been sleeping, he was so peaceful. He looked about seventeen again, every line, every care and worry washed clean.

"What was he like?" Sara asked me.

"He was a good diver, that's about all I can tell you. Not much at communicating. I see why now, of course. He always thought the sea would get him."

"Which it has in the end, hasn't it?"

"As clean a way as any. I'll be happy with the same when my time comes."

I lit a cigarette and moved to the rail. The boat rocked gently on the swell. Somewhere in the far distance, the navigation lights of a steamer gleamed in the night.

"Now what will you do?" she asked, leaning against the rail beside me.

"Oh, plenty of things for someone like me with a good boat under his feet."

"And no scruples?"

"To speak of."

"No regrets?"

"I've still got the boat, haven't I? It could be worse."

"But not much."

I managed a gay laugh. "That's the difference between you and me, angel. I've been poor before."

I left her there, went and lifted the hatch cover and told Hakim to come up. He emerged cautiously, his linen suit streaked with oil.

"Nothing to worry about," I told him. "I just want you to witness this."

Morgan had reached the neck and was about to cover Guyon's face for all time. Hakim looked down at the dead Israeli for a long moment and sighed.

"So, in the end it was all for nothing, Mr. Savage." He looked me straight in the eye. "I know every last detail of your background. Better perhaps than you know yourself. You are no Israeli agent, my friend. If you had looked the other way, minded your own business." And then there was something else in his voice, something personal. "In heaven's name, why? You've lost everything. Thrown it all away and for what?"

I laughed in his face. "The last of the big spenders, that's me. Now let's get him over the side."

I knew there was some kind of Hebrew prayer for the dead. The best I could do for him was a Hail Mary and an Our Father and I was pretty rusty on both. Hakim gave me a hand and we slid him gently into the water—so gently that he disappeared without even a splash.

Canayis was a tiny island three miles off the coast, mostly flat scrub fringed by long white beaches. There was a freshwater spring, sweeter by far than anything on the mainland, and fishing boats called in to fill their goatskins every day.

From the south, there was a clear run in to a curved beach, flat sand all the way and I took the *Gentle Jane* in close enough for her prow to bite. I had the hatch cover off without any delay and Ibrahim and the M.P. came up for air.

"Over the side," I said. "And don't try anything."

And they didn't, being more occupied with getting some oxygen into their lungs again. Ibrahim lost his balance scrambling over the rail and fell into the water which was about three feet deep at that point.

Hakim turned to me. "What about Lady Hamilton?"

"I'll see to her. Go on, over you go."

"You are a fool, Mr. Savage. A brave man, but a fool. I hope I never see you again, entirely for your own sake, of course."

He held out his hand which I took, for it would have
seemed churlish to refuse, then he went over after the
other two.

I turned to Sara Hamilton. "Well, this is it, the long
goodbye."

She said gravely, "What would you do if I refused to
go?"

"You've no choice. Not if you want to come clean out of
this business." I turned to Morgan who was standing at the
door of the wheelhouse clutching the Russian submachine
gun I'd taken from the M.P. "Cover me with that thing.
I shan't be long."

I vaulted over the side, waist-deep in water, turned and
held up my arms. "All right, let's be having you."

She stood looking at me for a long moment then reached
down and ripped open the skirt of her dress, scattering buttons with the violence of it, freeing her limbs. She moved
away from me and jumped over the rail into the water.

She lost her footing and went under completely and I
waded forward and pulled her to her feet. The dress clung
to her like a second skin, a nipple blossoming clearly on
each full breast. She might as well have had nothing on.

"Get your hands off me," she said fiercely in a low
voice, shoved me away with a stiff right arm and pushed
wet hair back from her eyes.

"I'm forty-two years old," I said. "This year, next year,
but not much longer than that, I go Guyon's way. Over
the side with fifty pounds of old chain round my ankles."

She stood quite still, water slapping around her thighs, a
hand to her face and then, God save us all, she actually
smiled.

I turned from her, heaved myself over the rail, went into
the wheelhouse and eased the *Gentle Jane* off the sand-
bank. Then I took her round in a great sweeping curve
and headed out to sea.

My hands were trembling, my whole body shaking. Re-
action, I suppose, or that's what I tried to tell myself.

I engaged the automatic pilot, reached for Morgan's
rum bottle and went on deck, avoiding his worried eyes.
What was left in the bottle was foul. I tossed it into the
sea.

Two hundred thousand pounds. Everything I'd sweated to build for eight long years, all down the drain and for what? Now I had nothing.

I had kept my head turned one way deliberately, but it was no good. Let me be honest at the end, whatever else might be. I went to the stern rail and looked back towards the beach.

The three men were on dry ground by now, but she still stood thigh-deep in the silver water, the thin crescent of the moon behind her. If I reached out, I could touch her, or at least that's what it felt like and I stayed there at the stern until she faded into the darkness.

CHAPTER V

DEAD MEN'S FINGERS

North from Kyros, I came awake from a deep, dreamless sleep and lay on the bunk staring up at the bulkhead, wondering who I was—a bad sign. Then things clicked into place and I yawned and swung my legs to the floor.

It was warm in the saloon, even with the air conditioning plant in full cry, but when I went up the companionway, the heat almost brought me to a dead halt. I took a deep breath and moved out.

It was a day to thank God for, a blue sky without a cloud in it reaching to nowhere, the Cyclades fading north into the heat haze, the great bulk of Crete far, far away to the southwest. We floated, motionless in a flat, copper sea, every line of the boat reflected as truly as in a mirror.

Morgan had rigged an awning in the stern and sprawled beneath it, snoring steadily. I kicked his feet, then dropped a bucket over the side on a line, sluiced myself and gave some thought to the afternoon.

We had several dozen sponges strung on a line to dry. They didn't look too good to me. Sponge divers are a dying breed and not only because synthetic have cornered most of the market these days. The youngers don't want any part of it. They've seen too many men old before their time, crippled by the bends. But for some men, it's a way of life—the only way, and you still get plenty of boats working the Aegean and the waters off the southwest coast of Turkey.

So, there was still a living to be had if you knew what you were doing, but only just. I'd had three weeks of it, working out of Kyros and just managing to keep my head above water. Eating money, fuel for the boat and not much left after that.

Morgan was having to manage on local wine which came cheap at around a couple of shillings a litre and the old lady who ran the *taverna* where he bought it always seemed to give him a little over the odds, so he was happy enough.

It was a strange kind of existence. A sort of limbo between old ending and new beginnings. We had the boat, enough to eat, the sun was warm. No word from Yanni Kytros which surprised me, but we managed.

He owned an old *taverna* on the waterfront at Kyros which he'd tarted up for the tourist trade. Yanni's, he called it. It was the sort of place that looked like something out of an old Bogart movie. Fishermen and sponge divers were encouraged to use it, preferably unshaven and with knives at their belts, to give the tourists a thrill, but it was mainly a big act and the local boys were strictly on their best behaviour and got their drinks cheap. The occasional fight added a little spice and even Yanni didn't mind that as long as it didn't go too far.

It was run for him by a fat, amiable Athenian named Alexias Papas who liked the quiet life and saw that things stayed that way by providing the local police sergeant with what amounted to free board and lodging and, as far as I could see, that seemed to include assuaging a pretty deep thirst.

As I said, there was no news from Kytros or perhaps Alexias was simply putting me off, so I gave up enquiring and concentrated on earning a living for a while.

We'd not had much luck earlier in the day and I had decided to try the area on the north side of a tiny island called Hios on the chance recommendation of an old Turk, crippled by the bends, who'd conned a couple of drinks out of me at Yanni's the previous evening.

Morgan got to his feet, yawning and scratching his face as I buckled on an aqualung. "Hope you do better than we done this morning, Jack. That lot we got drying ain't hardly worth taking in."

"You worry too much," I said and vaulted over the rail.

What he had said was true enough, but it wasn't exactly constructive. Sponges are funny things. The good and the

bad often look exactly the same, nice and black and shiny.
There's a definite art in being able to tell the difference
and the plain truth is that I was only fair at it.

I paused to adjust my air supply and went down in a
long sweeping curve. The water was crystal-clear and I
could see so far and with such definition that it was like
looking at things through the wrong end of a telescope.

I hovered for a while to get my bearings, aware with a
kind of conscious pleasure that I was enjoying this. There
were fish everywhere, dentex and black bream and just
below me, a group of silver and gold giltheads. I jackknifed
and went down fast, scattering them just for the hell of it,
and found myself part of an enormous shoal of tiny rain-
bow-hued fish. They exploded outwards leaving me alone,
suspended in the blue vault.

For a brief moment I seemed to become a part of it all
and it was a part of me, fused together into something
special. Man's oldest dream, free flight was achieved and
all things were possible. I experienced again the same incredible wonder I had known on the very first occasion
I had gone down in a self-contained rig.

It had been a long time since I'd felt like that. Too long.
I tried to hang on to the moment, to hold it tight. Perhaps
because of that fact it simply drained out of me, leaving
me wary and tense again and vaguely apprehensive.

I touched bottom at eight fathoms. It was suddenly
gloomier. For one thing, there were a lot of rocks around
which reduced visibility considerably and they reared up
out of a great carpet of marine grass that stirred uneasily.

I went over a spur of rock and found my first sponges,
but these were worse than useless. Bloated and horrible,
they were mainly black in colour and a tinge of green gave
them a suggestion of putrescence. Of some living thing
gone bad. No wonder the Turks called them dead men's
fingers.

I had been down perhaps ten minutes and had worked
my way round the western tip of the island. I went over a
great ledge of rock and got the shock of my life. Beneath
me, the chasm drifted into infinity. Across the gulf on a
large sandy plateau, a diver was working amongst as good

a crop of sponges as I had ever seen. He was wearing a
regulation diving suit, his air and lifelines snaking up to
the surface like an umbilical cord. He saw me at once
and paused in his work.

I had an idea who it might be, swam across the chasm
quickly and moved in close enough to peer through the
front window of his helmet. He was called Ciasim Divalni
and he was a Turk from Hilas in the Gulf of Kerma.

Now that the Cyprus troubles were really fading into the
past, Turkish sponge boats were beginning to be seen in
the Aegean again. I'd found Ciasim and his two sons on
the waterfront at Kyros a week or two earlier wrestling
with a faulty compressor. A serious business for poor men
for without it, they could not dive. It was a simple enough
fault if you knew what you were doing and Morgan had
a positive genius for that kind of thing.

We were accepted from then on which was quite something where Turks were concerned and when Morgan
spent a day overhauling the old diesel engine on their boat,
the *Seytan*, our stock rose even higher which was good
for his ego.

Ciasim reached out in slow motion, touched the empty
net hanging from my belt, then gestured to the sponges
scattered around the plateau, inviting me to join in. I didn't
need asking again. They were definitely the best I'd seen
and I filled my net very quickly.

He was ready to go himself, pointed upwards then gave
the regulation four pulls on his line which was diver's
language for *Haul me up*.

I ascended a lot faster than he did. There was no need
for me to decompress for I hadn't been down long enough
at that depth. It would probably be different for Ciasim.
Not that I believed for a moment that he would decompress properly even if it were necessary. Most sponge
divers treated the whole paraphernalia of modern diving
tables and decompression rates with the same good-hu-
moured contempt they reserved for all those who used
self-contained diving rigs. Their own remedy for the bends
and any minor physical aches and pains experienced after
diving, was to bury the sufferer up to his neck in soft

sand or get him to smoke a couple of cigarettes. The nicotine was supposed to have a beneficial effect, being absorbed straight into the bloodstream, which explains why every Turkish diver I've ever met is a heavy smoker.

I surfaced beside the *Seytan* which was a *trenchadiri*, one of those strange double-ended boats made from time immemorial in exactly the same way. It carried a large, patched, ochre-coloured sail and the diesel engine Morgan had overhauled gave it a top speed of four knots.

Ciasim's eldest son, Yassi, a tall, handsome youth of nineteen, kept a careful eye on the vessel's speed. It was necessary to stay on the move, not only to combat the effects of tide and current, but to keep pace with the diver down there on the bottom. It was also essential to keep the vessel in such a position that the engine exhaust was always to leeward of the compressor. More than one diver had died from carbon monoxide poisoning when someone had made a mistake over that one.

The compressor was banging away and Ciasim's second son, Abu, a bright, cheerful fourteen-year-old rogue, was acting as diver's tender, the most important task on board. I've known tenders who were so expert that they could work out what was happening below just by the feel of the lifeline. A bad one could be the death of you. Abu was a natural which was hardly surprising.

Yassi reached over the side with a big grin and gave me a hand up. I pulled off my face mask and held up my bulging net. We used Greek, for only their father spoke English and I had but a smattering of Turkish. He had a look at the sponges, picked one or two out and shook his head. They looked all right to me, but over the side they went.

"How can you tell?" I demanded.

"Easy," he grunted. "It's the size of the holes."

As his father rose, Abu was calling off the depth in *kulacs,* the Turkish equivalent of the fathom, roughly five feet. I unstrapped my aqualung, went and helped myself to water from a huge earthenware jar roped to the mast. It was Greek or Roman and a couple of thousand years old. Most of the sponge boats used the same. They were to be had with ease from the bottom of the sea in those parts from the many wrecks.

They had Ciasim over the rail a few moments later and I went to give them a hand. A diver in regulation dress is a clumsy creature out of water. The shoes weighed seventeen and a half pounds each and he had eighty pounds in lead weights strapped around his waist. And the great copper and brass helmet weighed over fifty pounds.

I unscrewed his face plate and he grinned. "Jack, my dear friend, how goes it?"

He was about forty-five, dark and handsome with a great sweep of black moustache. He should have looked older considering the way he lived, but he didn't.

"How long were you down there, idiot?" I demanded.

Abu had the helmet off by then and Ciasim grinned. "Don't start with your compression tables again. Just hand me a smoke. When I die, I die."

I gave him a cigarette from a little sandalwood box Yassi handed me. Ciasim inhaled deeply. "Wonderful. Where's your boat, Jack? Why not bring her round to join us? We'll go to the island and eat on the beach. I have been wanting to talk to you anyway. A business matter."

"Okay, I'll leave the sponges till later," I said and reached for my aqualung.

Yassi and young Abu helped me into it and I went back over the side. They accepted me because I was a *dalguc* like Ciasim—a diver. With him, it was something more for he had served with the Turkish infantry contingent sent to join the United Nations Force in Korea in 1950.

I had been there myself which was a bond between us. Had seen them arrive at the front, strange, fierce-looking men in ankle-length greatcoats who carried rather old-fashioned rifles with sword bayonets. They were just like something out of the First World War, but fight . . . Everything I'd heard about Johnny Turk was true.

Ciasim had been a prisoner in Chinese hands for nearly two years, subjected to the same brainwashing techniques as other allied prisoners. With the Turks it had failed completely and the Chinese had finally given up in some desperation and had placed them in an enclave of their own.

They were like rocks on which the sea breaks with no

effect. Hardy, utterly indomitable men. The best friends in
the world . . . the worst enemies.

They lit a fire on the beach and Yassi and young Abu
busied themselves with the cooking while Morgan, whose
Greek was about as broken as it could be, contented himself with watching while perched on a rock, a jug of
wine between his knees.

Ciasim and I went off some little way and sat by the
water's edge with a bottle of *arak* and a box of *halva,* that
unique Turkish sweetmeat made out of honey and nuts,
something to which he was particularly partial.

It was hotter than ever and very beautiful and on the
horizon, a *congoa,* the kind of boat that trawled for sponges
instead of using a diver, drifted by.

"Look at that," Ciasim said angrily. "They're ruining
the business, those butchers. They tear up the sea-bed and
everything that lives."

"Soon be impossible to make a living in the islands at
all," I said. "What with those things and synthetics."

I rolled a mouthful of *arak* around my teeth. It always
tended to make me feel about eight years old and sucking
aniseed balls again.

"I wouldn't be too sure, Jack," Ciasim said carefully.
"Plenty of ways a good diver can make a living around
here."

So now we were coming to it. "Such as?"

"Wrecks, for instance. Every kind of wreck from ancient
times up to ships that were torpedoed in the last war."

I shook my head. "If it's antiquities you're after, you
are wasting your time. Most wrecks of that kind aren't
visible. They're usually under a tumulus of sand and you've
got to be an expert to recognise them. Even if you do,
undersea excavation is one of the most highly technical
games there is. You need specialists, lots of money and all
the time in the world. On top of that, the Greek or Turkish
governments, whichever it happens to be, will have their
say in disposing of anything you bring up."

"No, it was something else I had in mind. I found a
ship last week, Jack, over towards Sinos in the Middle
Passage."

"Sinos?" I was surprised. "I didn't know they were letting anyone work that area."

The island of Sinos was a relic of the war. Only a couple of miles long and half that distance wide, it had enormous strategic importance during the war because of its position at the mouth of the Kasos Strait and the Germans had developed the old Turkish fortifications tremendously. It had recently acquired a rather more sinister reputation as a prison for political offenders from the Greek mainland.

"You know how it is these days?" Ciasim grinned. "Greece and Turkey are co-operating again, at least as far as things go at the official level, so all of a sudden, everyone is being friendly. A Greek Navy M.T.B. turned up to say we shouldn't be there, but they were nice and helpful when I explained about the wreck. Said I should apply through police headquarters at Kyros for a permit to work on her."

"And did you?"

"I saw Sergeant Stavrou that same night. He filled in a form for me and sent it off to Athens. He seemed to think I stood a good chance of getting permission."

"How much did it cost you?" I commented sourly.

"A drink, Jack, that's all. At Yanni's. One of those cold German beers Stavrou likes so much. He was fine." He shook his head and sighed. "Jack, whatever happened to you? You've got to start trusting people again."

"That'll be the day. Tell me some more about this wreck."

"An old three-thousand-ton coaster the Germans used to run supplies between the islands. Sunk by bombing in 1945 just before the end of the war. I made a few enquiries around the bars in Kyros and found someone who was in the crew. An old man called Constantinos. Has a farm on the south side of the island. He said they were on their way to the mainland from Sinos just after the Germans had evacuated. They even had the commander on board. Some S.S. general or other. Think of it, Jack." He prodded me in the chest with his forefinger gravely as the *arak* began to take effect. "Think of the loot. You know what the Nazis were like? There could be anything down there."

"Or nothing. How deep is she?"

"Twenty-six *kulacs*. I made an accurate recording."

A hundred and thirty feet. I shook my head. "You need good equipment for that kind of deal, Ciasim. At least two divers for a start."

"Exactly what I thought."

He grinned, dropping into the American English he'd picked up in that prison camp. "You and me, baby, we'll make a fortune."

But I wasn't so sure. Oh, there was a chance of sorts, a good chance, but there was more money to be made out of the wreck than out of sponging in the same period, which wasn't saying much. There had been a time when I wouldn't have thought twice about joining such a venture, but I wasn't at my best around wrecks these days. How could I tell a man who'd never had a nerve in his body in the first place that I'd lost mine?

"This afternoon, Jack. I take you there this afternoon. We go down together. You'll see." He lifted the bottle to his mouth and swallowed deep, *arak* spilling across his face. "Now we eat."

He pulled me to my feet and lurched across the sand towards the fire. There was *corba* to start with, probably the finest fish soup in the world, lobsters fried whole on the white-hot stones, fish steaks. You couldn't have done better at the Athens Hilton. Why, then, had I lost my appetite?

When I focussed the binoculars, the cliffs of Sinos jumped into view. They were two to three hundred feet high at that point and great concrete gun emplacements, relics of the German occupation, were clearly visible at every strategic point. Bare rock and grass and not much else.

"A hell of a place to die in," I said.

Ciasim shrugged. "Politics is for the insane, Jack. I just don't want to know."

Which expressed my own sentiments exactly. The *Seytan* was anchored about half a mile off-shore, the *Gentle Jane* was up alongside in a spot which he assured me was the correct one in spite of the absence of any marker buoy. I leaned against the mast and watched Yassi and Abu get him ready.

Diving dress is made of india-rubber between layers

of heavy twill which together makes for something pretty durable, but the gear Ciasim was wearing had definitely seen better days.

You can forget about moray eels and octopuses, sting rays and other terrors of the deep. Diving is a lot like flying. The danger comes from the very fact that you are doing something so completely against nature.

The pressure increases at up to fifteen tons for every thirty-seven feet you descend and air isn't just necessary to breathe. It has to be fed down to you at something like fifty pounds more than the pressure at the depth at which you are working. Once the air supply is cut off, the pressure of the water can collapse the suit and the diver is quite simply compressed. I've heard old timers say they've seen blood and flesh squeezed out of the end of the air hose up top. A nice way to die . . .

The only decent item of equipment Ciasim had was a massive copper and brass helmet which like most of the modern variety had a check valve which closed automatically when the air supply was cut off. The exhaust valve did the same, leaving the diver with the air in his suit, but it didn't leave him long to get to the surface.

It was crazy to take up this kind of work with the sort of gear Ciasim had. He was a good diver—none better, but he only had guts to go along with that and it wasn't enough.

"See you down there, Jack," he said as the helmet went over his head and they screwed the wing nuts on his breastplate tight.

I nodded and went over the rail to the *Gentle Jane* where Morgan was checking the aqualung. He glanced up, a worried look on his face as I stripped off my sweater and pants. Underneath I was wearing a full Neoprene wetsuit in black. It was going to be cold down there and I shivered involuntarily.

"How do you feel, Jack?" he asked in a low voice as I slipped my arms through the straps of the aqualung.

"Bloody awful," I told him and instantly regretted it. His face sagged and I put a hand on his shoulder quickly. "Nothing to do with the diving. Never bothers me these days. It's just that I don't fancy the idea of hooking up

with Ciasim on a thing like this. We don't have the right
kind of gear. An old blue-belly like you knows that better
than anyone."

But he didn't believe me—not for a single minute.

I gave Ciasim three or four minutes' start before going
over and following his lines down through the clear water.
It wasn't so bad at first and then I entered the neutral zone
from fifty feet on where all colours faded and things
started to move in on me. Visibility was nothing like as
good and for some reason, there didn't seem to be many
fish about. It was all rather sinister.

I checked my depth gauge and moved on. No reefs,
no undersea chasms—nothing. A mysterious green void
leading nowhere. I was sliding headlong into eternity.

A ship's stern moved out of the gloom with startling
suddenness and I straightened out and hovered, adjusting
my air flow.

She was tilted ever so slightly to one side, but otherwise
in a remarkable state of preservation. The anti-aircraft
gun on the fore deck was still in place on its mounting,
barrel tilted towards the surface. Ciasim stood beside it.
He raised a hand and beckoned. I went closer.

Black mussels grew on her rails and ventilators and
some of her surfaces were covered with vicious dog's teeth,
a razor-edged clam, which not only slice like a razor as the
name implies, but also carry enough poison to put you on
your back for a week.

The compass and wheel were encrusted with barnacles
when I peered inside the wheelhouse. Barnacles grew on
the winch. I went down through an open hatchway. The
interior of the hold at that point was like being inside the
nave of a church, light filtering down through ragged holes
in the deck, mainly cannon shells from the look of them.
She'd been strafed from the air before sinking, that was
for sure.

I moved into the gloom, looking for a way into the main
cargo area and ran into trouble at once. This was where
the bomb had landed, the direct hit which had caused all
the trouble. There was a jumble of twisted girders and

buckled deck plates, the whole encrusted with strange, sub-marine growths.

I moved closer, reached out to a metal spar only to hold myself in place. God in heaven, but it moved. Not only that, but everything in sight seemed to tremble with a kind of gentle sigh that seemed to echo through the water.

My very bowels twisted, the fear running through me like a living thing. I went up through the hatch and kept on going, leaving Ciasim to his own devices, going up just as fast as I was able. There was no need to decompress. I hadn't been down long enough and I came up into the clear light of day a few seconds later and kicked for the ladder. Yassi gave me a hand up. I wrenched off my mask and spat out the rubber mouthpiece.

"What about my father?" he demanded.

"Still down there. He'll be up soon, I suppose."

Morgan was with them and I don't think I'd ever seen his face greyer. I ignored him, stepped over the rail of the *Gentle Jane* and went below. By the time I heard his foot on the companionway, I had a bottle of Jameson out from under my bunk where I still had a secret hoard, and was on my second glass.

He stood there watching me and I shoved the bottle along the saloon table. "Okay, so I've been holding out on you. Go on, help yourself."

"Was it bad, Jack?"

"Christmas and New Year rolled into one."

I unzipped my wet-suit, towelled myself down and pulled on trousers and a sweater, ignoring his troubled gaze, then I filled my glass again and went on deck. Ciasim was back on board the *Seytan*, helmet off and in the act of lighting a cigarette from the match Yassi held out to him.

He waved, "Heh, Jack, come aboard. Let's talk."

I smiled bravely and muttered in a low voice to Morgan who had followed me up the companionway, "Make ready to move out. I've just about had it."

I stepped over the rail to the *Seytan*'s deck and leaned against the mast.

"You see, Jack?" Ciasim said. "You see what I mean? You come in with me?"

I shook my head. "I'd think again if I were you. I

thought the whole damned lot was going to come in on me down there."

He frowned. "I didn't notice anything to worry about."

Which I didn't like because of the implication, but I took a deep breath and tried sweet reason. "You were right about one thing. It's a hundred and thirty feet deep. Now that means that for every forty-five minutes worked in a helmet suit, you'll have to decompress four minutes at thirty-five feet, twenty-six minutes at twenty feet and twenty-six minutes at ten feet. A decompression time of fifty-six minutes for every forty-five worked and you can only get away with going down twice a day."

He was scowling now. "Why must you always talk in this way like a woman who fears every shadow. Always this decompression nonsense. Always these diving tables of yours."

"Ciasim, you'll kill yourself, it's as certain as that," I told him. "You need a team of divers down there. Half-a-dozen at the very least to get anything worthwhile done and at that, it could well be a waste of time."

He was good and angry by now, eyes touched with fire. "Talk, my friend, lots of talk and clever language, but when it comes down to it, I think you are afraid. Yes, you are afraid to go down there again."

He didn't mean it, not for a moment and when I cracked, I gave him the shock of his life. "Afraid?" I laughed wildly. "I'm scared to bloody death. I couldn't even hold my bowels down there. How's that for a laugh."

His eyes went wide and calm and very, very dark. It was as if in one single moment of revelation he saw everything. Really understood.

"Jack." He reached out to me quickly. "I'm sorry—truly sorry."

I went over the rail fast. Morgan was already casting off as I ran into the wheelhouse and pressed the self-starter. Those magnificent Penta engines roared into life instantly and I swung the wheel hard over and took the *Gentle Jane* away in a great sweeping curve.

I ran her hard for a couple of miles before slowing down. When I glanced over my shoulder, Morgan stood in the doorway.

"Feel any better?"

"Some," I said.

"Well don't get too happy. You left those sponges, the good ones, on board the *Seytan*."

We came into Kyros in the late afternoon. It was a spectacular little island, six or seven miles long by three across, and a single double-peaked mountain towered three thousand feet high into the sky at its centre.

A single-masted *caique*, sails bellying, slipped out through the narrow harbour entrance and turned towards Crete, passing so close that I could see the eyes painted on each side of the prow. The man at the tiller waved. I waved back and took the *Gentle Jane* into harbour.

There was one new arrival since the morning, a ninety-foot diesel motor yacht with gleaming white hull and scarlet trim. The kind of craft that must have set someone back all of fifty thousand pounds. She was anchored a hundred yards out from the main jetty and carried the Greek flag.

I passed her well to the other side of the harbour and made for my usual mooring beside the old stone jetty where there were no dues. Brightly painted *caiques* were beached on the white curve of sand and fishermen sat beside them mending their nets while children ran through the shallows, their voices clear over the water.

I killed the engines, we drifted in and Morgan jumped for the jetty and tied up. I stepped over the rail and joined him.

"You going some place, Jack?" he asked.

"I'll buy a few tins of something or other," I said. "I feel like stretching my legs anyway."

He didn't try to argue and I walked away quickly in case he did. There was more to it than that, of course. Much more. I had some thinking to do. The business down there in that old wartime wreck had really brought things home to me in a big way. I was finished.

To try with my kind of problem to earn a living as a diver could only lead to one certain end. A quick and messy death.

I came to that conclusion in a small *taverna* at the other

end of the waterfront after my third glass of *restina*. So be it. No more diving. But what was I going to do instead? That was the question. The only other thing I seemed to be much good at these days was drinking.

I walked back along the waterfront in a world of my own for a while as I considered every angle. It was one hell of a situation, that was for certain. I turned along the jetty and went towards the boat. There was no sign of Morgan, but when I went over the rail to the deck I could smell coffee.

For some reason, I felt better and went down the companionway briskly. "That's the ticket, Morg," I called as I entered the saloon and tossed my cap on the table.

Lady Sara Hamilton moved out of the galley and stood there, a coffee pot in one hand, a tin of cream in the other. She was wearing light blue linen slacks, a white shirt knotted at the waist and looked about as beautiful as any woman could ever usefully hope to.

And the face? God help me, that dear, dear face, the wide generous mouth lifting a little in scorn, but not at me, I knew that now. And the calm, grey eyes.

"Hello, Savage," she said crisply. "Pleased to see me?"

When she smiled, it was as if a lamp had clicked on inside, touching everything in sight.

CHAPTER VI

THE SMILE ON THE FACE
OF THE TIGER

Anything might have happened in that first golden moment if Dimitri Aleko had not appeared from the galley behind her. I don't know what he was supposed to be. He wore old denims, faded blue sweatshirt, scarf knotted carelessly at the throat and a battered and salt-stained cap. He looked every boy's ideal of a hard-line bosun off a Finnish windjammer.

For some reason he actually seemed pleased to see me and pushed out his hand in that rather stiff Bostonian way of his that was so alien to his Greek background.

"Good to see you, Mr. Savage. You certainly left more than a little confusion behind when we last met."

He slipped an arm around Sara Hamilton's shoulders in another of those little intimate gestures of his that was probably even for my benefit, just to let me know where we stood.

"It was something to see, wasn't it, Sara?"

In a way, she seemed to ignore him and gave all her attention to me. She poured coffee into a cup, added cream, then gave it to me, a deliberately personal gesture that carried its own intimacy. I was hard put to it to stop the cup from rattling in its saucer.

"Colonel Hakim sent a message," she said. "In case, as he put it, we just happened to run across you in the islands. He said it was a magnificent gesture and he hoped you never had cause to regret making it."

"He'd be an unusual man if he didn't," Aleko said. "Two hundred and thirty-seven thousand pounds. That's real money. To anybody, that's real money."

I showed my surprise at the accuracy of his figure and
he smiled in a slightly complacent way. "I hope you don't
mind, but I was interested enough to have a few enquiries
made in Alex. The figure I quote excludes good will. You
haven't any left, I'm afraid. Not in the United Arab Republic, and I'd keep well clear of their waters if I were
you. If they ever lay hands on you, they'll hang you out
to dry."

"Then I'll just have to see that they don't," I said.

Sara Hamilton sat drinking her coffee and smoking a
cigarette, saying nothing and there was a kind of hiatus.
We all felt it, but Aleko most of all. He was extra ballast
and didn't like the feeling.

He smiled brightly. "This is quite a boat you've got here.
I'm impressed."

I responded because it seemed the thing to do. "The best
around for her size. Built by Akerboon about six years
ago. Steel hull, twin-screw."

We kept it technical for a while. I showed him the
engines and then we went up top to the wheelhouse and he
had a look at the controls.

Sara followed us and sat on the stern rail looking out
across the harbour. She had tied a scarf around her head
and was wearing sunglasses of a style particularly in vogue
that year. Very large, so that virtually half the face was
covered. The whole combined to give her a strange remote
air.

It was not that she had turned inwards on herself. No,
it was more than that. It was as if she had stepped to one
side quite deliberately, putting herself on the outside looking in. In some curious way she seemed to be waiting for
something, though God knows what it could be and for
some reason, I shivered in spite of the warmth.

Aleko offered her another cigarette. As she took it, I
heard him ask her in a low voice if she was feeling all
right. I couldn't catch what she said in reply, but she definitely wasn't pleased.

He turned with that great, fixed smile of his on his face.
"I understand you're making a living out of sponge diving
at the moment?"

I wondered who he'd been asking, but let it go. "Of a sort. It isn't what it was in the old days."

"So I believe. I should have thought there would have been more lucrative openings for a man of your talents."

I kept pace with him all the way. "Such as?"

He smiled, a different smile this time, the smile on the face of the tiger just before the kill, but didn't attempt to give me an answer.

Instead, he said, "We'd be happy to have you dine with us tonight on board the *Firebird*, Mr. Savage. Seven-thirty, or would that be too early for you?"

I told him that would be fine by me and he said he'd send a boat for me. He put a hand under her elbow and brought her to her feet.

"Till tonight, then."

She didn't even nod and they went off along the jetty together. I watched her all the way to the end, the way her hips moved, the slant of her shoulders, the tilt of her head. Strange, but I could tell she was angry about something just by looking at her.

My guts ached and not from belly hunger. No, it was something else I needed—needed and wanted with a fierceness I had forgotten existed.

I went below, got a bottle from my private stock, found a glass and some ice and poured myself a large one. There was a fair view of the beach through the nearest porthole. Several children played tag in and out of the *caiques* which were drawn up out of the water and there was still plenty of net-mending going on.

Aleko and Sara Hamilton came into view walking close together just above the water line. He still had a hand under her elbow, but quite suddenly, she pulled free of him. They stood there talking for a second or two, or to be more accurate arguing. Yes, they were definitely having one hell of a row. She ended it by walking away from him. He didn't attempt to stop her; simply turned and went off in the other direction.

I sat at the table, gazing morosely into the bottom of my glass. It was very, very quiet, the children's voices remote and far away, an echo from another world.

"What do you see?" she said from the doorway. "Past, present or future?"

"The present," I said. "That's all there is."

"No future?"

"Not in my line of country. I won't make old bones as my grandpa used to say. What happened to Morg?"

"Dimitri gave him a couple of hundred *drachmae*. Told him to go and have a drink."

"Enough to keep him full for a week. Very generous of your Mr. Aleko. What goes on between you two?"

"Do you mean how much time do we spend between the sheets? Is that it, Savage? Does it bother you?"

She was still standing there in the doorway, one hand on her hip, the other on the wall. She started to come in and I stood up fast.

"Nothing doing, angel, you stay right where you are. Once in here and anything goes, I'm warning you."

I emptied my glass and made for the companionway and some fresh air. We came together in the entrance.

"I asked you if it bothered you?" she said. "Dimitri and me."

She moved very slightly and I got the full treatment from breast to thigh. What with that damned perfume and the whiskey, I was beginning to feel more than a little light-headed and that ache was back down there in my guts again.

I took her both arms just above the elbows and shook her. "All right, if it makes you feel any happier, it just about tears me apart. A humiliating confession for a man of my mature years, but I stand up on end the moment I clap eyes on you. Distance no object."

I released her and she stayed exactly where she was for a moment. When she removed her sunglasses, she looked rather complacent.

"Good," she said. "Can I have that drink now, please?"

"You come in here and I'll have the pants off you."

She raised an eyebrow and inclined her head. "Now that *does* sound interesting."

There was only one thing left to do. I slid my hand down across the flat belly and cupped it between her thighs.

She didn't even flinch. "What a technique," she said

calmly. "Now that really must be straight off the water-front. It has such an air of finesse about it."

It had roughly the same effect as a stiff right hook from Henry Cooper in his prime. She patted my face and kissed me on the mouth.

"But I like it, Savage. Yes, I definitely like it. A good year, nineteen forty-three."

She went up the companionway and was away before I knew what was happening. By the time I reached the deck she was already halfway along the jetty. She paused at the end to wave. I waved back, and then she was gone.

I took a shower and shaved and then had a look at my wardrobe. There wasn't much to go at, which was hardly surprising considering our hurried departure out of Egypt. I managed a clean white shirt and a rather exotic little Turkish silk scarf in place of a tie. Navy linen slacks and an old double-breasted blazer with Royal Marine buttons that had once cost me fifty pounds in a wild moment and still looked as if it had, completed the picture.

In the mirror, I looked about as good as I was ever likely to do. It was all downhill from now on, anyway, I told myself sourly and I went up on deck to wait for my transport.

There was no sign of Morgan which was hardly surprising. On two hundred *drachmae* the wine would be coming out of his ears. And why not? What else was there for him? Definitely my evening for philosophy.

The speedboat arrived with a showy flourish, one man at the wheel, another ready with the boathook in the stern. They wore white uniform slacks and their blue Guernsey sweaters had *Firebird* emblazoned across the chest. All very Royal Navy which was obviously the way Aleko liked things and they certainly had their drill just right. I found myself frowning. There was something not quite right here, something to do with the two sailors. These were no ordinary deckhands, I was certain of that.

Hard, tough looking men. Mountain Greeks from the south by the look of them, with sallow faces and crisp, blue-black hair and alike enough to be brothers. They had the confident air of the professional and looked as if they could handle most situations—but professional what? As we neared the *Firebird*, the one with the boathook leaned across in front of me and his jersey lifted disclosing a Smith & Wesson with a two-inch barrel in a spring holster at the small of his back.

Which was interesting enough. On the other hand, Aleko was a very rich man and needed looking after. And then there was the political situation. In Greece at that time, anything could happen and very often did.

We came in to the ladder and I found the captain waiting to greet me, resplendent in a uniform that wouldn't have disgraced the bridge of a Cunarder.

He saluted and said, in fair English, "Mr. Savage, my name is Melos. Would you come this way please?"

Everything was perfection, decks scrubbed, rails gleaming, and the steps down the main companionway were carpeted wall-to-wall as were the corridors below. We went into a largish saloon with a bar at one end. There was no one behind it. Melos asked me to wait a moment, saluted and went out.

I lit a cigarette and had a look round. The paintings on the walls were all reproductions, I was expert enough for that, but there were one or two nice bronze pieces that looked authentic to me. One of them was particularly good. A face mask, blank eye-holes gazing into eternity.

"You like it?" Aleko spoke from the doorway.

He wore a white tuxedo and looked extraordinarily handsome. I nodded. "First century Rhodian or I miss my guess."

He showed his surprise. "You know what you are talking about."

I had genuinely caught him off balance. "Not really," I said. "I tried my hand at archaeological diving for a while a few years back. I've seen stuff like this come out of plenty of Roman and Greek wrecks, off the Turkish coast particularly."

We had a reasonably interesting conversation for a while, talking around the whole subject, about which he certainly knew a great deal, but then he was rich enough to be able to afford that kind of interest.

I suppose I'd been expecting Sara Hamilton to make

some sort of spectacular entrance for my benefit, which
shows, on reflection, how much I still had to learn about
her, for when I turned as the conversation with Aleko
started to flag, I found her sitting on one of the high stools
at the bar.

She was wearing another of those simple little dresses of
hers. Black silk this time, cut in the style of a Greek tunic
of the classical period, no sleeves and straight across at the
neck. The pleated skirt was fashionably short and sheer
black stockings and gold sandals finished things off.

With that pale golden hair hanging straight to the shoulders, she looked marvellous and knew it. The one touch of
real ostentation was the pendant she wore on a silver
chain, a sapphire so large that I could only conclude that
somewhere in the depths of India, some temple god or
other was missing an eye.

"Is someone going to give me a drink?" she demanded
in that strange harsh voice of hers.

Aleko raised her hand to his lips. "As always, you look
magnificent," he said in Greek, and went behind the bar.

She took out a cigarette and I gave her a light. She
held my hand to steady it, only it wasn't shaking. For a
moment, there was real physical contact—real contact.
Not something superficial at all. She knew it and so did I.
She pushed her hair from her eyes and glanced up at me
and there was something else I hadn't expected—a touch
of sadness.

I could have taken her in my arms there and then. She
needed me, really needed me for some strange, dark reason of her own, but Aleko was watching us in the mirror
behind the bar, his face pale and tense. He knew then, I
realised that afterwards, but carried on fighting.

He smiled as our eyes met, passed Sara a tall glass and
produced a bottle of Jameson from under the bar. "I believe you prefer this brand, Mr. Savage?"

"You've been checking up on me," I said lightly.
"Why?"

"John Henry Savage," he said. "Born on a farm near
Sligo in 1927. Irish citizen. Joined the British Marine
Commandos in 1943 giving a false age. Promoted in the

field. Retired with the rank of captain in 1958. Lack of promotion due to Irish citizenship. A fair summary?"

He waited, the bottle in one hand, my glass in the other. "I could have saved you some time and told you that myself," I said.

"I'm sure you could. It is, of course, as false a picture as could have been presented and one you put about to suit your own purpose. Say when," he added pleasantly.

I raised a finger when the glass was half-full, aware that Sara Hamilton was watching gravely. I suddenly realised that whatever was coming, she knew about it.

"All right, I'll buy it."

Aleko was enjoying himself. He put the bottle away. "Would you like to know what it says on the confidential file of Captain John Henry Savage? What it really says?"

"Now that can't have come cheap," I said. "Admiralty clerks are a notoriously old-fashioned lot and a breach of security of that magnitude comes under the Official Secrets Act as I remember."

"You crossed the Rhine in 1945 about a week before anyone else. Underwater, of course. You were a sergeant then and that little exploit earned you the Distinguished Conduct Medal and promotion in the field to full lieutenant."

"Those were the days." I toasted him and took half the whiskey down in one go. I had an idea I was going to need it.

"Palestine, 1947. The Jews had a very efficient underwater sabotage unit."

"You don't need to rub it in. Some of them served with me during the war."

"You got a mention in dispatches for removing a couple of limpet mines from the keel of a destroyer in Jaffa harbour in the nick of time, as they say."

Had I done that? How old had I been? Twenty-one? No, that had been another Jack Savage entirely. An eager youngster with Irish mud still clinging to his boots, mad keen to astonish the wide world. And his information was incomplete, thank God. He'd missed the big one.

"More good work in Korea, the odd spell of security duty in Trucial Oman."

"The tribesmen were restless that year."

Sara choked on her drink and even Aleko smiled as if he meant it.

"Finally Cyprus. The D.S.O. in 1957. More underwater only this time the saboteurs were the E.O.K.A. variety." He produced the Jameson and topped up my glass. "And in 1958, you retired and went into the salvage game."

I turned to Sara. "So now you know. The mail got through. I was a hero."

"I never doubted it."

"A most promising officer with exceptional leadership qualities," Aleko put in. "That is a direct quote. Now why would anyone as highly thought of as that retire?"

I was suddenly tired of playing the game his way and showed it. "Why ask when you bloody well know?"

He put up a hand defensively. "All right, Mr. Savage, so you told a certain British general at a cocktail party in Nicosia who hails, I understand, from that part of Ireland which those who think like yourself still regard as disputed territory, that he was a blue-arsed baboon and not fit to be described as an Irishman. I believe you also added that you more than sympathised with the E.O.K.A. movement. Would that be a reasonably accurate description of what happened?"

"You've missed out the bit where I belted his aide on the jaw." I turned to Sara. "You should have been there. Saturday night at Cohan's Select Bar with the tables going one way and the glasses the other."

"Was it worth it?" she asked gravely.

"I thought so at the time. They didn't want a stink, of course. I was invited to resign quietly. Did you hear about poor Jack Savage? Been to the well too often, poor devil. Cracked up." I shrugged. "I got my gratuity anyway. Funny people you English. Always have to do the decent thing."

"Bred in the bone. It makes us feel superior."

I started to get up. "All right if I go now. It's been fun although I'm not sure who for."

"But we haven't mentioned your services to Greece, Mr. Savage."

So he knew after all and for that kind of information he would have needed to go right to the top.

"There's nothing about any service in Greece during the war on my records," I said carefully. "I know that for certain."

"I am speaking about after the war. May, 1946 to be precise, during the Greek Civil War. A Communist force was in possession of the old Turkish fort on the island of Pelos in the Gulf of Thermai. In other circumstances the Greek Navy would have blasted them out of the sea. In this case there was an added complication. A general named Tharakos who provided a more than adequate hostage. They threatened to hang him from the battlements if any move was made against them. All very mediaeval."

"It was a hell of a war," I said, remembering. "Things could be like that in those days."

"But Tharakos had the highest possible connections in the government and in any case, it would have been bad for morale if the Communists had been allowed to get away with it. And nobody wanted that, not even the British government." He smiled gently. "People knew which side they were on in those days."

"All right," I said. "So the Greek government asked for specialist help and got me and four Royal Marine Commandos. We landed on Pelos and got Tharakos out."

"A remarkable operation. Worth a Victoria Cross according to my information if it hadn't happened in someone else's war. Plus the fact that it had to remain top secret. I don't suppose the Russians would have been pleased."

"True enough," I said. "But don't let's exaggerate. It was the kind of small-scale, cutting-out operation the commandos handled all the time during the war. Nothing very special."

Nothing very special. Could I really dismiss it all as lightly as that, even after so many years? I sat there, trapped by memory, and stared blindly into the past.

CHAPTER VII

PASSAGE OF ARMS— MAY 1946

The old *caique* we were using had a diesel engine, but the captain, a Greek Navy lieutenant named Demos, was taking her in under sail. He'd spent the war working for the British in the Aegean with the Special Boat Service so there wasn't much he didn't know about landings at night on unfriendly shores.

The small cabin was hot and stifling. I'd slept, but not for long and when I woke, there was a dull, nagging pain at the back of my head that wouldn't go away. The smell of diesel oil was all pervading mixed in with fish and stale urine. An unhappy combination that came close to turning my stomach.

I wasn't in the right frame of mind for this business, that was the trouble. There had been a time when this kind of action by night was a whole way of life that one accepted because there was a war on and such things had to be done. But the war, in Europe at least, had been over for nearly a year. Certainly long enough for me to have got used to the idea that there was no longer the regular prospect that tomorrow might never arrive.

I swung my legs to the floor and sat there, head in hands. There was a knock at the door and Sergeant Johnson looked in. He wouldn't have gone down well at the depot in Pompey at all. He hadn't shaved for a week and was wearing an old cloth cap, the kind of patched, incredibly filthy suit that any self-respecting Irish tinker would have been ashamed to wear, and broken boots.

"Twenty minutes, sir. You asked me to call you."

Before I was commissioned we had served together as

sergeants, but these days he was very careful to preserve
the niceties of rank. Having said that, he knew me as
well as any man can hope to know another.

He said carefully, "Are you all right, sir?"

"Depends entirely on your point of view. I'm beginning
to wonder if it was wise of me to learn all that Greek.
Some other poor bastard would have been stuck with this
one if I hadn't. What about you?"

He shrugged. "It's what they pay me for."

Which was true enough and applied equally well to myself. For some unaccountable reason it made me feel
better. I got up and stretched.

"And the others?"

"Ready for anything. You know O'Brien. A fight a night
and twice on Saturdays. And young Dawson can't believe
his luck."

"I can remember when I couldn't believe mine," I told
him sourly, "but that was a long time ago."

The other three were waiting in the big cabin that
usually housed the crew. Like Johnson and myself, they
wore patched, shabby clothing and old boots. In other
words, the standing garb of the Greek peasant in the
poverty-stricken mountain area of the north.

O'Brien, a twice-a-day shaver, already sported a fair
beard and Forbes looked satisfactorily villainous. Young
Dawson was as clean as a whistle, mainly because there
was nothing he could put a razor to, so he'd had to make
do with a liberal application of dirt to the face.

He was the weak link in more ways than one. Still in
training when the war ended, he was certain he'd missed
out on life's greatest adventure, convinced as he was that
war was some sort of splendid game. In other circumstances I wouldn't have touched him with a bargepole,
but I'd needed a wireless operator and he was the best they
could do on such short notice.

They all stood up and I waved them down again.
"We've got about fifteen minutes so I'll make it brief. To
recap. Phase One of the operation, we go in by dinghy
to Thrassos Bay where we're met by a guide waiting to
take us to this farmer, Mikali. Phase Two, we arrive at

Mikali's place and sort out the situation with him. Phase Three, we get Tharakos out of the fort." *Good, positive thinking that.* "Phase Four, we get ourselves and Tharakos out by the same way we got in."

They knew it frontwards and backwards in detail, but there was no harm in rubbing it in.

"Any alternatives, sir, in case things go wrong?" Dawson asked.

And that question alone made me almost decide to leave him for intelligent improvisation was supposed to be one of the most important products of commando training.

"Alternatives are something we make up as we go along," I said, which wasn't entirely true, but was good enough for him.

Johnson did an equipment check. Each man carried a submachine gun, an automatic pistol and four grenades and Dawson had his radio transmitter in an old German military haversack, the sort of thing Greek partisans used all the time. And that was it, apart from individual emergency food packs.

I left them to it and went up on deck. It was the right kind of night for it. No moon and plenty of cloud so that even the stars only glowed intermittently. A couple of Greek Navy boys dressed like fishermen were inflating the dinghy and Demos was leaning out of the window of the wheelhouse, speaking to them softly.

"How does it look?" I asked.

"Oh, it's you." He shook his head. "Not good. Not good at all. There is a very strong current running into the bay here which is what we want, but tonight of all nights there has to be a snag. The wind has turned unexpectedly. An easterly, which means it's driving straight into the bay."

"A lee shore?" I said. "No good for a sail boat. You'd end up on the rocks."

"Exactly and if I use the engine they hear us come in."

"So what do we do?"

"We could always try another night."

I shook my head. "No good. The navy won't wait. The central government in Athens had a hell of a job stopping

them from blowing that fort off the top of the cliffs
before now. It's tonight or not at all."

He nodded. "All right, if you are willing to have a try,
then so am I. I'll take you into the bay making my run
from the southeast, but I'll have to turn to come out again
almost immediately which leaves you a quarter of a mile
to cover in the dinghy."

"We'll manage," I said.

He chuckled grimly. "Let's hope you can all swim."

It was a cheerful thought and I left him there and went
below to prepare them for the worst.

The *caique* was low in the waist which made disem-
barking simpler than it might otherwise have been, but it
was still a tricky business. The run-in to the bay wasn't
too bad although there was little doubt now that conditions
in the water were going to be worse than I had anticipated.

We were all waiting in the waist and the inflatable dinghy
was already over the side and held in close by the two
sailors. Each man carried his own gear and wore a lifejacket. The time to go was when Demos started to turn
away from land to commence his run out to sea again because it was then that the boat's speed would drop though
only for a minute or two.

Demos gave a sudden sharp whistle, the prow of the
caique started to turn into the wind and she shuddered
and heeled over, almost coming to a dead stop, the great
sail fluttering wildly.

Johnson needed no order. He went over the side briskly
followed by Forbes and O'Brien. Dawson snagged his
haversack on the rail and hung there for a couple of
violent moments, struggling desperately while Johnson
cursed him.

Already we had picked up speed. Soon it would be too
late. I lifted him over the rail bodily, dropped him into the
darkness and went after him. A second later and the
caique was a ghost ship fading into the night as silently
as it had come.

I'd made a mistake, I knew that as soon as I felt the
dinghy heel, water pouring over the gunnel. I adjusted

my weight and grabbed for a paddle, but the wind was
lifting the waves into whitecaps and it was impossible to
keep it from slopping in over the sides.

We were waist-deep in the stuff within seconds, but still
floating which was the main thing. I told them to paddle
like hell if they wanted to live, which sounds dramatic at a
distance of years, but was a reasonably accurate state-
ment in view of what happened.

We moved in fast which didn't surprise me as Demos
had warned of a five- or six-knot current and the land was
plain to see now, partly because the low cloud seemed to
have moved away, but mainly owing to the surf white
in the darkness as it pounded in across the beach at the
bottom of the cliffs.

We were moving faster now, the waves dipping in great
shallow runs like a moorland burn in spate the morning
after heavy rain and we were caught in a current of such
strength that there was nothing to be done except try to
keep floating and hang on.

The sea filled the night with its roaring, the waves
pounded in across the rocks, tearing the shingle from the
beach with a great, angry sucking and the surface of the
water trembled and shook, a hundred different cross-cur-
rents pulling every which way, spinning the dinghy round
and round so that we lost control altogether.

A long comber rolled in out of the darkness, a six-
footer with a white, curling head on it that would have
warmed the heart of any surf-rider. It was exactly what
we didn't need at this stage. The dinghy shook violently
and Forbes went backwards over the stern. O'Brien
reached for him desperately and managed to catch him by
the top of his lifejacket. Better for him if he had missed,
for a second later, the dinghy bucked violently to one side
and Forbes was swept into the darkness pulling O'Brien
in after him.

The current had us then and took us into the final line
of breakers at a frightening speed. A great wave swept
under, rolling in to dissolve into a cauldron of froth and
white spray that boiled for about fifty yards between us
and the shore. Another wave took us in so fast that we
were suddenly halfway across. For a moment, I thought

we might make it and then a giant hand simply tipped us over.

My feet touched bottom at once for it was no more than five or six feet deep. I was aware of the dinghy spinning beside me upside down, reached out blindly and grabbed hold of one of the handlines. There was no sign of Johnson or Dawson and in any event, it was all I could do to help myself.

The world had turned upside down, darkness and spray, no clear way to go and I floundered there in bad trouble for a moment and then a light flashed briefly three times. I thought it my imagination until it came again. I kicked out desperately, in three feet of water.

The sea poured in again, a great final wave that seemed determined to have me back, but I hung on, clawing into the shingle with my right hand for all I was worth. And as it flooded back again, someone grabbed me under the arm and pulled me to my feet. We splashed forward into the darkness and then my feet stumbled in soft, dry sand and I fell on to my hands and knees and vomited what felt like half the Aegean.

The sea was in my head, my heart, my brain, its roaring filled the night. I took a deep, deep breath and it stopped and then a dim light dazzled my eyes. I blinked a couple of times to get things into focus and a woman's face loomed out of the darkness. Great flat cheekbones, slanting eyes, wide nostrils, a mouth that was far too big. She was almost a Tartar. Pure peasant. The most beautifully ugly woman I have ever known.

"You are all right now?" Her voice was low and rough in the way you get in the mountains of the north.

"I'll do," I said. "But who in the hell might you be? I was expecting to be met by Mikali—John Mikali."

"He was killed yesterday at the fort," she said calmly. "One of the guards shot him by mistake. I am his daughter Anna."

"And you know what all this is about? You'll help us?"

"I know what is to be done," she said, "and I will do it. For my father's sake I will do it."

I crouched there, trying to make some sense of it all,

aware of the stale, unwashed smell of her, pungent on the clean salt air and then Sergeant Johnson and Dawson staggered out of the surf hanging on to each other for dear life and collapsed beside me.

Both of them had lost everything in the surf. Radio, submachine guns, even their supply packs which left them with only a commando knife apiece and the .38 Smith & Wesson automatics we each carried in a shoulder holster. I still had my submachine gun and haversack slung round my neck. I gave them a couple of grenades each and we split into two groups and spent a fruitless half-hour searching for Forbes and O'Brien. It was a hopeless task, so dark that you could hardly see your hands in front of your face and the surf seemed to be getting worse all the time.

So, now there were three of us which raised all kinds of new problems, but they would have to wait. The girl indicated a shallow cave where we left the dinghy ready inflated against a quick departure and we moved out, following her across the beach to climb the cliffs by means of a track so narrow and crumbling that it was probably best for all concerned that we had to manage in almost total darkness.

Once out of the bay with its enclosing cliffs, things improved considerably. The low cloud had cleared and the dark night sky was a blaze of stars. The girl didn't hesitate and started to lead the way across a plateau of short close-cropped grass without the slightest sign of caution.

There was a movement in the bushes ahead of us. I swung, crouching, the submachine gun ready. There was the dull clanking of one of those home-made bells that peasants make to hang around the necks of their animals. A goat brushed past me, the stink of it tainting the air.

"It is nothing," she said calmly. "They wander at will."

"What about patrols?"

"They stay in the fort," she said. "They don't like it out here at night. This is a bad place. There was a city here in ancient times. They say the cliffs crumbled beneath it and the sea swallowed every trace of it in a single night."

Which was a hell of a thought. Forty or fifty good men

and I could have taken the whole damned island. So much
for Greek military intelligence.

"It is not far now," she said. "Half a mile, no more."

She carried on, leading the way across the plateau and
we climbed a boulder-strewn hillside. Not another word
was spoken for the next fifteen minutes and quite suddenly, we came over the shoulder of the mountain and saw
a house in a grove of olive trees below.

A dog barked hollowly in the far distance. The girl said,
"I will go down alone, just to make sure. Sometimes I
have visitors. Men from the fort."

"Is it likely?" I said. "Do they come often?"

"As often as they feel the need," she said gravely. "I
am the only woman on the island."

Which was honest enough, however hard to take, but
when she was out of earshot, I whispered to Johnson, "I'm
going after her. If anything goes wrong, get the hell out
of it."

He didn't argue and I went down the hillside. The house
was small and obviously very old and the yard between
the back door and the barn was cobbled, the heavy smell
of manure everywhere. I crouched beside a small haystack
and waited.

There was a slight, eerie creaking as the barn door eased
open and someone said softly in Greek, "The gun—on
the ground, quickly now."

I laid the submachine gun down carefully and stood up.
The muzzle of a rifle prodded me in the back. It was all I
needed. I swung to the left which meant that the muzzle
of that gun now pointed into thin air, kicked him under
the knee-cap and had him face down in the dirt in a
second.

The door opened, light flooded out, picking us from the
darkness and I saw that my antagonist was not much
more than a boy. Perhaps seventeen or eighteen, with a
thin, earnest face and a mass of curling black hair. He
turned his head awkwardly to glance over his shoulder.

"Anna!" he cried desperately. "It's me, Spiro!"

She touched me briefly on the shoulder. "It's all right.
Let him go."

"Who is he?"

"One of them," she said. "A Red, but he loves me. He'll do anything for me." She gave a short, contemptuous laugh. "Men. Always the same, like children who can never have enough sweets."

The plan of the fort Greek military intelligence had given me, the only one they could find, was about fifty years out of date and Spiro soon put me right on a few things.

"The walls are mostly in ruins," he said. "Especially on the land side and there is no gate any more. Just the open archway."

"What about sentries?"

"There is someone on the gate at all times. Usually just one man. Most of the building itself is not habitable. They keep Tharakos in the central tower on the first floor."

"Have you seen him lately?"

"Every day. They take him out on the ramparts, just to show he's still alive in case they're watching from the ships. Mind you, I've never been very close to him. I'm not important enough. The officers see to him."

"And what about guards in this tower?"

"There's usually someone on his door at all times. They've turned an old cell next to the entrance on the ground floor into a guardroom."

"Why do you say usually? Are there times when there isn't a guard up there?"

"You know how it is?" He shrugged. "Tharakos is locked in and his window is only one of those old arrow slits. How can he go anywhere? We aren't like the national army. Sometimes men want to please themselves. Stay down in the guardroom and play cards and so on."

I had another look at the map and thought about it all. Sergeant Johnson said, "It doesn't look too difficult, sir."

"That's what we thought about landing from the *caique* in the planning stage."

I didn't get a chance to take the argument any further because there was the sound of an engine out there in the darkness. Johnson was already at the window, peering through the curtain.

"Some sort of truck," he said. "Coming down the track

now." He turned to Anna. "Looks as if you're going to have company."

Young Dawson already had had his automatic out, his face pale and tense. I grabbed him by the arm and shook him roughly. "Put that away. So we shoot them from cover and what good does that do? They go missing and our friends out at the fort start turning the island upside down."

"The loft," Anna said. "You will be safe up there."

There was a ladder in one corner leading up to a trapdoor. Spiro went up quickly, shoving the trap back and Johnson and Dawson went after him.

As I put my foot on the first rung, the girl placed a hand on my arm. Funny, but somehow that smell didn't seem anything like as unpleasant, the face not ugly, but strong and full of character.

"I will get rid of them as soon as I can."

"They might want to stay," I said.

She shook her head. "They never stay long. What they want, they take very quickly."

A hell of a time for this kind of discussion, but I had to say it. "And this doesn't bother you?"

"It has been a long time. It doesn't really happen any more. Not to me. You understand this?" She smiled briefly, but sadly. "One thing life has taught me above all others is that one can get used to anything."

Spiro jammed the trapdoor open slightly with a piece of wood making it possible to see a little of the room below, mainly the table and the area around it.

There was laughter, the door banged and three men moved into view. Two of them were dressed in the usual shabby peasant clothes, bandoliers at the waist, machine pistols hanging from their shoulders. The third wore an old khaki uniform which in spite of its filthy condition still managed to give him a certain military air when combined with the peak cap on which he wore a red star.

"Major Ampoulides," Spiro whispered. "He is in charge at the fort this week."

What happened then, took place with extraordinary

rapidity as violent events often do in life. There was hardly even time to think.

Ampoulides simply grabbed Anna Mikali the moment he came in and kissed her. Then he laid her across the table and lifted up her dress. He was between her legs before any of us realised what was happening.

It wasn't even particularly brutal, that was the terrible thing although it was rape of a kind, no matter how much that wretched girl had come to accept it as a fact of life. It was animal-like, something out of the cow byre, but there was still the girl to consider, gazing blindly past his shoulder, beyond him, beyond any of us, trying to pretend that this wasn't happening to her.

A sob rose in Spiro's throat, he had the trapdoor back with a crash and dropped through. Which left me with no choice, but to go after him. I landed badly and rolled for the wall. Spiro had Ampoulides by the tunic and went over backwards, tearing him away from the girl. She pulled down her dress and started to get up.

And then all hell broke out as one of the other two men cut loose with his machine pistol, firing from the waist, trying to catch me as I rolled against the wall. He was too high, way too high, but not for Sergeant Johnson who dropped right into the line of fire. As he fell to the floor, the girl was knocked off the table by a burst in the chest and fetched up against me.

Her eyes rolled up in a kind of surprise and she died as calmly as she had lived. I shoved her away and fired one-handed from the floor, sending the man who'd done all the execution back into the far wall.

The third man was having trouble with the sling of his machine pistol which had caught in a tear in the shoulder of his old jacket. On such small turns can a man's life go one way instead of another. He died struggling, for young Dawson leaned out through the trapdoor and shot him in the head at close range with his automatic pistol.

Ten, perhaps twenty seconds was all it had taken to turn the world into a bloody shambles. As I got to my feet, Spiro and Ampoulides rolled against the door struggling violently. Ampoulides ended on top, his hands wrapped

round the boy's throat, but a kick in the side of the head
soon took care of him.

Johnson was still alive, but not for long as far as I
could judge. His left arm was badly shattered and he'd
taken at least two bullets through the chest. He was in
deep shock, eyes glazed, quite unable to communicate. I
did what I could for him, binding him up with two or three
field dressings and gave him a morphine shot.

The girl was beyond anyone's help and I told Dawson
to get a blanket to cover her with. Poor lad, he'd aged
ten years in as many minutes. Forbes and O'Brien and now
this. I wondered just how much more he would be able to
take. This was make-or-break time with a vengeance.

Spiro had taken a pretty hard knock on the head and
blood oozed from a gash above his left temple. He appeared to be dazed and very badly shocked and dropped
to his knees beside the girl, pulling the blanket down from
her face.

He crouched there looking at her as if not really taking
in what had happened and I examined the two dead men.
We were certainly well fixed for arms again now for both
of them had been carrying a Schmeisser submachine gun,
presumably picked up during the war after some German
column or other had been ambushed.

I put them on the table and Major Ampoulides groaned
and tried to sit up. Spiro's head turned and suddenly, the
face, the eyes, were filled with what I can only describe
as burning hate.

"Bastard! Filthy scum!"

He pulled a knife from his belt and jumped up and it
was Dawson who got in the way first, his Smith & Wesson
surprisingly steady as he pointed it right between Spiro's
eyes.

"None of that, now." He turned to me. "I presume you
want Ampoulides in one piece, sir?"

"You presume right." I moved to join him and said to
Spiro, "I'm sorry. I know how you must feel, but I've got
a job to do and it looks as if Ampoulides could be helpful
so I don't want any rash moves from you. Understand?"

There was agony on his face. "He killed Anna."

"The war killed Anna," I said bluntly. "Now, are you going to help us get Tharakos out of there, or aren't you?"

He passed a hand wearily across his eyes. "It was what Anna wanted."

I patted him on the shoulder and gave him a cigarette, then turned and walked across to Ampoulides who was sitting up now, his back against the wall. His eyes were watchful and wary, no fear there at all.

I squatted beside him. "You are alive, your friends are dead. You wish this happy state of affairs to continue?"

"What do I have to do?"

"I want Tharakos. Out of the fort, alive and well."

"You must be crazy."

"I don't see why. We drive in through the gate in your truck. We get him out of his cell with your assistance and come out in the truck again. Five minutes at the most."

"And what happens to me then? Face-down in a ditch with a bullet in the heart."

"You'll have to take your chances on that one," I said. "But for what it's worth, I give you my word you'll survive."

"Your word." His tone of voice indicated the extent of his recovery.

"I could always turn Spiro loose on you," I pointed out.

Ampoulides turned and met Spiro's burning eyes briefly. He looked back at me hurriedly. "Okay," he said. "I'll do whatever you want."

Whatever happened next had to take place that night because it would only be a matter of hours before Ampoulides and his men were missed. Under the circumstances, it seemed sensible to strike while the iron was hot and I decided that three o'clock in the morning was as good a time as any to go in. Even the card players should be asleep by then.

The truck was an old three-tonner, a British army Bedford. Spiro did the driving and I sat next to him and poked the muzzle of my submachine gun into the major's side. Dawson lurked in the shadows at the rear with one of the Schmeissers.

The road up to the fort was very rough, more a track than anything else, and had obviously deteriorated considerably over the years. The final quarter of a mile crossed a flat, boulder-strewn plain that sloped up to meet the edge of the high cliffs at that end of the island. It was certainly a hell of a good site for a fort strategically speaking, or must have been in the old days when the Turks ruled this part of the Mediterranean.

A hurricane lamp hung from a hook at the main gate and beneath it, a sentry, if that was what he was supposed to be, squatted against the wall, a rifle across his knees, and slept.

As we slowed to negotiate the gate, he came to life and staggered to his feet. I nudged Ampoulides in the side and he leaned out of the cab for his face to be seen.

It was enough. The sentry called something and waved and Spiro drove across the dark fort towards the door at the bottom of the tower over which another hurricane lamp hung. He turned the Bedford back towards the gate, ready for a quick exit, braked to a halt and left the engine running.

We'd been through what was to happen, in theory at least, half a dozen times, but I still had my doubts about Ampoulides.

I said, "If there's a sentry up there, you'd better make it good for all our sakes. If anything goes wrong, you'll be the first to go. I'm warning you."

Perhaps it was a miscalculation, the final straw that pushed him towards the course of action he chose, although I suspect that he expected a bullet in the head whatever happened for that is exactly what he would have given me.

In any event, we moved towards the door, myself on one side of him and Dawson on the other and Spiro waited by the truck. I opened the door gently and light drifted into the dark passage from the hurricane lamp.

It was as quiet as the grave. Dawson slipped inside and flattened himself against the wall, his Schmeisser covering the door to the guardroom on the left.

The flight of stone steps opposite was wider than I had

expected and turned to the right some way up, light flickering on the rough wall, presumably from another lamp on the landing outside the general's cell.

I said to Ampoulides in a whisper, "All right, up we go."

He took a slight, hesitant step forward, spun round and jumped out through the door and ran for it. He didn't stand a chance for Spiro had been waiting, probably hoping he would do exactly that. There are twenty-eight rounds in a Schmeisser's detachable magazine and I think Spiro must have pumped the lot into Ampoulides, driving him back towards the entrance with terrible force.

There was a sudden shout inside the guardroom, a chair went over with a crash.

"They're all yours," I said to Dawson. "I'll get Tharakos."

I went up the steps on the run and reached the corner at the same moment a burly peasant appeared on the way down. He lurched into me with a cry of dismay, an old Lee Enfield rifle clutched to his chest and I rammed the muzzle of my Thompson into his belly and blew him away from me with a short burst.

The door opened in the passage below and whoever emerged walked straight into a burst of fire from Dawson's Schmeisser. I kept on going round the turn in the staircase and found myself on a small stone landing.

There was a battered oak door opposite, heavily strengthened with bands of iron. In the light of the hurricane lantern hanging from a hook in the wall, I saw that it was held in place by two great iron bolts. I eased them back quickly and kicked the door open.

There was heavy firing downstairs now, but up there, it was calm and still and nothing moved in the darkness of the cell. I took down the hurricane lamp and stepped inside.

"General Tharakos? I've come to get you out."

He emerged from the darkness like some pale despairing ghost, a man whom I knew to be forty-nine years of age and who looked seventy. He shambled forward, reached out and clutched at the front of my coat.

"Are you all right? Can you walk?" I said.

He moaned horribly, tightening his grip on my jacket, then opened his mouth and pointed inside.

The bastards had cut out his tongue.

As I got him to the turn of the staircase, there was what seemed like a considerable explosion and the whole damned tower seemed to shake, dust rising everywhere in clouds. It was Dawson who, as I learned later, had thrown two grenades in through the door of the guardroom one after the other to finish the business off.

He rose to meet me as I came down the stairs, supporting Tharakos with one hand. Dawson grabbed him by the other arm and we stumbled to the door.

Spiro was waiting at the tail of the Bedford, his Schmeisser ready. "Get behind the wheel. Let's get out of here," I said and Dawson and I heaved the general up and over the tailboard and dumped him inside.

Dawson climbed over after him and Spiro slung his Schmeisser over his shoulder and ran to the cab of the Bedford. I was no more than a couple of yards away as he started to climb up behind the wheel. He never made it because a single, well-placed rifle shot drilled into the base of his skull, killing him instantly.

I loosed off a great rolling burst into the shadows on the far side of the square from where that shot had come, pulled Spiro's body back out of the cab and scrambled up behind the wheel.

As we started to roll, the shooting increased considerably, lights flashing on and off in the darkness like some macabre firework display. Bullets thudded into the bodywork of the Bedford, ripped through the canvas, for we presented a target as big as the proverbial barn door.

The arched gateway loomed out of the night and the sentry appeared dead in the centre, rifle levelled. I put down my head and increased speed. The windscreen shattered, showering me with glass, there was a sudden jolt, a desperate cry and we were through and darkness was our friend.

We were about a quarter of a mile from the farm when the engine coughed asthmatically and died on me. I could smell the petrol as soon as I jumped down and went to the rear.

Dawson dropped the tailgate. "I thought she caught a few down there," he said. "What happens now?"

"We walk," I said. "Run if possible. If those characters back there get their hands on you, they'll roast you alive."

"I can believe anything after tonight," he said. "But I'd say we'll be lucky if we get the general to move more than a hundred yards under his own steam, sir. I don't know what they did to him back there, but it must have been bad."

"They cut out his tongue for a start," I said. "And I hope that pleasant item of news puts an edge on you."

And it did, for he responded magnificently to the challenge of the hour that followed. He had been absolutely right about the general. He was virtually a dead-weight and after the first few yards, we had to carry him between us. When that didn't prove any more satisfactory, we took turns at carrying him on our backs, moving at a steady jog-trot all the time.

I had never felt so grateful for the extreme physical fitness that was a product of commando training and yet, when I turned into the farmyard, Tharakos across my shoulders apparently unconscious, I felt almost at the point of collapse.

I laid him down none too gently and said to Dawson, "A cart—any kind of handcart. There must be one round here somewhere. I'll see to Johnson."

The room, when I lit the lamp, was exactly as I had left it. A bloody shambles, the smell of death everywhere, and it had touched Johnson also with its dark hand, for when I dropped to examine him, I saw at once that he had been dead for an hour at least, his face already cold.

The door swung open with a crash and Dawson appeared. "I've found a cart, sir and there's somebody coming. I heard voices down the track."

"Get Tharakos on the cart and move out," I said, I'll catch up with you."

He appeared to hesitate. "Sergeant Johnson, sir, we're leaving him?"

"I'll see to Sergeant Johnson. Now get to hell out of here."

There was lamp oil in a five gallon drum in the back room and I emptied it across the floor, the bodies themselves. It was Johnson I was thinking of. We'd soldiered together for a long time now and I owed him something, one Marine to another. I couldn't take him with me, but I was damned if I was going to leave him to the bunch who were on their way here looking for us.

When I tossed the lighted lamp into the room from the doorway, it exploded like a bomb and I turned and ran across the yard and followed Dawson along the narrow track. I caught up with him within a few yards and took one handle of the cart and we put our backs to it.

When we reached the shoulder of the mountain, we paused to look back. The farm was burning well now, a beacon in the night and I wondered what they were thinking on the bridges of those ships out there. I could see figures, a dozen, possibly more, black against the flames, but no one saw us, or at least there was no shooting.

"A Viking's funeral," Dawson said softly.

"Something like that. Now let's get out of here."

The rest was mainly anti-climax. We pushed the cart to the edge of the cliffs above Thrassos Bay and got General Tharakos down to the beach between us, although it was a hell of a struggle and he remained unconscious for most of the time.

The sea was calmer now which helped when we put out in the dinghy, for the paddles had been lost in the upset on the way in and we had to make do with our hands and a piece of driftwood Dawson found on the shoreline.

We were sighted by an M.T.B. which picked us up just after dawn and radioed the news at once to the destroyer that the admiral in charge of the task force was using as his flagship. They also reported on the general's condition which explained what started to happen within a matter of minutes.

I went out on deck and found young Dawson standing at the rail in a duffle coat someone had loaned him.

"How are you doing?" I said.

"All in a day's work, sir."

I suppose he thought I expected that kind of remark. In any case, he tried to smile and started to cry helplessly instead. I put an arm around his shoulders and we stood there together at the rail. The destroyers of the task force, line astern, opened up with their big guns and started to blow the island of Pelos out of existence.

CHAPTER VIII

A KNIFE IN THE HEART

Dicky Dawson. Sergeant Major Richard Emmet Dawson, D.C.M., shot in the back by an E.O.K.A. gunman while shopping with his wife in Nicosia, January 1956.

Instantaneous recall is the psychologist's term for it, just like the events of a lifetime flitting through a drowning man's mind in a matter of seconds. It took something of an effort to bring me back to reality. To the present that was the sumptuous lounge of the *Firebird*. To Sara Hamilton and Aleko.

I turned to her and said, "All right, I'll buy it. What's it all about?"

"He'd like you to do a repeat performance. For money this time."

"Twenty-five thousand dollars, Captain Savage," Aleko said calmly. "Paid into a Geneva account."

It was beginning to take on all the qualities of a privileged nightmare. He produced the Jameson, one eyebrow raised, and I pushed my glass across.

"I think I'd better," I said.

"May I start by asking what your attitude is towards the present regime in Greece, Captain Savage?"

It was captain all the way now. We had moved to a room next to the saloon that he obviously used for business judging by the Queen Anne desk and the filing cabinet and telephone.

"I don't have one," I said. "Politics don't interest me. I've had a bellyful or hadn't you noticed? So you've got a military junta running things and they don't like the mini skirt. I've been in worse places than Greece, believe me."

"Political prisoners by the thousand, the educational system used as a weapon to indoctrinate children, the Left almost stamped out of existence. Come now, Captain Savage, does this sound like the home of democracy?"

"Nothing is ever that simple," I said. "I was here during the civil war, remember. The worst things I've seen anywhere in war I saw in Macedonia when I was with our military mission. I've seen whole villages wiped out by the Communists—women, children, even the bloody animals. People don't forget that kind of thing."

"So, you are a fascist by persuasion?"

Which was such a stupid remark that it was hardly worth answering, but I tried.

"I'm John Henry Savage—me, no one else," I said. "I don't take sides."

And as always with him, he did the unexpected. He smiled, looking extremely satisfied. "Excellent, Captain Savage, a first-rate mercenary who knows what he's about is worth ten idealists any day of the week."

Sara sprawled in the big leather chair in the corner, legs outstretched, head back. She was smoking, eyes closed, as relaxed as a black cat and yet alert to everything that was said. Her eyes gleamed for a moment beneath the dark lashes, an unspoken communication. When I turned, Aleko was watching me, that strange, set look on his face.

"I don't think I've met a revolutionary millionaire before," I said. "Who are you working for? The D.D.?"

"The Democratic Defence are not having a great deal of success," he said, "and the Patriotic Front aren't doing too well either. No, I represent a rather more powerful organisation. Many are men like myself. Their names would surprise you. Industrialists, shipping magnates, politicians, artists. Men who are leaders in various walks of life. All brought together in the common cause. The fight for democracy in my unhappy country."

Words, empty words mouthed by fanatics on both sides while the ordinary people in the middle got squeezed.

"An interesting list," I said. "Greek military intelligence would give a lot to get hold of it, if it existed."

He straightened in his chair, his face suddenly rather

pale. "But it does, Captain Savage, which is the purpose of the exercise, as they say."

And now it *was* getting interesting. There was a large map of the Eastern Mediterranean on the wall behind him. He stood up and turned to it.

"About four weeks ago there was a meeting of certain interested parties at a village near Pilos in the Peloponnese. As a result of that meeting, a list of over two hundred prominent men hostile to the present regime was compiled. A list which the headquarters of the organisation, which operates from Crete, needed badly if they were to be able to plan the overthrow of the present government with any certainty. The list was entrusted to a special courier, a man named Apostolidis, who carried it in a briefcase chained to his wrist. He was flown out by night from a private airstrip near Pilos. The plane was a Piper Aztec and the pilot, a young man named Andreas Paylo."

"The briefcase doesn't sound much of an idea to me," I said. "I'd have thought they could have done better than that."

"An explosive device in the lock ensured its destruction if the wrong person attempted to open it."

"Along with Apostolidis?"

"He was what one would term a dedicated revolutionary."

"I see. So he didn't make it?"

"Unfortunately the Aztec had engine trouble in a heavy rainstorm somewhere off the coast of Crete. It seems that Apostolidis was either killed or knocked unconscious in the crash. In any event the plane sank almost immediately and he was still inside the cabin. Pavlo only just managed to get out himself."

"Then what happened?"

"He drifted round in a dinghy for a couple of days which didn't help his general condition. He was finally picked up by a fishing boat which took him into the nearest island at once. He was delirious and apparently dying."

"Which brought the police into it?"

"Unfortunately for Pavlo there isn't a police station in

Greece which doesn't have a poster on him. They've been snapping at his heels for a year or more now."

"And down came the bright boys from Athens in a hurry? Where is he now?"

"They took him to the political prison on Sinos. There is a small hospital there."

"And do they know what he was up to? About Apostolidis down there in the Aztec off Crete somewhere with that briefcase chained to his wrist?"

"Not yet." He shook his head. "That will come later when they start to squeeze him. I understand it was touch and go for a while. He almost died on them. A broken arm, smashed ribs, a punctured lung."

I nodded slowly, thinking about it all very carefully. "One thing I really don't understand. How did you manage to find out in such detail what happened when the plane went down?"

He smiled gently. "That mate of the fishing boat that picked him up after his two days in that dinghy. Pavlo had said a great deal in his delirium in the man's hearing —things which he had kept to himself."

"Why?"

"Partly out of fear, I suppose. Like most ordinary people he just didn't want to be involved in this kind of thing."

"And you persuaded him to change his mind?"

"For a consideration."

"And now you want me to get Pavlo out?"

He nodded eagerly. " I have certain contacts on Sinos. Naturally, I can't disclose who they are even to you, but it means that I can furnish any necessary information. I have maps, plans. I can show you exactly where Pavlo is, who is guarding him."

He opened a door in his desk and started to take out a rolled-up map. I said, "Don't bother, I don't want to see it."

There was genuine shock on his face as if he realised at once that I really meant it and his American accent slipped a little, the Greek peasant poking through.

"But compared to the Pelos affair this would be a picnic."

"You're a businessman, Aleko," I said. "And unless I miss my guess, you got where you are today by following one golden rule. Buy cheap, sell dear. If you're willing to offer me twenty-five thousand dollars to go in after Pavlo, then it's worth a lot more than that and if it is, then it's too damned hot for me."

He leaned across, hands flat on his desk, frowning at me. "All right, I'll make it thirty thousand."

"Apparently you didn't get the message," I said. "I'm just not interested. I've got my health and the boat. That's a whole lot better than being dead."

He gave a sudden, sharp laugh as if making a discovery. "By God, I see it now, Savage. You've lost your nerve."

"That's it exactly," I said cheerfully. "Frightened to death."

Sara stood up and yawned. "You know there are times when you're four different kinds of a fool, Dimitri. Now can we eat, please?"

"Not me," I said. "I've suddenly lost my appetite for the finer things."

"All right," she said. "Give me five minutes to change and I'll meet you on deck. You can show me the sights."

She went out quickly and Aleko stood glaring at me, his face whiter than ever, a muscle working in his right cheek. I wondered for a moment whether he intended taking a swing at me, an unhealthy prospect when you considered the sheer size of the man. I turned and started into the saloon. He called my name and appeared in the doorway behind me when I was halfway across the floor.

"You're wasting your time, Savage. She isn't for you."

I turned to face him. "Your opinion, not hers."

I started to turn away again. He said, "She's dying on her feet, Savage. A little bit more each day."

"Aren't we all?"

I tried to sound flippant, but the coldness was there in my belly and my heart began to pound and it was going to happen, whether I liked it or not, whatever it was he was going to tell me, the thing that would explain so much that had bothered me about her.

"Chronic leukaemia," he said and there was a vindictiveness in his voice as if he must hurt, had to cut through at all costs. "Does that satisfy you?"

I struck out like a child does in anger and frustration at the nearest thing. My fist grazed his right cheek, he staggered back against the bar and stayed there, staring at me wildly, making no attempt to return the blow. I turned and walked out.

It was out of this world down there on the beach as darkness fell, a full moon lighting the sky, more stars scattered across it than I had ever seen before. A night when it was good to be alive.

The very thought was a knife in the heart and I glanced at her briefly. She had changed into a linen skirt and white sweater and had tied her hair back with a ribbon. It was the first time I'd seen her really look her age and suddenly, the whole thing, the sheer blind pity of it, swelled up inside, threatening to choke me.

I lit a cigarette hurriedly, offered her one as an afterthought. She refused and we moved on past the boats, leaving the harbour behind, following the white strip of sand leading towards the cliffs.

"You still haven't told me your interest in all that back there," I said. "Or are you simply trying to be a latter-day Lord Byron?"

She shook her head. "Dimitri took me into his confidence, that's all. I've known what he was up to for some time now. All this political nonsense of his. He wanted my opinion about you—about how I thought you'd react to his offer."

"Did you tell him?"

"Pretty accurately." She laughed. "I didn't think you'd be hungry enough and I was right."

"So you don't think I'm just too scared?"

"You'd be a fool if you weren't. Like you said, you've got your health and the boat and that's a whole lot better than being dead."

"He'll hang himself," I said. "You know that, don't you? Sooner or later they'll catch up with him."

"I know and I sometimes think he does. God knows why he's doing it. Something that happened in his youth,

I think. He lived in a village in the Peloponnese in the mountains. His mother and father and two sisters died in the fighting when the soldiers came. He won't talk about it, but he has this thing about the military."

She was surprisingly cheerful and took off her sandals to walk in the shallows. "But you—you surprise, me, Jack Savage. Whoever heard of an Irishman who wasn't interested in politics."

"They killed my father," I said. "He lived and breathed for Ireland. When he was sixteen he was out in the Easter Rising. Three years later he was carrying a gun for Michael Collins. By the time he was twenty-one he'd lost count of the men he'd killed and all for the Cause. Always the Cause."

"How did he die?"

"He was a Republican to the last. Fought for the I.R.A. in the Civil War after your lot were kicked out. Refused to surrender even when De Valera called it a day. He spent his whole life on the run one way or another. They caught him at my mother's place. She had this farm near Sligo that her uncle left her. The officers in charge of the soldiers were all men who'd fought alongside him over the years."

"And they killed him?"

"He wouldn't stay inside because of my mother and the children. I was a babe in arms at the time. Anyway out he went, a gun in each hand, shouting 'Up the Republic'. They wanted to take him alive. There were young men there to whom he'd been a name over the years, a legend, but he was too good with a gun thanks to Mick Collins. Shot two of them stone dead so they emptied a Lewis gun into him."

"And that put you off politics?"

"At a very early age. Oh, I was raised on the hero bit. We had his photo on the mantel with a rosary hanging from the frame and a candle always on the go. My mother never let that candle out. She loved him till the day she died. Poor lass, she had a hard time finding it in her heart to forgive me for joining the bloody British Army."

"But she did?"

"In the end." I hesitated, aware of something that had

to be said. "It isn't that I hate him or the memory of him and the things he did. A man has to do what is right for him, I know that. It's just that I think we needed him a damned sight more than that God-almighty Cause of his."

She reached up to touch my face. "Poor Savage, you love him like hell, always have done and it hurts to admit it."

And that was the plain truth of it. "Something like that," I said.

"No more sad songs now. It's too beautiful. Far too beautiful."

We were almost at the cliffs now, the boats far behind us. The night was warm, the slight breeze perfumed. She paused, her hip touching me, and I put an arm about her waist. She looked up and I kissed her gently.

She pulled away and turned in a circle, arms outstretched. "Oh, but I feel good. I feel alive. A hundred per cent alive."

She stood there, hands on hips, smiling at me. "You know what we're going to do? We're going to celebrate being alive. We're going to go for a swim and then I'm going to let you make long and very slow love to me."

Her hands were already at the zip on the side of her skirt. As she stepped out of it, I said quickly, "I don't think you should, Sara. It's damned cold out there when the heat of the day has gone. It wouldn't be good for you."

She went very, very still, standing there in the moonlight, the skirt in her left hand.

"You know," she whispered. "You know. But how?"

"Aleko," I said.

The language that erupted in one vicious deadly stream was as bad as I'd ever heard in any barrack room or waterfront saloon. She stepped into the skirt and zipped it up quickly.

"Listen to me, Sara." I reached for her. "Just for a minute."

She sent me back with a stiff right arm. "Not pity, Savage. Do you really want to know what I was after? You, all the way, and you wanting me. To be possessed, to feel you inside me, one inside of two, something warm against the darkness. And you didn't even need to love me.

I could have taken that as long as the part of me you did want, you wanted honestly and truly. But not now—now, it's all spoiled. Now, I could never be sure it wasn't out of pity and I've too much pride for that."

She turned, then, running through the moonlight, and disappeared into the shadows. I didn't go after her.

If Aleko had been there or anywhere within striking distance, I think I'd have taken a knife to him, so great was the anger I experienced after she had gone. Anger at the world, at life and the sheer, senseless cruelty of it, but most of all, anger at Aleko. It was as if he was somehow responsible, which was absurd for it was better to know, whatever Sara thought. Better for her—better for me.

But now more than anything, I needed a drink and I walked back along the beach towards the harbour. Someone had lit a fire of driftwood beside the boats. They were cooking lobster from the smell of things. There was laughter, a young girl of sixteen or seventeen ran past me, a boy of around the same age hot in pursuit.

They didn't notice me, a shadow in the darkness, and I stood there for a moment watching the group at the fire, feeling completely apart and outside of things and lonely.

And then I thought of her and realised, quite suddenly, that this was how Sara must have felt. With people, yet apart from them, branded clean to the bone with no possibility of escape. Alone—really alone.

I hadn't cried since I was a boy in short pants. My grandfather's funeral. Rooks lifting out of the trees like black rag bundles, calling to each other through the heavy rain. Father Fallon's clear gentle voice, the rattle of the soil that we threw in one after the other.

A long time ago. Strange, but the same lump the size of my fist threatened to choke me now and my eyes were stinging. There was the Celt in me if you like and I turned and stumbled away through the darkness.

I could hear the *bouzoukis,* plaintive in the night as I turned on to the waterfront and approached Yanni's. The door was wide, light flooded out across the tables on the front terrace and most of them were occupied.

Inside, it was at first sight a typical waterfront *taverna* with stone floor, whitewashed walls, beamed ceiling and the food being cooked on the spot in copper pans over charcoal in a kitchen area on the left. The resemblance ended there as the prices indicated.

It was about half-full for it was early in the season for tourists, but there were a couple of dozen in there, mainly German from the sound of them and most of them were women of the well-preserved variety or perhaps mature would be a kinder word. Typical products of a class to be found in most countries. The ones who have everything and who find, in the final analysis, that they have nothing.

If they were looking for excitement, they'd come to the right place. There was an atmosphere about things in there that night. I could sense it in the laughter from the rougher element who kept to the tables on the other side of the small dance floor. Fishermen, and sponge divers in the main, they were wholly Greek for the Turks had still not returned in substantial numbers. The few who did work these waters stayed clear of Yanni's to avoid trouble, except for Ciasim Divalni, who was very much a law unto himself, feared nothing on top of earth and didn't think much of anything Greek at the best of times.

Greece is a man's country and this is especially true of the islands and old-fashioned codes of behaviour still apply. A man does not take his wife to the *taverna*. He goes there to drink with his friends in what is essentially a man's world and any woman—which usually means tourist—who invades that world, must expect to be looked upon as fair game.

On the other hand, the plain fact was that most women of the type who were there that night, rich, bored, eager for excitement, knew the rules of the game to a nicety and if their present aim in life was to find themselves flat on their backs in the sand under some muscular specimen off a sponge boat, then that was all right by me.

Loukas, the police sergeant, was seated on a wooden stool at the very end of the long bar talking to Alexias Papas, the manager. They were drinking *ouzo* and helping themselves from a plate of *mezes* which had been placed between them. Scraps of *fetta* cheese, whitebait, chopped octopus and similar delicacies. Definitely an acquired taste and certainly not mine.

Papas noticed me at once and waved. "Ah, Mr. Savage, I was hoping you would come in. Mr. Kytros is back. He would like a word with you."

"Here I am," I said.

"Good." He put a bottle of Fix on the bar which is a very passable beer they produce in Athens. "I will tell him you are here."

The beer was ice-cold which is the way they always serve it in Greece, even in the winter. Very refreshing, but I needed something stronger. I swallowed it down and Sergeant Loukas filled a spare glass with *ouzo* and pushed it across.

"You will join me, Mr. Savage?"

I didn't care for the stuff, but to refuse would be like insulting the Greek national flag. He was a small, insignificant-looking man in a shabby, sun-bleached khaki uniform. He badly needed a shave and there was an expression of settled melancholy on the narrow face. Nothing about him impressed, not even the automatic in its black leather holster on his belt.

And yet there had to be more to him than this, for according to Yanni he had been an area commander with the old E.O.K. in Crete during the German occupation. A man with an awesome reputation who had stayed one step ahead of the Gestapo for the entire war.

He smiled gently, this quiet little man, this simple island policeman who must have cut an untold number of throats in his day.

"How are things, Mr. Savage? For you, not so good, I think."

"Don't worry about me," I said. "I'm surviving."

"I am happy to hear it." He swallowed another of the tiny glasses of *ouzo* and stood up, making no attempt to straighten his uniform.

"Making your rounds?"

He nodded. "Perhaps I will look in later. We have another drink together, eh?"

"I wouldn't bother," I said as laughter roared out at the other end of the bar and a glass broke. "They'll have burned the place down by then."

He smiled politely as if not understanding and then the smile widened. "But of course, you are joking. The British are always joking. I remember this from the war."

"Irish," I said.

"The same thing, is it not so?"

He saluted and moved off which was as well. One hell of an exit line and there were places I knew where they'd have had the arms and legs off him for making a remark like that.

I helped myself to another *ouzo*. Funny, but it was beginning to taste better already, then Papas appeared and lifted the flap for me to go through to the rear.

Yanni Kytros met me at the door of his office and embraced me like some long lost brother. "Good to see you, Jack. Good to see you."

Which meant that he wanted something. "It's going to cost you, whatever it is," I told him.

There was a small bar in one corner. He went behind it, produced a fresh bottle of Jameson and almost filled a shot glass.

"There you are, Jack, a drop of the Paddy, isn't that what you call it?"

"Now I know you want something."

He smiled, that beautifully self-deprecating smile of his, and lit one of his Turkish cigarettes. "I only arrived this afternoon, but from what I hear, you aren't doing too well. On the other hand, what can you expect. Who needs real sponges these days? A dying trade."

"What have you got to offer that's any better?"

"Rum," he said. "They are paying a lot for rum on the black market in Turkey these days."

"They've also got a very old-fashioned attitude towards people who break the law," I said. "They not only put them away for rather lengthy periods. They throw in hard labour as a bonus."

"I'm not asking you to land, Jack. You rendezvous with a Turkish fishing boat five miles out on the other side of

Nisiros. They'll transfer your cargo and off you go. Nothing could be simpler."

"How much?"

"A thousand dollars plus expenses."

Which was more than I could make in a month and he knew it. "All right, when do I go?"

"Tomorrow night," he said. "I'll give you details later." He grinned and clapped me on the shoulder. "Nothing to it, Jack. Just like falling off a log."

"Then why don't *you* go and save yourself some money?"

He laughed heartily and pushed the bottle of Jameson across. "You'll be the death of me, Jack. Here, take this. Go and enjoy yourself. I'll see you tomorrow. We'll talk some more then."

It was noisier than ever when I went back in. Three *bouzoukis* were going full blast and half a dozen couples were dancing in the cleared area in the centre of the floor. I got a glass from the bar on the way through and found myself a table. I wasn't ready to leave yet. Time for that when I was too drunk to think straight, or think at all.

Ciasim came in through the entrance like a strong wind, paused, his eyes scanning the room, and saw me. He came through the crowd in a straight line, shrugging people to one side carelessly, a grin on his face.

He produced an envelope and waved it in my face as he sat down. "My licence, Jack. My licence to work the wreck. It's come through. Loukas saw me when I got in."

"Good for you." I shoved the bottle across. "Help yourself."

He reached for someone's glass from the next table, emptied its contents on the floor and filled it with whiskey. Down it went. He closed his eyes in bliss and smiled as he opened them again.

"Maybe you change your mind now, Jack?"

I shook my head. "Not a chance. You don't need me. I'd be no good to you."

His face was grave. There was sympathy there—real sympathy. "So, you meant what you said. It is that bad, eh?"

"I'm afraid so." I filled my glass again and shoved the bottle back to him. "To you, Ciasim. Good luck and no foul-ups."

The glass went to my lips and stayed there. Aleko was standing in the entrance, wearing, for some obscure reason, his bosun's outfit again. Everyone was looking at him, astonished at the sheer brute size of the man, and the clothes rounded things off nicely, so that he looked capable of clearing the place out on his own if the need arose.

Sara Hamilton moved in to join him. She stood there full of the arrogant assurance of her kind as if totally unaware that everyone in the place was looking at her. Her eyes found me, moved on with never a sign and Aleko took her by the elbow and led her to a table at the edge of the dance floor. Papas himself hurried to serve them.

"In the name of heaven, who is she?" Ciasim demanded.

"I would have thought that was obvious," I said. "The most beautiful woman in the world."

The drink talking? No—no, the truth for once. The great admission. She was into every part of me, every fibre of my being and the final irony was that I had lost her.

Ciasim, as if realising the situation, or at least the essence of it, handled me like a master.

"My luck is turning, Jack," he said. "Now we eat. Good food, good wine, all on me."

And eat we did. *Bourtheto*, a specialty from Corfu, his favourite Greek dish, which was fish cooked with lots of onions and all the red pepper in the world. To wash it down, a couple of bottles of *Demestica* and Ciasim finished it off with *baclavas*, a sweet made from sheets of pastry stuffed with nuts and soaked with honey.

I had never seen him drunk although he was halfway there that night. "Now I feel like a man again," he told me at one point. "All I need is a woman. That one for preference."

He pointed across the floor to a buxom German lady of forty or so with short blond hair and good breasts. She was sitting with two other women and didn't seem particularly put out by Ciasim's obvious interest.

"Now that's my kind of woman, Jack. What a body and the backside—magnificent. Something for a man to get hold of there."

"You'll need to be good," I said. "From the look of her she's just getting her second wind."

He laughed uproariously so that people turned to look and slapped the table. "Jack, I love you. Like a brother I love you. Now I go and dance with her. I rub her belly a little and see what happens."

He got to his feet, the most magnificent rogue I've ever known and looking it, every inch of him, swayed there for a moment, then plunged across the floor. The German woman was fast in his arms before she knew what was happening.

By now I was in no pain. The Jameson was nearly all gone which was quite extraordinary, even when you took Ciasim's bottomless thirst into account. I emptied the bottle deliberately into my glass and glanced across the room. Sara was watching me, a serious expression on her face. No, it was more than that. She looked genuinely concerned. But then the mother in most women floats to the top at the drop of a hat.

I toasted her gravely then emptied my glass spilling no more than half of its contents down my shirt front. She looked away, Aleko frowned and said something to her. She nodded, they got up and started to dance.

By then I was feeling good and sorry for myself. Aleko danced surprisingly well for such a big man and she moved like an angel, gazing through people like glass, the mouth hooked up at one side into that expression of perpetual scorn. I closed my eyes, inhaling that perfume of hers, or the memory of it. When I opened them again, there was trouble.

CHAPTER IX

FUGUE IN TIME

The man who had pushed his way through the crowd was not Aleko's size, but he was big enough. He was also good and drunk as were the group of half a dozen or so that he had left at the bar. His name was Andrew something-or-other. Big Andrew, they called him. He was captain of a *congoa* and had served a term of imprisonment on the mainland for stabbing a man in a fight.

It seemed he fancied his chances with Sara, but Aleko simply shrugged him off and continued dancing. Andrew tried again, grabbed him by the shoulder this time so violently that Aleko's shirt ripped. I waited along with everyone else in the silence which followed, for Aleko to break his jaw. Instead, he and the girl walked back to their table.

Andrew gave him a kick up the backside and Aleko went staggering forward to sprawl across the table. Everything was grinding to a halt now, the music dying in antic-ipation of the slaughter to come. What happened then was one of the most surprising things I have ever seen in my life.

Andrew went in on the run as Aleko started to turn, de-ciding I suppose, that his only hope was to get in first, or perhaps he had some inkling of what was to follow. In any event, as he got close, Aleko put his hands up defensively and cried out in fear.

A lot of things made sense to me then as the big man cowered back in his chair. The outfit he was wearing that made him look like a hard line bosun or some bucko mate off a sailing ship was all a front, a defensive mechanism to hide the true state of affairs which was quite simply that

in spite of his enormous size and strength, physical violence or its prospect, frightened him to death.

Andrew stood there looking at him, hands on hips. Then
he started to laugh, turned and made an obscene remark
to his friends. He followed this with what, in the circumstances, was the supreme insult. He patted Aleko on the
cheek as if he were a child and told him not to worry. That
he wasn't going to hurt him. Sara Hamilton tossed the
contents of her glass right into his face.

Island Greeks are very like Sicilians in one major respect. Humiliation in public by a woman is unthinkable.
The most deadly insult imaginable. So he did what was to
him, the obvious thing. He slapped her in the face, so hard
that she lost her balance and fell back against the table.

All the frustration, the pent-up rage at the whole lousy
world, burst through to the surface. I crossed the dance
floor in two quick strides and delivered a thoroughly dirty
punch to his kidneys with everything I had.

He gave a cry of pain they must have heard on the other
side of the island, his body jerking and turning in time to
get my right fist in the mouth. I followed it with my knee
delivered well below the belt and he went down like a tree
falling.

A woman screamed in the silence that followed. I was
aware of Aleko's face frozen like marble and then Sara was
very close, brushing the hair from her brow, so fierce.

"What are you trying to do?" she demanded. "Commit
suicide?"

"I love you," I said. "I just wanted you to know that.
Anyway the package comes, you're the girl for me. Now,
this minute, tonight. Tomorrow can go to hell its own
way."

She turned pale as if in shock and then she smiled, all
the way down to her toes. And as quickly, that smile
faded as she glanced beyond my shoulder.

When I turned, there were five of them moving in a
semi-circle. All good friends of Big Andrew and distressed
to see him on the floor like that. Hard, rough men as
sailors of any kind tend to be and with drink taken. It
didn't look too good, particularly when one of them picked
up a bottle and smashed it across the edge of the bar.

There was a stampede to the door by a proportion of the customers and if I'd had any sense I'd have been there with them, but I was too drunk for that kind of logic. Whatever happened, I couldn't run. Not in front of her.

I grabbed Aleko by the shoulder and pulled him up. "Go on, get her out of here."

He seemed confused and dazed, unable to think straight. She pushed him out of the way and said fiercely, "Not without you, Savage."

But by then I had no choice for the entrance was jammed with people. "Too late to run, angel," I told her and turned to meet the enemy. "Come on, you bastards, let's be having you."

The whiskey coursed through my bloodstream, inflating my head like a balloon. I was ten feel tall, I could take on the whole damned world. The man with the bottle came in first. When he was close enough, I kicked a chair at him and gave him the other foot in the face as he fell.

A moment later and the other four swarmed over me. A fist grazed my cheek, another landed hard under my ribs. I started to go down in a flurry of punches, then quite suddenly the man immediately in front of me was plucked out of the way and catapulted into the crowd.

Ciasim Divalni was roaring with laughter. He pole-axed another of the fishermen with a hammer blow delivered with his clenched fist and lashed out with his foot, sending a third staggering across to the bar.

Which was when it turned nasty for Ciasim was a Turk and this was Greece and no Greek worth his salt was going to stand by and see a Turk walk all over his fellow countrymen. There were angry cries and at least half a dozen men moved out of the crowd shouting threats.

"This doesn't look too good," I said to Ciasim as we backed towards the kitchen area.

He didn't seem to be able to stop laughing. "What a night, Jack, I haven't enjoyed myself so much in years. As for my *hausfrau*." He kissed his fingers. "Her belly scalded me through her dress. I shall make love to her all night. All night, I tell you. Who needs sleep?"

He picked up a chair, smashed it across a table and

wielded one leg like a club. "Come on, Greek pigs," he cried.

Which was not the wisest thing he could have said. There was a roar like an angry sea and half the crowd decided to join in, but so did Yanni Kytros. I'd been wondering what had happened to him.

There was one hell of a bang and lead shot spattered the ceiling. Everybody froze and Yanni came round the end of the bar clutching a Winchester automatic shotgun. He looked as genial as usual except around the eyes. The crowd didn't need telling twice. People started to fade rapidly, some returning to thier tables, others leaving altogether.

Yanni tucked the shotgun under his arm and turned to me with a sign. "The art of enjoying oneself, my dear Jack, lies partly in knowing when to stop. Please remember that in future."

Trust him to have the last word.

There was no sign of Sara Hamilton or Aleko by the time I'd finished with Yanni Kytros, but Ciasim's *hausfrau*, as he rather unkindly called her, was hovering near the door. He went off with her, an arm about that ample waist. Suddenly, I was alone.

The waiters and kitchen staff had already cleared the debris, the *bouzoukis* were playing and strangely enough, no one seemed to be even looking at me. I was the one on the outside looking in again.

I left and walked along the waterfront to the jetty and as the effects of the whiskey started to wear off, I began to ache all over and there was blood on my face from a cut beneath my right eye. Still, a fine time was had by all. A fine, lovely time. *But you might have waited, Sara Hamilton. You might have waited.*

I dropped to the deck of the *Gentle Jane* and went below. No sign of Morgan. Probably sleeping it off in the corner of some *taverna* or other. Would I ever end up like that? A distinct possibility on tonight's showing.

I sat there on the edge of my bunk, head in hands and after a while, there was a foot on the companionway. I should have known, I suppose, but the emptiness moved in me again and my mouth went dry.

"Savage?" she whispered. "Are you down there?"

She fumbled for the switch. I glanced up, eyes half-shut against the sudden brightness and there was dismay on her face. She dropped to her knees beside me and touched my cheek.

"Oh, the pigs, look what they did to you. What happened to your friend?"

"Ciasim?" I grinned wryly. "Hard at it on the beach somewhere with a German lady."

"I thought he looked a man of parts."

"Very definitely." I held her wrists lightly. "I'm glad you came."

"I know. About what happened on the beach . . ."

"To hell with that. This is all that counts. Where's Aleko?"

"He's all right now. He's gone back to the *Firebird*." She hesitated and said slowly. "He has a thing about physical violence. Some psychological disturbance or other. I believe he's had psychiatric treatment, but it didn't do any good. He can't help it. It isn't that he's a coward in the normal sense. You understand what I'm trying to say?"

"I think so. In a way, I have the same kind of fear down there at depth. But tell me about you and him. Anything you think I should know."

"He'd do anything for me," she said. "Since my sister was killed he seems to have turned all the love he had for her on to me. Not in any sexual way. I can honestly say he's never put a foot wrong that way. He needs me, I suppose that's about the size of it."

"And you? Do you need him?"

"I don't need anybody," she said and then added, "or thought I didn't."

She got to her feet, then sat down beside me. "I'm a wealthy woman, Savage. Just about all the money in the world. Left to me by my favourite uncle who had the good sense to marry a rich American lady who fancied being a countess. The thing is, I don't get to touch it till I'm twenty-one. Just over a year to go and Dimitri is my trustee. The uncle in question never did like my father."

Which explained a great deal. I stood up and groaned as pain hit me in half a dozen different places. She was immediately all concern.

"Are you all right?"

"I'm getting old, that's all. What I need is a swim. Are you interested?"

"If you think you're up to it."

She stood there, a hand on my hip, her mouth lifted in that strange, scornful way of hers and it wasn't swimming she was talking about. I knew it and so did she.

"You'll just have to take your chances, won't you?" I said. "Now if you'll come on deck and cast off when I tell you, we'll go and find a little peace and quiet."

I took her out to Hios where I had eaten earlier that day on the beach with Ciasim, mainly because it was uninhabited and I wanted to get away from people. As far away as possible.

It was a wonderful run at any time, but especially so on a night like that and visibility was excellent because of the bright moonlight. I gave the *Gentle Jane* her head and Sara leaned in the doorway of the wheelhouse and watched me.

"You love this boat," she commented after a while. "You're a different person in here."

"I suppose I do in my own twisted way," I said. "It's the sea as much as anything."

"*Gentle Jane*," she said. "Was she an old girl friend?"

I laughed. "That's what she was called when I bought her. The original owner was from North Cornwall. Believe it or not, but there's a hamlet in those parts that's actually called Gentle Jane."

I allowed her to take the wheel for a while after that, but not for long because at the speed we were going, we were approaching Hios within half an hour. I stopped the engines and dropped anchor in the same tiny bay I had already visited earlier that day.

I got some blankets together, coffee, a pot to go with it and some tinned milk and we went ashore in the dinghy. There was plenty of driftwood still on the beach, all dry as a bone after the heat of the day and flames roared up into the darkness when I put a match to the brushwood.

"Our own private island," she said. "Now that, I like."

"Do you want to swim now?"

"No, later if it's all the same to you. Let's talk."

"What about?"

"Anything. Cabbages and kings, love, war, life, death. You name it."

And now she was getting too close for comfort and for a little while I staved off the big question, the one I really wanted to put to her. Instead, I said, "You told me you weren't interested in your brother-in-law's involvement with present Greek politics. Did you really mean that?"

She seemed surprised. "I thought I made it clear enough when you asked me earlier. I'm not interested in politics. In all the hopeless stupidity of men's affairs. I'm interested in the now. In me. I'm living for as long as I can hang on."

At last, the big question and there was no avoiding it. "And how long would that be?"

"I've got chronic leukaemia and there are worse varieties. At least five years in my case. Ten, if I'm very lucky, but that would be exceptional." There was one of those silences again and finally, she said, "Well, what have you got to say to that?"

"What do you want me to do?" God knows how I kept my voice steady. "Start feeling sorry for you? In my game, angel, I could die tomorrow. I take a chance whenever I go down. Tears are a waste of time. You've got to make every minute count. That's the important thing."

Her eyes were shining in the firelight. I didn't dare touch her, not at that precise moment for the emotion was too close to the surface of things. Instead, I stripped off my jeans and shirt and ran down the beach into the sea without saying a word.

It was cold out there and the salt got into the various abrasions I had sustained in the fight and stung like hell. I swam around to the other side of the *Gentle Jane* and turned for the shore. When I went back up the beach, there was no sign of Sara, but her clothes were in a neat pile on the blanket. I was aware of a splashing out there beyond the boat, but it was impossible to see her for a cloud had crossed the face of the moon, killing all light.

The fire had died down into a great pile of glowing

embers so fiercely had the dry wood burned. I crouched over it, raking through it with a stick and heard a movement behind me. As I turned, she stepped into the light.

She was quite naked and water ran from the firm breasts, glistening in the light of the dying fire and her body was a thing of mystery, shadowed in the secret places, more beautiful than anything I had ever known.

She stood there for what seemed the longest moment in my life, a fugue in time, and then she smiled, that wonderful smile and dropped to her knees beside me. I reached for a blanket to cover us. When we came together, it seemed like the most natural and inevitable thing that had ever happened.

CHAPTER X

HEADLONG INTO ETERNITY

It was a little after seven when I awakened, but already sunlight was drifting in through the portholes of the cabin.

Sara Hamilton slept easily in the bunk opposite, all very right and proper, the pale, straw hair spread across the pillow, the face in repose, washed clean, no longer scornful at the whole world.

The blanket had slipped down from her shoulders in the night, exposing the left breast, which added a certain piquant charm to the general picture, but was calculated to disturb at that time in the morning.

A couple of minutes spent looking at that was all that flesh and blood could stand. I tiptoed out, taking my clothes with me and went on deck. It was going to be a hot one. I stood at the rail for a moment, the warmth of the sun pleasant on my skin and was aware that I was hungry and there was only one answer to that.

I checked the two aqualungs. One was empty and the other was about as low as it could be, which was a pity because I suddenly remembered that our portable compressor had packed up the previous day and Morgan simply hadn't had the time or opportunity to put his mechanical genius to work. Still, one good fish was all I needed and that shouldn't take long in a spot like this where they weren't used to spearfishmen.

I went over the side quietly clutching a harpoon gun, adjusted my air supply and went to work. Within ten minutes I found exactly what I was looking for, a fine sea bass weighing a good five pounds from the look of him. Perhaps it would be more accurate to say that he found me, for he came in to meet the harpoon as if greeting a long lost friend.

When I surfaced at the boat, I caught the wood smoke scent at once and swimming round to the land side, found the fire burning well on the beach and Sara a few yards away gathering driftwood.

She saw me as I waded from the water, dropped her wood beside the fire and came to meet me. She wasn't wearing her denim skirt. Just the white sweater and black nylon briefs.

"The longest legs I've ever seen," I told her.

"Like me to cover them up?"

"In a pig's eye, you will." I got an arm around her, wet as I was, and kissed her good and hard.

"There's passion for you at this time in the morning." She prodded the bass. "What do we do with him?"

"We eat him," I said, "for breakfast, or would you prefer lemon tea and three fingers of toast?"

But she didn't, because at least half the bass disappeared into the lovely mouth just as fast as I could get the steaks out of the pan as they were done. She sat cross-legged on the blanket, licking her fingers and looking very satisfied with herself.

"You know, Savage, you're something special. You can cook as well."

"As well as what?"

I ducked to avoid the plate she threw and any idea of retaliation was foiled by her quickness with the coffee pot. I was clutching a full cup before I knew it.

"Beachcombing has a lot to be said for it," she remarked.

I nodded. "Who needs people?"

She lay back on the blanket, hands behind her head, one knee raised, presenting a disturbingly erotic picture. I was filled with a strange sadness but also a perverse desire to bring her back to reality.

"All right in dreams," I said, "but the present is rather different. Maybe five minutes of air left in my aqualung and enough fuel in the tank for forty or fifty miles at the most. I need people all right. People with money who'll help support me in the manner to which I've become accustomed."

She turned her head sharply and her voice was gravel and ice. "Why do you talk such balls?" As usual, her language was peculiarly her own. "Jack Savage, the unscrupulous adventurer, mercenary to the trade. Anything considered as long as the price is right."

"An accurate enough picture. I'll take a couple of hundred handbills of that one. Gothic script, black edging."

But she wasn't smiling. "If money is what you want, you could have had thirty thousand dollars last night. You turned it down."

"Hollywood adventure stuff," I said. "I got away with it once and that was once too often. Anyway I like living."

Which was a bloody stupid remark to make because she flinched and said bitterly, "Don't we all?"

It was the first time I'd had even a hint of what she must be feeling about three layers down. There was an awkward silence and I couldn't think of anything to say. Any way in which I might comfort her.

I poured myself some more coffee and said lightly. "You never did tell me anything about your family. You said you had brothers the first time we talked."

"Phil and Roderick. They're at Eton."

God save us all. "And your parents?"

"My mother died some time ago. My father remarried a couple of years back. He's a dear, lovely man and his wife is fine, but two women in a house. You know what I mean?"

"I should have thought you could have kept fifty or sixty rooms between you," I said. "You told me last night that your favourite uncle left you a pot of gold, but didn't like your father. What was the trouble there?"

"Simple," she said. "They were twins and Daddy pipped Uncle Gavin at the post for the earldom by eleven and a half minutes. Poor old Gavin never forgave him."

Hambray House. The Earl of Hambray. Major General the Earl of Hambray as I recalled.

"I served under him in France," I said. "Your father, I mean. Not that he'd remember me. I was a sergeant at the time."

"Oh, no you don't," she said "To hell with your peasant pride." She came close and leaned against me. "You'll like him, Savage, and he'll like you which is exactly as it should be."

"And when does this merry meeting take place?"

"When you go to ask him for my hand," she said complacently. "It's an old family tradition."

"I know," I said. "You told me. All seven hundred years of it."

"I want everything to be right and proper," she said lightly. "Isn't every girl entitled to that when she gets married?"

My heart pumping loud enough to hear, I swallowed and said with some emotion, "I don't know about that, angel, but if I'm it, you can have me anyway you want."

She came into my arms then and I held her close, rocking her gently as if comforting a child and a small, chill wind rippled the surface of the sea as I gazed blindly out to the horizon.

Coming through the Middle Passage towards Kyros just before noon, I gave Sara her head and left her at the wheel on her own.

The morning had been wonderful. We'd explored the island, gone swimming, talked in a way I had not talked to anyone for years, or to be more honest, a way in which I'd never talked to anyone before.

But everything had to end and we had to put in an appearance at Kyros some time. There was Aleko to see, various arrangements to be made if I was to return to England with her which was very definitely what she wanted. I had responsibilities again. From now on Sara came first. It was simple as that. A favourite phrase of mine and a curiously empty one, for if life had taught me anything it was that nothing ever was as simple as it looked at first sight.

I had just finished making a pot of tea on the galley when the phone buzzed. She said calmly, "I think you'd better get up here. Someone is trying to signal us and it's all Greek to me."

Which was intriguing, but I found time enough to put the pot of tea on a tray along with a can of milk and a couple of mugs before going up to join her.

We were slap in the centre of the Middle Passage now, about half a mile south of Sinos and three hundred yards to starboard of Ciasim's *trenchadiri*, the *Seytan*. I put the tray down and picked up the binoculars. Yassi jumped into view, waving an old piece of red cloth vigorously. Abu was standing by the compressor and from the looks of the lines disappearing into the water, Ciasim was already working on the wreck.

Something was wrong, I knew at once. Instinct, or was it simply that I had been expecting it? I pulled Sara out of the way and took over the wheel. "We're going in. The big Turk who saved my neck last night, Ciasim Divalni, that's his boat."

"What's he doing, diving for sponges?"

"Not this time. Salvage job. Wartime wreck about a hundred and fifty feet down. Too deep and too damned risky with the gear he's got. I told him it was no go, but he wouldn't listen."

"Is that your fault?" she asked with real perception. "I don't know much about diving, but that sounds a fair way down to me."

We were already coming close and I throttled back and cut the engines to run the *Gentle Jane* in against the *Seytan*'s starboard rail. Yassi had a couple of old tyres over as fenders and grabbed the line Sara threw to him. He was scared—scared all the way through and Abu turned from the compressor, tears streaming down his face.

"Please, please, Mr. Savage." His Greek was broken and disjointed. "Help my father. Something bad happen down there."

I turned to Yassi. "How long?"

"Half an hour, maybe forty-five minutes. Everything fine and then something go wrong. Just before you come he gives three fours."

Four quick pulls on the line by the diver repeated three times meant *Get me out of here*. It usually meant things were about as bad as they could be.

"What happened then?"

"We tried to haul him up, but the line, she won't budge. No more signals since."

Abu plucked at my sleeve. "You go down now, Mr. Savage. You bring him up."

Which was fine except for the fact that my aqualung was just about empty. "Did you get any of that?" I asked Sara.

She nodded. "What are you going to do?"

"I've no choice, I'll have to go down."

She frowned. "But you said the aqualung was almost empty."

I didn't even argue. Simply went over the rail to the *Gentle Jane* and got my gear on fast. No time to put on a wetsuit so I left my denim pants and shirt on.

As I buckled on the aqualung and turned, I found Sara talking to Yassi in fast, fluent Greek. I went back over the rail and he got in my way, a hand to my chest. "No, Mr. Savage, not this way. My father would not want this."

I shoved him to one side and vaulted into the water. I paused barely long enough to adjust my air supply and went down fast, following the curving lines into the green mist.

I swerved as a steel mast pierced the gloom, and hovered over the wreck. There was something wrong, something different, I knew that at once and in the same moment realised what it was. The old anti-aircraft gun which had been mounted on the foredeck was missing.

I found it when I went down after the line, hanging over the starboard rail of the hulk along with about fifty tons of scrap iron and the air hose and lifeline disappeared underneath.

Which could have been the end of things if something hadn't made me take a look on the other side of the pile where I found Ciasim flat on his back on firm sand, pinned like a fly by his fouled lines, helpless, unable to aid himself in any way at all.

It was a miracle that his air hose had not parted, but whatever happened, he could not last long like that. A couple of lengths of old iron drifted down from above in slow motion. I put my mask up against the face plate of his helmet and he actually smiled. The cavalry arriving in the nick of time was how it must have looked to him, but then, he didn't know about my lack of air.

His face suddenly seemed distorted, my mouth was dry, my heart pounding. I had stayed too long already. I went up fast. I barely made it and broke through to the surface beside the *Seytan's* ladder just in time. I spat out the rubber mouthpiece and gulped in lots of clean sea air.

Yassi and Abu hauled me over the side and I unbuckled the aqualung and slumped to the deck. Sara dropped to her knees beside me. "You look awful, what happened?"

"I think I made the last fifty feet on a dry tank." I turned to Yassi. "He's still alive, but not for long. About half the ship seems to have come down across his lines."

Muslims are supposed to be cheerful about that kind of thing and leave it all to Allah, but when your father is going to go the slow way, inch by inch, nobody is much good at keeping a stiff upper lip.

Abu dropped to his knees, hands together as in prayer and screamed at me hysterically in Turkish. I didn't need any translation to know what he was saying.

"Can we get help from anywhere?" Sara asked.

"No one near enough with the right equipment and he can't last long in any case. Bits and pieces were still coming down when I left him. The whole damn lot might collapse at any moment now that it's started. I've seen this kind of thing happen before."

I'd spoken to her in Greek, mainly for Yassi's benefit, his English being almost non-existent. Now, he straightened and said calmly, "Then there is nothing to be done. It would have been a kindness if you had severed his air hose with a knife, Mr. Savage."

It took a moment for it to hit me, the one possible solution I got to my feet. "That helmet of your father's, it's a lot newer than the rest of his equipment. It's got a check valve—right?"

"That is so, Mr. Savage."

I turned to Sara and said in Greek, again for Yassi's benefit, "The more modern type of helmet has a safety check valve. It automatically shuts off if the air supply stops and the exhaust valve does the same. It means the diver still has whatever air there is in his suit."

"And how long will that last?"

I frowned, trying to remember the tables. "In shallow

water eight minutes or so, but it goes down rapidly the
deeper you go. A hundred and thirty feet. He should be
good for two minutes." Suddenly I was excited. "And two
minutes should be ample."

"For what?" she looked puzzled.

"To get him to the surface," I explained patiently. "All he
needs is a fresh lifeline, then I cut his air hose. The check
valve closes automatically as I've explained and Yassi and
Abu haul him up just as fast as they can."

It was Yassi who was frowning now. "But how do you
get to him, Mr. Savage, I don't understand?"

"I'll free dive," I said. "I've cleared a hundred feet plenty
of times in the past."

And come straight up again. But I didn't tell him that
because there was already hope in his eyes. But Sara knew
me better, I think, than I knew myself.

She pulled me round to face her. "That was a lot of
drinks ago, Savage, am I right?"

"No good arguing, I've got to try," I said.

But she was right. I'd be lucky to get down half that
distance under my own steam and then, as I turned from
her, my foot caught in an old sand anchor, half a hundred-
weight of stone worn smooth by the years with a ring hole
through the top for a line. It was all I needed.

"I'll use the stone to take me straight down like the *petra*
divers," I told Yassi. "Get a rope through it for me and
have another line ready for me to take with me."

A *petra* diver uses a heavy stone to take him straight to
the bottom, thus saving his energy for the task in hand. A
technique as old as time and still used extensively by pearl
divers in Japan and the Polynesian islands. There were still
a few Arab divers operating that way in the Red Sea working regularly at around a hundred feet although I'd never
seen them myself.

"You must be mad," Sara clutched at my arm. "This
isn't Alexandria. This isn't your doing."

Which was fair enough. I'd warned Ciasim and he had
not listened, but that wasn't the point. "He's a friend of
mine, angel," I said. "A man I like more than most people
I've ever met. If I don't go down there, if I leave him to

go the hard way, then I'm finished. I might as well cut my throat."

Her eyes went very wide. She stared at me blankly and then sighed and the sound was like a small wind through trees at nightfall. "I should have known."

"As long as you do. Now come with me. There's something I want you to handle, something very important."

I called to Yassi to join us and went over the rail to the *Gentle Jane* and entered the deck house where I stored my diving gear. I switched on the generators, plugged in the portable decompression chamber that some engineering marvel in Switzerland had produced, and dragged it forward.

"The moment he surfaces, get him out of that suit and into here." I turned to Yassi. "I want your promise on it. He will die otherwise."

"I swear it, Mr. Savage. How long?"

I found a note pad and pencil and did a quick calculation. At a hundred and thirty feet he would have needed at least fifty-six minutes of decompression time. He'd been down there over an hour and I had to consider the speed at which he'd been coming up. His blood would be bubbling like soda water.

"Three hours," I said, "and be careful to alter the pressures in the chamber as I've indicated. That's important."

Sara's face was very white now. "And you? What about you?"

"I won't be down there long enough to worry about decompression if I come up."

A slip of the tongue, that.

She took a deep breath and said in a harsh voice, "How long are you good for?"

"With that kind of weight, I'll touch bottom in a few seconds. A minute down there is all I can afford if I'm to stand any chance of reaching the surface again."

Which was being about as direct as I could be and she accepted that now with her own brand of fatalism. "I hope you find time to check your watch."

"You could help me there, just in case I don't."

She followed me into the wheelhouse and I pressed the

button to release the secret flap under the chart table and
handed her the Walther automatic.

"Time the minute exactly from the moment I go over,
then fire this into the water twice."

"What's that supposed to do?"

"It's an old trick of Cousteau's. The shock waves can be
felt quite distinctly, I assure you," I added, with a feeble
attempt at humour. "Don't forget to take the safety catch
off."

Her answer was completely in character. "Damn you,
Savage, I'll never forgive you if you die on me."

There was nothing I could say to that, nothing at all. I
went back across to the *Seytan*, pulled on my flippers and
adjusted the nose clip. I wore goggles as well as a mask
simply because there was less likelihood of their being torn
off in my rapid descent. Abu had the new lifeline coiled
ready. There was a spring clip at the end which would help
and I snapped it to my belt. Yassi brought the sand anchor
across. He'd run about four feet of manilla hemp through
the ring and had knotted it into a loop which was fine.

I was aware of Sara standing behind me, her watch in
one hand, the Walther in the other, and then I lifted the
anchor in both hands. I balanced it on top of the ladder
breathed in three times to really fill up my lungs, then I
simply leaned forward and let the great stone take me
down.

*The pressure increases at up to fifteen tons for every
thirty-seven feet you descend.* Strange how that interesting
snippet of information ran through my head as I fell headlong into green darkness; for that is what it seemed like, so
fast was my rate of descent.

I passed through a great shoal of silver fish, scattering
them on either side, the stone plummeting down like some
live thing. There was a story I'd read as a boy about Beo-
wulf, the great Saxon hero, diving down through the dark
waters to Grendel's lair. I used to wonder what he'd done
for air because he'd lasted a damned sight longer than I
was going to do down there.

The mast loomed out of the gloom to spear me, flashed

to one side, and the stone disappeared into the dark mouth of the centre hold as I released its grip on the rope.

I grabbed at one of the deck rails to steady myself, then started to swim forward across that great, twisted mass of old iron that hung across the side of the ship.

The weight of the whole world bore down on me, I was making no progress at all and yet, by some miracle, he was there beneath me and I went down and clutched at him.

I was close enough to see that he was still alive, to see the dismay on his face. He reached out to touch me and I was aware of a strange, tingling sensation like electricity running through my body. I felt it again almost at once. *The shock waves as Sara fired into the water.*

So I was too late? For me, perhaps, but not for Ciasim. I snapped the link of the new lifeline to his body harness, pulled out my knife and slashed through the old one. He knew then what was to happen. He raised a thumb and I jerked four times on his lifeline and sliced through the air-hose. A great stream of silver bubbles rushed out and in the same moment he started to rise.

Everything had happened in slow motion, part of some strange dream and I followed him up, kicking rhythmically, though I knew it was no good.

A strange thing happened then. Sara Hamilton's voice seemed to echo inside my head with surprising clarity. *Damn you, Savage, I'll never forgive you if you die on me.* It had been a long time since anyone had needed me like that. Really needed me like she did.

I hung on to that thought and fought like hell, my eyes never leaving that small, doll-like figure, far, far above me. And then she seemed even farther away like something at the wrong end of a telescope and then she disappeared altogether and I drifted into warm darkness.

CHAPTER XI

THE RUM-RUNNER

Her perfume filled my nostrils and I floated up from the darkness into light very, very slowly, broke through to the surface and breathed again.

I was lying flat on my back on my bunk in the main cabin, no pillow at my neck, wondering who I was. I had been here before, felt exactly like this then, trapped in some strange limbo of the mind. Was it then or now? Time was a circle turning endlessly on itself. No beginning, no end.

But the perfume—that damned perfume? I moved restlessly and she was there, the golden hair brushing my face. She wore a blue cotton dress cut square at the neck. It gaped wide as she leaned over me and I put my hand inside and touched a breast.

"A hell of a temptation for any man."

The voice echoed inside my head, the voice of a stranger. She managed a smile, but only just. "Oh, you bastard, don't you ever frighten me that way again."

She turned and went out quickly and I lay there, watching the pale sunlight drifting in through the porthole, alive and accepting that fact without any particular surprise. After a while the door opened and the local doctor came in. His name was Karakos, a nice little man with a goatee beard and round steel spectacles. We'd had dealings a couple of weeks earlier when I'd gashed my left leg rather badly on a coral out-crop and he'd put five stitches into it for me.

He put down his bag and felt my pulse. "Good," he nodded. "Very good."

"How long have I been out?"

"Just over four hours."

"I didn't expect to wake up at all. For a while there I thought it was the last act."

"And so it would have been had it not been for Lady Hamilton. When you surfaced, you had stopped breathing. After the Turks had got you out of the water she gave you mouth-to-mouth resuscitation."

So, I had been dead in effect and she had brought me back to life? It was a hell of a thought to cope with.

"What about Ciasim Divalni?"

"The Turk?" It was there in the way he said the words, that ancient antagonism so deeply rooted that it seemed that nothing could eradicate it. "I released him from your decompression chamber after three hours as she had instructed me. He seemed his usual animal self."

I ignored that. "What about me?"

He produced a bottle of pills from his bag and put them on the side. "You will undoubtedly feel the effects for a day or two. Severe headaches, nausea. The body has been subjected to an intolerable strain for a man of your age." I loved him for that one. "These pills will help you with the pain. Stay on your back for a day or two and no alcohol."

"What do I owe you?"

"Not a thing. I came at Mr. Aleko's request. My bill is to go to him personally. He was most insistent on that point."

He went out without closing the door and I shut my eyes. When I opened them again Sara was standing beside me. I smiled. "The kiss of life, that's what the man said."

She shuddered visibly. "When you came to the surface, you weren't even breathing. It was horrible—really horrible. At first you didn't seem to be responding . . ."

She started to shake and I took her hand and squeezed it hard. "All right, let it go. Just let it go. How is Ciasim?"

"Fine. We got him into the chamber like you said. He was kicking to get out after the first hour. I had to be pretty firm with him."

"And how did we get back?"

"To Kyros?" She smiled. "I brought you and Yassi and

Abu followed in the *Seytan*. I'm afraid I spoiled your paint-work coming in to the jetty."

"Angel, you can spoil my paintwork any time you like," I said.

We spent an emotional couple of minutes locked to-gether and finally, she pulled free and said, "Dimitri was waiting on the jetty. He'd seen us coming in, of course. He had the doctor there within ten minutes."

"That's what comes of being a multi-millionaire."

She frowned at that and ruffled my hair. "Try to like him, Savage, for my sake. It would make things a lot easier."

"Who for?"

There was a difficult moment during which her eyes flashed with temper and an explosion threatened. I was saved by Morgan who appeared hesitantly in the doorway and stood there twisting his cap in his hands. He badly needed a shave, his eyes were tinged with yellow and I could smell the stink of that cheap wine mingled with his sweat, acrid and unpleasant. He waited, uncertain as a dog that seeks a kind word and I gave it to him.

"How goes it, Morg?"

He shuffled forward. "Hell, Jack, you had us worried. I thought you was for the deep six."

"Not me, Morg, indestructible, just like you."

I dug my fist into his shoulder and he wriggled with pleasure. "Yanni Kytros was here, Jack, about tonight's run. I didn't know about that."

"You wouldn't, Morg, I only took it on last night. What did he say?"

"He figured you wasn't in no fit state. He said he'd look elsewhere."

I sat up and swung my legs to the floor. "Like hell, he will. You go find him, Morg. Tell him to get those cases down here and loaded. A thousand dollars is a thousand dollars."

He went out fast, bobbing his head at Sara, who ignored him. "What are you up to?" she demanded.

I was beginning to feel a whole lot better and pulled open a drawer and found a clean pair of denims and a shirt. "Oh, a little business I've arranged with Kytros. Nothing to get worked up about. A milk-run."

"I can just imagine what your version of a milk-run is." She came very close and started to button my shirt. "Would it do any good for me to point out that you ought to be flat on your back for the next two days?"

"Not in the slightest." I put my arms around her and pulled her close enough to feel every line of that wonderful body all the way down. "You know, I thought I knew women, and God knows I've had enough of them in my time, but now, with you, I feel as if I've been missing out on a damned good thing all my life."

She kissed me hard, her mouth opening, and beyond her, Aleko appeared in the doorway. He watched gravely for a moment, betraying no emotion worth mentioning, then moved forward as we came apart.

He held out his hand. "If there's one thing I admire above anything else, it's guts, Captain Savage. You certainly have your share."

There was an awkward silence and he turned to Sara. "We should really be going, my dear, we've guests for dinner, remember." He hesitated, then said to me, "Perhaps you'd join us? It would seem appropriate under the circumstances. Sara has signified her intentions to me. I understand you'll be going to England together as soon as possible."

He was so solemn, so pedantic, that I could have laughed out loud, but I would have been laughing at him, not with him, and that wouldn't do at all.

"That's very kind of you," I said formally. "But I'm afraid I've already made other arrangements for tonight."

"A pity. Some other time, perhaps."

He went up the companionway without a word. Sara said, "What time will you be leaving?"

"I'm not sure. Sometime after dark, but not too late. It's a three- to four-hour run."

She nodded in a strange abstracted manner, then reached up and patted my face. "Look after yourself."

She started up the companionway, paused and turned. "You did pretty well for a man who's supposed to have lost his nerve. I'm rather proud of you."

And then she was gone and I stood there, taking in exactly what she had said and realising the implication. I could have shouted out loud, so great was the release of energy—energy which had been locked-up in that strange involuted pattern of neurotic fear ever since Alexandria.

Was it that deep in my subconscious, I felt that I had expiated my guilt for poor old Morg? There could be no real answer to that one. The only really important thing was that I was no longer afraid. At least, not in the same way.

I went up on deck and stood there in the pleasant warmth of late evening looking out across the harbour. In some strange way life began again and I was alive again.

Ciasim called to me from the beach and when I turned I saw that the *Seytan* was drawn up out of the water and he was standing barefoot in the shallows. I climbed to the jetty, moved towards the stone steps that would take me down to join him, but he was too quick for me. He embraced me, finishing off with a kiss on each cheek, then held me at arm's length.

"What do you want—a hand, my right arm?"

It was an old Turkish saying and meant pretty much what it implied.

"Maybe you'll listen to me another time," I said. "I told you that wreck was bad news."

"I was unlucky, that's all. It can't happen twice."

"So you're going to try again?"

"Why not?"

Any attempt at argument would obviously have been a complete waste of time so I accepted one of his cheap Turkish cigarettes and we sat on the low stone wall.

"You feel all right now?" he asked. "Okay for a man who's supposed to have lost his nerve."

"Don't let's start digging into that one."

He didn't attempt to pursue it, but said instead, "The girl—The English milady—she loves you, Jack, the way a woman should love a man, with everything she has."

For some reason I felt uncomfortable. "Oh, I don't know. She's young. You know what they're like. This time next week, she'll fancy someone else."

"Not that baby."

Another of those quaint Americanisms of his and yet it was what I wanted to hear. Why, then, did I feel so restless? So uncertain?

But such thoughts were swept away completely when an old three-ton truck turned on to the jetty and rolled towards us. When it braked to a halt. Kytros got down from the passenger seat. He was wearing a white linen suit and a smile on his face to rival the Cheshire Cat's as he advanced on me.

"So, the dead can walk after all, Jack?"

Behind him, half a dozen labourers got out of the back of the truck and started to unload the cases of rum.

Just before we left, I went along to Yanni's place by arrangement to collect my thousand dollars in advance. We'd already filled the tanks at his expense which was part of the agreement and when I got back to the jetty, Morgan had the engines ticking over ready for a quick departure.

It was already dark and a slight drizzle drifted down through the yellow light of the lamp at the end of the jetty. Faintly in the distance as a door opened I heard the sound of a *bouzouki* that was as suddenly stilled. It was as if no one else in the world existed and in the yellow light, Morgan looked like a walking corpse, old and used up and past everything there ever was.

He seemed nervous and strangely jumpy and that worried me. Maybe he really was getting past it. Had I the right any longer to involve him in this kind of affair where the consequences, if anything went wrong, could be disastrous?

I pushed her hard for the first couple of hours running northeast into the Dodecanese against a freshening east wind that brought rain to rattle against the wheelhouse windows like bullets.

It was your own small world in there, enclosed, cut-off from everything and a world I liked, the wheelhouse a place of shadows, the only light the glow from the instrument panel and the compass. Things became sharper, clearer, problems, even the more serious variety, less important or perhaps it would be closer to the truth to say that the sea cut them down to size.

I sat back in the seat, my hands on the wheel when I could have had her on automatic pilot and didn't because I enjoyed handling her in conditions like this. In fresh weather, she came alive, like a woman does under practised hands and it was a good feeling—a feeling that the one was part of the other.

Morgan had gone to make tea and I was thinking of Sara, a subject which tended to occupy my mind most of the time then. When the door opened, I didn't turn my head until I sensed the perfume, heavy and quite unmistakable on the fresh salt air.

"Two sugars or one?" she said, and put the tray down on the table.

She was wearing an old reefer coat of Morgan's, I could make that much out, and her hair was tied back. So now his agitation back there on the jetty was explained.

"I'll have the old soak's scalp for this," I said.

"Oh, no you won't. I told you he'd do anything for me. He was frightened to death—but just as afraid to say no. He's like a child."

I switched-on to automatic pilot and took the mug of tea she passed to me. "All right, so I take it out on you."

"Now that sounds much more interesting." She pulled down the other seat from the wall. "First I'll have a cigarette, then you can tell me what you're up to."

Which I did and when I was finished, she said, "So now you're what they call a rum-runner?"

"Prohibition," I said. "The twenties. You've got the wrong decade."

"The same thing when it comes down to it. What will they give you if you're caught?"

"Seven or eight years with hard labour."

"And for this you get all of a thousand dollars?"

I managed a small laugh. "All right, rich girl, so some of us have to work a little harder than the rest."

"I'm glad you can joke about it."

"Like Yanni said, easy as falling off a log. We go in, we come out. No trouble—no trouble at all."

"Which is why you keep this little lot so handy, I suppose?"

She reached under the chart table, pressed the button and the flap containing my small armoury dropped down.

"What have we got?" she went on. "A submachine gun, an automatic pistol and a revolver. Nothing like the quiet life. No self-respecting motor yacht complete without this interesting collection."

I shoved it back into place with the toe of my boot. "Are you going to rattle on like this at breakfast every morning?"

Which appealed to her and she struck out in that sudden wild way of hers, laughing, punching me on the shoulder. "All right, but I just don't want to lose you. It's been one hell of a day, that way, or had you forgotten?"

And now it was my turn. "So what do I do for money? Live off you?"

"And why not? Would it offend your peasant conscience?"

So now we were scratching. But she was right, of course. Money, as the economists would say, was only a medium of exchange. Hers or mine? What difference did it make? And these were special circumstances after all. Time was limited and not just for her. For the both of us.

But the awkward silence remained, the constraint was there. For the first time we had clashed—really clashed, with something important underlying it. It was the sort of situation where mutual pride is involved and best solved by going to bed, but this was neither the time nor the place and after a while, she went out quietly and left me to it.

Five miles on the other side of Nisiros on the inner curve of the Dodecanese, I hove to and gave the agreed signal. A white light flashed five times, a clear interval of a second between each light. The reply was instantaneous. Three red flashes repeated twice.

We waited, the *Gentle Jane* rolling considerably in the heavy swell and the other vessel slid out of the darkness, her deck lights on.

She was larger than I had anticipated, a fifty-footer, with diesel engines from the sound of it. There were five men on deck, all Turkish fishermen, another leaning out of the window of the tall and rather old-fashioned wheelhouse. A

trawl was set up in the stern and there were nets festooned
all over the place. Either they were genuine, which was
possible, or else it was a damned good front.

They slipped alongside surprisingly neatly for such a
large boat in that sea and the man in the wheelhouse came
down and clambered across. The others stayed where they
were for the time being, presumably waiting for credentials
to be established.

The one who had boarded us was large and squat and
wore a black oilskin jacket that glistened in the rain. I
didn't like him and not just because of the greasy moustache and pockmarked face. It was the eyes mainly. Restless, cunning, constantly moving.

He said in good English, "I am Amer—Captain Rasi
Amer," and held out his hand.

I didn't like the feel of it, soft and warm and the look on
his face as Sara moved out of the shadows didn't do anything to improve matters. His tongue flipped along the edge
of his lips and then he smiled and it was entirely the wrong
sort of a smile.

"You have the cases ready?"

"In the hold," I said. "You can start unloading as fast
as you like. I want to get out of here."

"But why bother, my friend? To unload, I mean," he
added by way of an explanation.

"I don't follow you," I said although I was already most
of the way there.

"The boat." He tapped the rail. "It is a fine boat. And
the girl." He grinned, looking about as depraved as any
human being could reasonably expect to do. "I can find a
use for the girl, too."

He raised his right hand and snapped his fingers negli-
gently and the two men who had been standing aft of the
wheelhouse on the Turkish boat, whipped some nets aside
and disclosed a light machine gun mounted on a tripod.
One of them got behind it as if he knew what he was doing.

The other three came over the rail to cover me and
Morgan, who looked as if he might pass out at any moment. Sara had stayed exactly where she was in the entrance of the wheelhouse, her hands thrust deep into the

pockets of her reefer coat. Her face was very calm, even when Captain Amer advanced on her.

He put a hand under her chin. "Beautiful," he said. "Exquisite."

His other hand got about as intimate as it possibly could. Her mouth lifted in that superbly contemptuous way of hers and she backed into the shadows of the wheelhouse. Amer, shaking all over from what I could see, went after her.

He gave a sudden cry of dismay and came out backwards very, very slowly, the barrel of the Walther rammed up under his chin and from the look on Sara's face, she had every intention of using it.

The boys with the machine gun were in something of a quandary. I solved it for them by moving across quickly and relieving her of the Walther. I got a strong grip on Amer's greasy hair and shoved the barrel another half-inch into his throat.

"Tell them to toss that machine gun over the side fast or I'll blow the top of your head off."

He was no hero which helped because there were still six of them to deal with. The machine gun went into the water with a splash and I told Morgan to take the controls and move us apart.

By then I had Amer and the other three lined up at the rail. As our engines rumbled into life, the gap between the two boats widened. I waited till it was a good twenty yards and told them to start jumping.

Amer was the last to go, shaking like a leaf, sweat on his face. I think he believed to the end that he was going to get a bullet in the back of the skull which was, after all, exactly what he would have given me.

I rammed the barrel of the Walther into the back of his neck just to frighten him some more, then said in his ear, "I hope you can swim, you bastard."

I put my foot to the base of his spine and shoved him over the rail. Morgan had been watching from the wheelhouse and now, he boosted the engines and started to take us away.

Sara crossed towards me and at the same moment, one of the men on the trawler's deck, dropped to one knee, produced an automatic rifle from beneath the nets and started firing.

I pulled Sara down fast and fired three times in reply, just to keep his head down for considering the range and conditions, I couldn't expect to do much else with the Walther. He managed to get ten or twelve rounds off. One of them shattered a couple of panes of glass in the wheel-house and several more chipped the woodwork here and there, but that was all. By that time, Morgan had taken her past twenty knots anyway and we were streaking into the darkness.

"Can I get up now?" Sara asked from beneath me.

"It's a nice position, but if you insist."

She stood up and leaned on the rail, breathing deeply as if to steady herself. "Straight in and straight out, the man said. Easy, like falling off a log."

"See this little item?" I tapped the side of the Walther with my fingernail. "It's called a safety catch. Next time you want to shoot somebody under the chin, I'd make sure it was off if I were you."

I was at the wheel and alone again an hour later when for the second time that night, she appeared with tea on a tray. We were making time, the sea calm and still and only a feather of spray came over the rail pushed by a small wind.

"How's Morg?" I asked.

"Not too bad. He's only had three drinks. I made him promise. What happens now?"

"To the rum? That's Yanni's headache. I got paid in advance."

"That seems fair enough."

She sat there sipping the scalding tea, holding her cup between both hands. I said, "You know something, you're quite a girl. You handled a gun as to the manner born back there, safety catch or no safety catch."

"I had my thumb on it the whole time," she informed me. "My father had me out with a shotgun when I was barely strong enough to lift it."

"Grouse on a Yorkshire moor is one thing. What you've

NIGHT JUDGEMENT AT SINOS

just been through back there, quite another. You'll never be as close again to being raped. The most I can say is that our good friend Captain Amer would probably have kept you to himself."

She said quietly, "The first time we met you made a few cracks about the kind of life I'd probably been leading and you couldn't have been nearer the truth. I got kicked out of a very superior school for young ladies near Geneva when I was sixteen and I jumped into the swinging London scene so hard, I went in over my head. I'll miss a hell of a lot out and move to the morning after my eighteenth birthday when I woke up in bed with someone I didn't even recognise. I suddenly started wondering what it was all about."

"What was your answer?"

"As always with me, I went to the other extreme. Social work in an East End mission. Drop-outs, junkies, meths, drinkers wetting the bed five times a night. The terrible thing was that it didn't move me. Not one little bit. I just found it disgusting so I looked elsewhere."

"And did you have any luck?"

"Oh, I think you could say that. My step-mother has a cousin, a Chuch of England bishop, God bless him. He was organising a group of relief workers to go to Biafra. People who would be willing to turn their hands to absolutely anything that needed doing."

"And you went?" I said incredulously.

"I spent nine months there. Only came back because I began to show the first signs of my illness. Believe me, poor old Amer back there with his sweaty hands and bad breath was very small beer compared to some of the things I saw out there."

She went out, closing the door behind her. A small wind lifted the charts like a sail, then died. Not for the first time, I began to wonder what life, the whole cock-eyed business, was all about.

We were back in Kyros just before dawn and the first thing I did was to get Morgan to run Sara across to the *Firebird* in the dinghy in spite of her protests. I told her she needed a bath and at least ten hours' sleep which was partially so, for she was looking drawn and tired. The truth was that I wanted her out of the way before I saw Yanni Kytros, just in case there was any trouble.

I marched up to his place with blood in my eye and had him out of bed double-quick. Surprisingly, the whole thing was something of an anticlimax. He was horrified at my story. Unfortunately, the quality of the hired help at that end was not under his direct control, but he would certainly see that Captain Amer was dealt with as he deserved.

He insisted that I have an early breakfast with him while Papas rounded up a few of the boys and afterwards, I drove down to the jetty with them in an old truck and watched while his men emptied the hold of the cases of rum.

I felt a whole lot better as the truck moved away along the jetty. Admittedly in daylight, there were one or two more bullet holes in the superstructure than had been apparent during the night, but I was still one thousand dollars in pocket. It could have been a great deal worse.

I felt quite pleased with myself as I went down to the saloon. Morgan was already snoring in one of the bunks. I started to take off my reefer and heard a step on the deck.

"Mr. Savage, are you there?"

I went back up to the companionway and found Sergeant Loukas standing by the wheelhouse. "Anything I can do for you?" I asked.

"Indeed there is, Mr. Savage." He looked as mournful as usual. "I am afraid I must ask you to accompany me to police headquarters. I am placing you under arrest."

CHAPTER XII

FORCE OF CIRCUMSTANCE

I had a cell to myself, a fine and private place with white-washed walls, stone floors, straw palliasse on an iron cot and a bucket into which I could relieve myself should the need become urgent.

There was a small barred opening in the oaken door, giving a reasonably clear view of the passageway outside. After I'd been in there for an hour, I heard steps, the drone of voices, the sound of a key in the lock.

I went to the door and looked out. A couple of constables stood by a cell at the far end of the passage. As I watched, Morgan shuffled out looking anxious and bewildered. They shoved him along in my direction. When he got close enough, I called to him.

He turned, his rheumy eyes widening and stumbled towards my cell. He was frightened, I could tell that much from the tone of his voice alone.

"What do they want, Jack? What shall I say?"

Anything I told him would have been a waste of time. He was like an old, rusting padlock, ready to snap at the first pressure of the crowbar.

"Whatever it is, you tell 'em, Morg. Tell them anything they want to know. Look after yourself."

The two constables got a grip on him between them and one of them poked the end of his truncheon at my fingers. I moved out of harm's way quickly and they ran Morgan out through the end door.

They'd taken everything. Not only the thousand dollars in hundred-dollar bills which I had received from Kytros, but also cigarettes, matches, loose change. I sat on the cot, my back against the wall, and wondered what it was all about. Even if Loukas had caught me with the booze on board he would, in normal circumstances, have done nothing. The lawbreaking was strictly at the Turkish end of the line and since when did a Greek policeman start worrying because someone was putting one over on the Turks? No, there was more to this than met the eye—much more.

The *graffiti* on the whitewashed wall opposite had a certain political interest. As well as the usual sexual passages and the various unsuccessful attempts at drawing the more private portions of the human anatomy to scale, there were a great many anti-government slogans. The military junta and the prime minister didn't come out of it at all well and would have found most of the suggestions a physical impossibility.

Toughest of all was an inscription which read *Spadakis was here. Keep his gun oiled. He'll be needing it. Up the Patriotic Front.*

I wondered what had happened to Spadakis. He sounded a pretty hard nut, and then the door was unlocked and I was ordered outside.

They took me up to the ground floor where Loukas had his office. Morgan was sitting outside on a bench, his hands shaking, the fingers plucking at his old cap. They took me straight inside without giving us a chance to talk.

Like everywhere else in the place, the walls were whitewashed, mainly for cheapness, but also because it made it a little cooler in the heat of high summer. It wasn't much as offices went. A couple of metal files, a cupboard and the old desk behind which Loukas was seated.

He was writing away busily, waved me to a seat with hardly a glance and told the two constables to leave us. He kept on writing, so I helped myself to a cigarette from a packet on the desk, leaned back and waited.

He finally loked up. "I've just been completing my report. There are twelve separate bullet holes in the superstructure of your vessel, are you aware of that fact? We may also presume that several more were fired. There are three panes of glass shattered in the wheelhouse."

"Some crazy fisherman took a shot at us near the Turkish line," I said. "You know how touchy they are about Greeks fishing their waters? It happens all the time."

He shook his head very deliberately. "No nonsense, no pretty stories, Mr. Savage. I know what you were doing in Turkish waters. Plenty of other boats are engaged in the same trade and I can turn a blind eye and do, as you are perfectly well aware, as long as there is no trouble."

"And what trouble have I caused you, exactly?"

"This is a nice quiet little island and the tourist trade is very important. We can't have boats coming into harbour in the condition yours is in. It would alarm the ladies. It is bad for our image."

I couldn't quite see where all this was leading. I said, "Have I actually committed a crime?"

"An offence," he corrected and tapped a fat leather tome that lay before him. "Under two different statutes in here, I have the power to insist that you behave in an orderly and reasonable manner where you have been guilty of conduct likely to cause public distress and alarm."

"Fair enough," I said. "Do you want my assurances in writing?"

"No, I'm afraid that wouldn't do." He sat back, looking definitely distressed. "You see where the individual concerned is an alien, it is necessary for him to find some reputable Greek citizen to act as a surety for his behaviour. A citizen of some standing. Someone, to take a good example, like Mr. Dimitri Aleko, who is, I understand, known to you."

Some sort of light was beginning to dawn. "Let me get this straight. What happens to me and my boat in the meantime?"

"You personally are free to go, Mr. Savage, to seek what help you can. As for your boat," he sighed, "I am afraid I must impound it until you can produce the kind of surety I require. You do understand, I'm sure. I have my duty to perform."

"Oh, I understand all right." I got to my feet, the anger poking around in my guts like a living thing. "Can I go now?"

"But of course and you may take your mate with you. Your boat will naturally be under guard until this unhappy affair is resolved. You may return on board once only to pick up clothing or any other personal items of an essential nature that you may need."

"Very liberal of you."

He pushed an envelope across the desk. "I think you will find everything intact. Ten hundred-dollar bills, some loose change, cigarettes and a leather wallet."

I grabbed it and made for the door. As I got it open, he added, "There is nothing personal in this, Mr. Savage."

Looking back on it all now, I think he was deliberately needling me, but whether he was or not, he certainly succeeded.

"Why don't you get stuffed?" I said and slammed the door hard enough to shake the entire building.

It was still barely mid-morning when I went into Yanni's, Morgan trailing behind me, and trade was hardly brisk. I slipped him enough loose change for a couple of drinks and asked the barman for Yanni. He was on the roof, it seemed, so I left Morgan to it and went looking for him.

A flight of stone steps led up from the courtyard at the rear of the building to a kind of Moorish roof garden, all potted palms and tinkling fountains. Yanni was seated at a wrought-iron table by the parapet at the far end, drinking coffee and reading a newspaper. He was wearing a rather exotic robe in gold and red stripes, the whole thing held together by a golden cord around the waist. It was obviously one of his Egyptian mornings.

"Ah, Jack, you will join me?" He waved me to a seat and poured coffee into a spare cup.

His smile was of the instant variety. It wasn't that he was worried. He wasn't the kind, I'll say that for him. He always did have all the guts in the world when the chips were down in spite of the stone and a half of excess weight he carried.

It was more subtle than that. He knew why I was there, had known in advance. To make it even more complicated, I think he knew that I knew.

"How much did Aleko pay you to set up last night's little affair, Yanni?" I asked.

"Are you going to be angry, or reasonable, Jack," he

said and I noticed that his right hand was hidden under a
fold of the newspaper.

"All I want are a few answers," I said. "Then I'll go and
see the man myself."

He produced a .38 magnum revolver from beneath the
paper and slipped it into one of the wide pockets in his
robe, then he opened a sandalwood box on the table and
offered me a cigarette. Egyptian on one side, Turkish on
the other. *So we were going to be civilised about this?*

"Aleko is a powerful man, Jack, in Egypt as well as
Greece. He has friends at government level in both countries and money talks, you know that as well as I do. He
as good as has a licence to print his own."

"Get to the point," I told him. "I'm in a hurry."

"All right, give me a chance. He came to see me the
day before yesterday. He'd discovered that we'd had a
working relationship in the past and he knew about most
of my more clandestine affairs in Egypt as well as here.
He was polite, but firm. Either I helped him as required or
he would see that the squeeze was applied to me in both
countries and he meant it, Jack. You don't rise from barefoot peasant boy to multi-millionaire by the age of thirty-
seven unless you consider people to be expendable when
the need arises."

"What was the set-up?"

"He wanted you to lose your boat. To be on the beach.
He told me he had asked you to work for him and that
you had refused. This way, you wouldn't have any choice."

"So this latest effort is strictly improvisation?" I said.
"My boat impounded until I find an upright citizen to
vouch for my good conduct?"

"Everything went wrong. We didn't expect you to get
away, Jack, and no one expected Lady Hamilton to be
with you."

"What did Aleko have to say about that?"

Yanni shuddered. "I have never seen a man so angry.
He is arranging personally for something extremely unpleasant to happen to Captain Amer."

I can't say that prospect worried me particularly. "What
was supposed to happen in the original plan?"

"The Turks were to take over the boat and dump you on the beach outside Tatca. My agent was to pick you up there, lift up his hands in horror, cry Allah's curse on them for stealing your boat and his rum, and arrange for your return to Kyros."

"To go cap in hand to Aleko, willing and eager to accept his proposition."

"You have it exactly. Neat enough, Jack." He had recovered himself completely by now. "I think you must admit that."

"His proposition," I said. "Did he tell you what it is?"

"No, that didn't enter into our conversation. In fact I think I prefer it that way."

"To hell with that," I told him. "If I'm going down then I'm taking you with me. Our millionaire capitalist is a fanatical leftwinger at heart. He wants me to break a political prisoner out of Sinos for him. How does that appeal to you?"

He crossed himself involuntarily, horror on his face. "Mother of God, Jack, if you are caught. The secret police . . ."

"Will be rather unpleasant and not only to me, Yanni. You know what those boys are like when they get moving? They'll pull everyone in. Everyone I ever knew." I reached over and patted his face. "Just think about that. The sweating will do you good."

I might as well have kicked him in the lower stomach for the effect was the same. His face sagged, turned yellow and there was fear in his eyes which was exactly the way I wanted it. Why, as I crossed the garden and went down the steps, I was actually smiling although in the light of future events, I suspect that if I had been able to see his face at that moment, he would have been smiling too.

I left Morgan in the bar and went along the waterfront towards the jetty. The *Seytan* was still down there in the old harbour, drawn up on the sand and Yassi and Abu were working on the hull. Yassi saw me and looked up, shading his eyes from the sun. I heard him call out and a moment later, his father appeared on deck.

"Heh, Jack, you wait for me?" he called.

He vaulted the rail and ran across the strip of beach to the old harbour wall. He came up a rusting iron ladder no more than twenty yards away and I sat on a capstan and waited.

"What's happening?" His face was serious. "I went along to the boat to see you and was turned away by the police. You're in trouble?"

"In a way. Kytros asked me to run some booze to Turkey for him last night. The characters at the other end tried to take over the boat. I objected. There was a little shooting before we parted."

"So I noticed. The wheelhouse doesn't look as pretty as usual."

"That's what Loukas said. He's impounded the boat until I mend my wicked ways and find an upright citizen to stand surety for me."

He frowned and his eyes narrowed. "There is more here than appears on the surface. I am right?"

"Absolutely, but I can't talk about it now. I've got to see Dimitri Aleko."

"Your upright citizen?"

"All that money can't be wrong, surely?"

He laughed and gripped my left arm above the elbow tightly. "You remember one thing, Jack. If any throats need cutting, you come to me. You understand this?"

And he meant it, which was a comforting thought. He went back down the ladder and I continued along the waterfront towards the jetty, wondering what I was going to say to Aleko. What Aleko was going to say to me. And then there was the minor problem of actually getting to him for the *Firebird* was anchored a couple of hundred yards out in the centre of the harbour.

I needn't have worried for when I went down the ramp to the lower jetty, I found *Firebird*'s speedboat tied up there, the two specimens who had picked me up that first night, lounging against the padded seats.

They didn't say a word when they saw me, but simply went to work. One of them slid behind the wheel and started the engine and the other prepared to cast off.

So, they had been waiting for me, or rather, Aleko had.
I got into the rear seat without a word and was taken
away.

I was conducted to the main saloon by Captain Melos
and left at the bar with a drink in my hand. Aleko, it
seemed, was on the radio telephone to Athens and would
be with me shortly. In fact, it was Sara who arrived first.
She entered casually, a magazine in her hand and came to
an abrupt halt at the sight of me.

"This is nice. Why didn't someone tell me?"

She wore a white shirt cut like a man's and knotted at
the waist and the tightest pair of pants I've ever seen in
a kind of black velvet material. She sat on the stool beside me and reached for my hand. I kissed her fingers.

"I'm here to see Midas, king of all the world."

She went very still, eyes quite blank, face expressionless.
"What's happened? Tell me."

"Soon told. Last night's little affair was rigged. A set-up.
I was supposed to lose my boat. Without the boat, I have
nothing. That way I'd come crawling to Aleko, willing and
eager to take on his dirty work. When the plan misfired
they had to think up a subtle variation fast. I must say
they came up with a beauty. I'm a very reprehensible
citizen and a danger to the community. At least that's
the police version of things which means that my boat is
impounded until I can find a fine, upstanding and upright
Greek citizen willing to go surety for my good conduct. I
don't know whether you can think of anyone like that
off-hand."

"Nothing?" she queried gravely. "Without the boat you
have nothing?"

Strange how that was the one thing she had seized on
and I saw at once that I had hurt her without meaning to.
I reached across quickly, my fingers fastening in her hair.

"You know what I mean—must know. With the boat
behind me I can keep my head above water, stay off the
beach. Only just, but that's a big thing because it still
leaves me, Jack Savage, personally in charge. No orders,
no arms twisted. Without the boat I'm nothing. I either
sink to what Morgan is or become someone else's man.
Aleko's man."

"And will you do that?"

"Tell me something," I said. "How did he react this morning when he discovered where you had been last night?"

"You're avoiding my question," she said. "But all right. As a matter of interest, he hasn't mentioned it and I certainly haven't discussed it with him. When Morgan rowed me across this morning I went straight to bed. I slept for five hours, showered and had some breakfast. I've seen Dimitri once and he was busy. He gave me the ritual kiss on each cheek, asked me how I was today and went about his business."

"Which means Yanni Kytros must have told him." I looked beyond her to where Aleko had appeared in the doorway and raised my voice. "Did you get all that? Am I right?"

He moved towards us, grimly elegant in blue linen slacks and one of those cream doeskin jackets that only millionaires can afford. There was a certain anguish on his face and when he put a hand on her shoulder, it was shaking slightly.

"Before God, Sara, I didn't know you would be there."

She glanced up at him and her own face actually softened. She put her hand on his hand and said quietly, "I know, Dimitri, the best laid schemes . . ."

I suppose it was that which really set me off. The sheer illogicality of her attitude. The anger boiled up inside and I got to my feet.

"And this is supposed to make it all right, is it? Damn you Aleko, have you any idea what they had in mind for her?"

Something of the real man still buried deep inside broke through all that neurotic fear. His rage and disgust were at himself but he directed it straight at me. The unexpectedness of the attack caught me off guard.

He delivered a short and very expert right hook to my face. I tried to move, but was already too late. It landed on my right cheek and sent me back over the bar stool. Those beautiful carpets of his cushioned the shock, but the force of that punch seemed to rattle the brains inside my head.

I took a deep breath, came up fast and grabbed a bottle from the bar. Several things happened right about then. Sara cried out sharply, "No, Jack, no!" In the same moment Melos appeared in the doorway flanked by his two bully boys holding a submachine gun apiece.

It seemed an unnecessary amount of hardware to carry in the circumstances, but was as effective as the big battalions usually are. I looked from Melos and company to Sara who still stood between Aleko and me, arms wide in a strangely defensive attitude as if she would protect him from me. *And she had called me Jack for the first time.*

There was what can only be described as an air of expectancy to things. I had the stage, it was all mine, so I took my time about it, walked round to the back of the bar, found the Jameson and poured myself a large one. I took a tiny sip, savoured it for a moment, then emptied the glass. I put it down carefully on the bar and looked straight at Aleko.

"One hundred thousand dollars paid into a Geneva bank of my choosing in advance, now, today, and the boat returned to me when everything has been satisfactorily concluded. That's what it's going to cost you, Aleko."

And he still managed to surprise me.

"Excellent," he said. "I knew you would be sensible in the end. In exactly one hour you will be able to pick up the telephone, ring the bank of your choice, and confirm that the transfer has taken place. I guarantee it."

He turned and went out taking Melos and his boys with him with a wave of the hand.

I poured myself another whiskey and said to Sara, "Some days you just can't win, have you ever noticed that?"

Her fists were clenched, she was angry and afraid at the same time. "You fool," she said. "You bloody, pig-headed fool. Marry me and money would be the least of your problems or hadn't that occurred to you?"

"A good point."

"Then why are you doing it?"

"As the Americans say, stick around and I just might tell you, but only if you behave yourself."

She went out raging under full sail. I toasted the empty doorway and sighed. *Why was I doing it?* A good question. The trouble was, I didn't really know myself—or did I?

CHAPTER XIII

GOOD LOVING AND A LONG LIFE

Aleko was as good as his word and better, for no more than forty minutes had elapsed when he sent for me again.

"My agents in Geneva are standing by to make an immediate transfer to the bankers of your choice. I could, of course, give you my word that the transmission will go through today as planned, but it occurs to me that this may not satisfy you."

"A reasonable assumption."

"So I had concluded. If you will pick up the telephone, you will find they are holding a direct line to Geneva. Ask for the firm of your own choice. I wish you to feel one hundred per cent satisfied."

Which was fair enough. I asked for Steiner and Company, a firm of merchant bankers I had used in Geneva in happier days. The younger son, Hans, had visited Alexandria in connection with a salvage job in the Suez Canal that I had been involved in. I spoke to him briefly, then passed the phone to Aleko who told him exactly what to do in about thirty seconds flat, prefacing the address with the magic of his own name, then put the receiver down.

"Ten minutes, Mr. Savage, no more. Better to sit down."

I did, choosing a comfortable club chair in black leather and spent the time watching him closely. He was a different man, this big business Aleko, working his way through a mountain of paper at a quite incredible speed.

The ten minutes came and went. He glanced at his watch and the phone rang as if on command. He nodded to me, I picked it up and found Hans Steiner on the other end. It was signed, sealed, delivered. For good or ill, dead or alive, I was a man of substance again.

"Satisfied?" Aleko demanded.

I replaced the receiver. "Perfectly—what happens now?"

"You do what I have paid you to do. You get Andreas Pavlo out of Sinos." He appeared to hesitate. "Captain Savage." *So it was Captain again?* "Captain Savage, words are empty things. I do not ask for promises. I think that in spite of the impression you attempt to give, you are if anything, bedevilled by man's greatest curse. Moral integrity."

"God save me from that."

"I have been honest with you. I require, indeed believe, that you will be honest with me. One thing is sure. If anyone can get Pavlo out of that prison, you can."

"I'll try and earn my keep," I said. "Don't worry about that."

"I have arranged accommodation for you on board although naturally, you may come and go exactly as you please. Any equipment, any facility you need, just ask. The important thing to remember is that time is of the essence. Pavlo, though still on his back, has improved so much that there is a possibility they will move him to Athens this weekend."

Which gave us four days. "And all the information you promised me?" I asked.

"Is waiting in your cabin."

The door opened and Melos entered. "One more thing," I said. "This contact of yours on the island. Can they be used?"

"For information and guidance, yes, but not personally."

I nodded. "All right. I'll have a look at the general situation and then I'll come back to you."

I turned to the door and he said, "Your mate—Morgan Hughes. I don't think he's up to this sort of thing any more. I'm sure you agree. I have made arrangements for him to stay in a small *taverna* on the waterfront."

Which took care of Morg nicely. Funny, but it was somehow as if he'd been swept into the corner out of the way and I didn't care for that. Most of all, I didn't like the fact that I hadn't given him a thought. Aleko had taken him into consideration—I hadn't. I didn't feel too proud of myself as I followed Melos along the corridor.

The cabin was in the luxury class with the usual fitted carpets a couple of inches thick and its own bathroom. There was a large modern desk with a teak top and a swivel chair to go with it. Half a dozen foolscap files and several rolled maps and charts waited for me, Aleko's background information.

I lit a cigarette, sat down and started to work through it. He had been incredibly thorough. There was a file on Andreas Pavlo for a start that detailed everything about him from the day he was born and included the exact position and appearance of his appendix scar as well as his grades in Philosophy and Mathematics at university.

It ended at four p.m. on the previous day which would seem to indicate that Aleko's contact was getting daily information to him. The medical report was impeccable in its detail. Left arm fractured, three ribs cracked, laceration of the right lung. He had also suffered badly from exposure and severe sunburn and had been in shock for several days. He was still in intensive care, whatever that meant in a prison hospital.

There was a report on prison security, guard rotas, alarm systems and so forth which couldn't have been more thorough if it had come from the governor's office. Come to think of it, it probably had.

Most important was the island defensive system. The fortress itself had never held more than three or four hundred prisoners in the past, but under the present political regime, at least five thousand political detainees had been added who were housed in encampments outside the fort itself.

Because of this, the island's general defenses had been considerably strengthened. A radar system kept track of vessels in the area which were required to keep on the move in the Middle Passage on the south side of the island which was the main shipping route through to Kyros and Crete. This explained why it had been necessary for Ciasim to obtain a special license to work on his wartime wreck.

But there were other hazards. Not only was the coast

constantly patrolled by two M.T.B.s. Most beach approaches were mined as were the beaches themselves. *The bloody war all over again.* And yet, far from feeling dismay, my interest stirred. This was going to be one hell of a problem and that was putting it mildly. Difficult, but interesting, just like the old days.

The thing fell into four main parts. Landing on the island without being detected. Getting inside the fortress and reaching Pavlo. Bringing him out and finally, getting him off the island.

I started sorting the information relevant to each part of the operation to start with and the door opened and Sara entered. She closed it behind her and leaned against it watching me rather sullenly.

"Isn't there anything I can say to stop you going through with this?"

"Not that I can think of. It's too late, anyway. I've taken his money. It's already waiting for me in Geneva being carefully guarded by some thoroughly trustworthy Swiss merchant bankers."

"I hate you," she said bitterly. "I hate all men, but you in particular."

After that she came and stood so close that I ended up breathing pure Intimacy instead of oxygen, leading to another wild couple of minutes which ended with both of us shaking in our shoes and showing it.

"I love you, too," I said, "but work comes first. You can help me sort this stuff out if you like. I'll show you what I'm after."

Which I did and she came straight back at me with the first thing she picked up, a folded map of some description which I'd missed as it had fallen to the floor.

She opened it and frowned. "Well here's something that doesn't fit for a start."

"Why not?" I said impatiently.

"I don't understand it. It's in German."

I must have sensed how important her find would prove to be because my stomach went hollow with excitement as I reached for it. It was old, it was creased so badly that in places the paper had worn through, but it was still quite unmistakably the Germans' plans of their improvements

to the old Turkish fort in 1942. I examined it carefully,
then turned to the official plan of the prison produced the
previous year and it hit me right between the eyes at once.

Phase 2 of the operation was taken care of which
wasn't a bad start.

I smiled and Sara said, "Can I join in? It must be good."

I didn't see why not, so I showed her. Strange, but she
wasn't anything like as enthusiastic as I was.

Two hours, that's all it took, for the skeleton of an
idea to form in my mind. A little more thought and it
would all be there, but for the moment, I'd had enough.
What I needed was fresh air.

We took the speedboat round to the quiet side of the
island and ran her into a quiet little cove at the bottom
of high cliffs. It was pretty well inaccessible from the land
and just what I was looking for.

I ran the prow of the boat firmly into wet sand and
we went for a swim. Afterwards, we lay in the shade of
a semicircle of massive boulders and made love.

Which was marvellous, or almost marvellous. The trouble was that Sinos and Andreas Pavlo and the old German
ground plan kept clicking through my mind at a rate of
knots at the most inconvenient moments.

"Not bad," Sara said afterwards, "but not good. I object
to you having anything else on your mind at what should
be one of life's great moments."

"I warned you I was over the hill."

"That will be the day." She smiled. "A little more concentration, that's all you need."

I saw the chart, the Middle Passage, the south side of
the island again in my mind's eye. She said, "I wish you
could see the look on your face. Come on, spit it out."

"All right. Phase One is actually landing on the island.
Phase Two is getting into the fort. I've already explained
Phase Two and it means coming in from the Middle
Passage on the south side of the island."

"All right, what are the hazards?"

I went through them quickly. "M.T.B. patrols to be
evaded, underwater minefield to negotiate, guards to avoid

on land itself. Guards *and* dog patrols. And a constant radar check."

"All of which could be avoided by an underwater approach, you stressed that when we discussed Phase Two in the cabin."

"But you have to make your underwater approach from somewhere," I explained patiently, "and any vessel stopping in the Middle Passage must always accept the chance of being checked by those M.T.B.s."

"But Ciasim was working there the day before yesterday and nobody bothered him."

"He has a licence to work on that wreck from the Ministry in Athens," I said and stopped short.

A gull wheeling high over the cliffs, darted down through the shadows, a flash of white against the grey. She had that sombre look on her face again.

"The thing is," I said slowly, "do I have the right to involve him?"

"I'd let him make his own mind up on that one."

"No." I shook my head. "It wouldn't be fair. He owes me too much. He's bound to feel beholden. I'd be putting him in a hell of a position."

"You saved his life, didn't you?" There was a hard edge to her voice. "Why shouldn't he save yours? He's the only man I've seen around here who looks as if he might be of some real use to you."

And then I saw. She wanted me to have the best chance there was. The best chance of coming through alive and if that meant involving Ciasim, well and good. There was the female of the species for you, cold-blooded as hell and utterly ruthless where their own was concerned.

I sighed and reached out for her hand. "All right, I'll go and see him."

"I think you're being wise."

Was I? Perhaps, but I already felt as guilty as hell about it.

We left the speedboat at the ramp by the old jetty and I went looking for him. He wasn't at the *Seytan*. I found Abu and Yassi working away at the hull stripped to the waist, bodies shining with sweat, but no Ciasim. He had gone for a drink and they mentioned three strong possibilities, smiling shyly, but with complete admiration, at Sara.

We found him at the second place we tried, playing dominoes with two very old white-haired men, both famous divers in their day. He didn't notice at first and we sat in a corner under the vines and left him to finish his game.

His laughter was like a volcano's rumble or thunder far off beyond the mountains. One of the old men won, I suspect as much by Ciasim's design as anything else.

"Too good for me," he roared and got up, slapping a handful of loose change on the table. "Drinks on me and good health with it."

Turning to leave, he saw us and his face lit up with genuine pleasure. "Heh, Jack, baby! I'm glad to see you in decent company." He called to the waiter inside, crossed to our table and reached for Sara's hands. "I kiss your fingers," he said, and did just that. "The most beautiful woman in the world."

"I believe you," she said. "No reservations."

The wine came, a bottle of *Marco* served ice-cold. He filled the glasses himself and raised his own to toast us. "I wish you good loving, dear friends, and long life."

It was an old Turkish saying and unintentionally carried its own poignancy. Sara took my hand under the table and held it tightly.

"Not very likely, I'm afraid," she said and drank some of her wine.

Dear God, for a moment there I thought she intended to tell him about herself, but no. As he lowered his glass, a frown on his face, she added, "Jack, here, seems absolutely determined on getting his head blown off."

When I was finished, he sat there, his face very dark suffused with passion, his right fist tightly clenched.

"This Aleko, this Greek pig. Why not let me handle him, Jack, in my own barbaric Turkish way?"

He produced a knife from a sheath under his left arm, the blade razor-sharp, gleaming in the sunlight, as wicked a looking implement as I have ever seen.

Sara was genuinely horrified. "No, not that, for God's sake!"

Ciasim raised a hand to calm her and put the knife away. "I was forgetting the dog is your kind." He sighed. "And you, Jack, you feel bound to your bargain with him?"

"I'm going through with it if that's what you mean."

"Then I have no choice. I must help you."

"Ten thousand dollars, Ciasim, for the use of your boat as a base for just a few hours."

He shook his head. "You go too fast, dear friend. Tell me, who goes in to Sinos with you? Aleko's men?"

I shook my head. "I've done this kind of work before, with the commandos. It only works when you have absolute trust, complete confidence in your associates, whoever they are."

"And you do not care for Aleko's men?"

"Not particularly. I can get away with this on my own— just. I'd rather have it that way."

"Don't be a fool, Savage," Sara put in sharply.

Ciasim nodded. "She is right. On your own, you are a corpse before you begin. No, Jack, I am afraid I will not let you use my boat, even for ten thousand dollars. I will not take your money."

"Not mine, his," I said.

"You miss my point. It is not that I have any objection to improving my fortune. It is just that I refuse to allow you to commit suicide. It is against the tenets of my religion. No, there is only one way I can be persuaded to change my mind."

"And what would that be?"

"I must go with you," he said. "Into Sinos. Into the prison to bring this poor devil out." I stared at him, mouth open in astonishment. He added in a slightly injured tone. "You do not think me competent?"

I was unable to reply. And Sara? If ever I saw relief on a face it was on hers.

Ciasim swallowed his wine and patted her cheek. "You are really very, very beautiful. It is a good thing Jack is my most loving friend. Now I think we go and see this bastard Aleko."

CHAPTER XIV

PLAN OF ATTACK

The aquamobile is a bullet-shaped, underwater scooter driven by battery-operated propellers. Designed to operate at up to a hundred and fifty feet, it carries its own spotlight and is capable of a speed of just over three knots an hour. I needed two and they were absolutely essential to the success of the entire operation. Number one on the list I gave to Aleko.

He accepted it without question just as he had accepted Ciasim without any hesitation when I had explained about the *Seytan* and the licence to work on the wreck, in the Middle Passage. He had obviously really meant it when he had said that I was in charge. The only thing that interested him was getting Andreas Pavlo out of Sinos and everything that led to that end was all right by him.

"The uniforms you ask for," he said. "They are essential?"

"Absolutely."

He nodded. "All the additional diving equipment you mention here, we already have on board except for the underwater scooters."

"Lots of skin diving clubs in this part of the Mediterranean use them now," I told him. "There's an outfit in Athens who deals with them all the time. I've written the address on the back of the list. You shouldn't have any difficulty."

"If they are in Athens, they will be here first thing in the morning. I will have them flown in."

"There's no doubt about it," I told him amiably. "Money talks."

"Always." There was the ghost of a smile on his lips.

"I was exactly fourteen when my uncle took me to America. The land of the free, Captain Savage. An ironic phrase. My English was almost non-existent. We were so poor that we ate on alternate days and no one cared. No one took any notice. You understand me?"

"And you decided to change all that?"

"Have I not done so?"

Suddenly, he was all Greek, the Bostonian veneer stripped away, about seventeen different people staring out at me from those dark eyes. He spread his hands in a vaguely Continental gesture as if indicating everything around him. The boat, the luxury, the evidence of vast wealth.

And then the other Aleko peered out for a moment, the real man he might have been if things had not happened to him in the way they had. He smiled, a genuinely engaging smile, ruefully like a small boy caught out.

"Naturally, a small meed of thanks is due to the Texas oilfields that gave me my first million."

"America, America," I said and got up. "Ah, well, I've got work to do. Have that gear here in the morning and we'll go tomorrow night."

"So soon?" He seemed surprised.

"No sense in hanging about. I'd like to get it over with."

"You've really worked the thing out to that degree already?"

"I think so. I'll go over the details with you later on. Right now, I'd like to have a look at that diving gear of yours."

I had my hand to the door when he said, "One other thing—Sara."

I turned, suddenly wary. "What about her?"

"I'd be obliged if you would involve her as little as possible in this business from now on."

"Isn't that for her to decide?"

He sat there staring at me for a long, quiet moment, then he got to his feet, went to a corner cupboard and produced a decanter of brandy and two glasses. He was grave, and very, very dignified. Whatever was coming, was going to be good, that much was obvious.

He handed me one of the glasses and poured a generous measure. "I deal in facts, Captain Savage, because they are the only things that pay off. That is why I am where I am and who I am. Because I can accept things as they really are without any illusions."

"Sounds reasonable," I said. "On the other hand, what about the Pavlo business? A strange kind of knight errantry for a man who deals only in facts, in things as they really are."

He seemed surprised. "The present government cannot last, surely you see that? Any sensible man must see that. Read the history of my country. An object lesson to would-be tyrants."

Which was all nice and flowery, but didn't really get us any further.

"And Sara?" I asked. "Where does she fit in to all this?"

He held his glass rather tightly and it was the one sign of stress as he spoke. "My wife was everything to me. For her sake, I love Sara. Love her as dearly as if she were my own sister."

He could have meant every word of it. It was impossible to be sure, but there was certainly great emotion of some kind in his voice as he carried on.

"Chronic leukaemia is unusual in a girl of Sara's age. The symptoms first became apparent when she was working in Biafra with a relief mission."

"I know about that," I said and suddenly, didn't want to hear any more. Did not want to know what I sensed was now to come.

He carried on relentlessly, his voice a little calmer now. "To you, she must appear as you would expect any normal, healthy girl of her age to look, but you have not seen her as I have. As she was last year at the first real onset. She almost died."

"But she didn't," I said and my throat was dry.

"No, the doctors obtained what they call a remission. She was luckier than most. In her case, the drug worked. Her blood count gradually returned to a reasonably normal level. She has now joined the fifteen per cent who can expect to survive five years."

And he was telling me the truth, the absolute clinical truth, I was certain of that.

I remember losing my air once during a job at the bottom of the Suez Canal, the sudden choking sensation like great fingers wrapping themselves around your throat and squeezing. It felt exactly like that now.

I said, "And that's it?"

"There have been cases in which the patient has survived ten years. Anything can happen, of course. New drugs are being developed all the time. Who knows?"

"Only you don't think so, do you?" I put down my glass. "Why are you telling me all this?"

His voice was urgent and he moved closed. "She needs what I can give her, Savage, don't you see that? Constant care, every attention. Everything money can buy she will have. The right doctors, the rarest medicines. I can give her all these things, but you, Savage? What can you give her?"

His eyes were wild and there was a smell on him like an open grave, cold and damp, cutting to the bone, the touch of death. It sent my heart pounding wildly.

"Go to hell," I said, hoarsely, turned and got the door open, running as if all the devils in that place were snapping at my heels.

When I went into my cabin she was sitting in the swivel chair at the desk examining the old German plan that was the key to the whole operation. She swung round to face me and smiled.

"Ciasim's gone back to the *Seytan*. Says he wants to get her floated by this evening. Did you see Dimitri?"

"I saw him."

It was in my voice, I couldn't help it and her face changed, altered before my eyes, the skin tightening over the cheekbones. She knew, by instinct, I suppose, or perhaps on past knowledge of him.

"What did he say?" she said calmly and got to her feet. "What did he tell you?"

"I love you, Sara Hamilton, whatever that word is supposed to mean, but is it enough?"

She frowned as if not understanding and then, I think, suddenly saw it all. She smiled, that delightful smile that was herself alone. She started to laugh, came close, grabbed a handful of my hair and shook it vigorously.

"It's everything there is. Do you mean to tell me you've got this far without realising that fact?"

I could have died for her at that single moment in time, an absurdity if you like, but as I took her in my arms, it did occur to me that to *live* for her sake might be of more use. How strange life was. And she seemed so alive. It was beyond belief.

Allowing for the traditional contempt to be expected from any self-respecting Turkish spongediver for skin divers, Ciasim had, in fact, had plenty of aqualung experience at one time or another. In spite of that fact, Sara and I took him out beyond the point in the early evening in the speedboat after the *Seytan* had been successfully floated.

We used some of Aleko's diving equipment and I gave the big Turk a thorough briefing on the technical side of things again, just in case he'd forgotten anything. It wasn't really needed. He was like one of those great early pilots of pioneering days. The men who flew by the seat of their pants. In the same way, he dived by instinct, using his senses like an animal. To go under the surface of the sea seemed the most natural thing in the world to him.

I think he was probably the most likable man I have ever known. On the run back to harbour after we had changed, he had Sara laughing hard at one outrageous story after another, most involving his many encounters with women like his German *hausfrau* of the night before last.

"Ciasim Divalni, you are a rogue—King Size," she told him.

He simulated bewilderment. "But I render such excellent service, dear lady."

Dear lady. He always called her that and there was something different in his voice, in his manner, when he was with her. I think he sensed in some way that she was different from other women. One apart. Perhaps that animal instinct of his hinted at the reason. One thing is certain. I would not have given much for the chances of any man who insulted her or gave her hurt in his presence.

"The operation can be divided into four main areas," I said and turned to the maps pinned on the board behind me.

We were in the main saloon of the *Firebird*. My audience consisted of Sara, Aleko, Ciasim, Captain Melos and the two hard-faced young men who never seemed to stir far from his side. They were not, as I had first imagined, brothers, but cousins. One was named Christou, the other Kapelari.

"Phase One," I continued, "involves actually landing on the island. We make an underwater approach from the *Seytan* which will be anchored at this point half a mile south of Cape Heros just below the outer walls of the fort."

"A long swim," Melos put in.

I think that was the first moment it struck me that his status might be very different from what was pretended. The intervention had a quality of authority about it. In a way, he had made a slip and knew it, his eyes darkening as I turned to him.

"The aquamobile is good for just over three knots an hour. A ten minute run to the Cape at the most. There is a static minefield to negotiate, but they're well spaced, if the map I've been provided with is accurate, and shouldn't give us much trouble. Not if we take care."

Ciasim bared his teeth. "I love you too, my friend."

"Aren't the beach approaches mined?" Aleko demanded.

I nodded. "But that won't bother us. If you look at the official plan of the fort and the prison area produced last year and compare it with the German military plans of their improvements in 1942, you'll notice a significant difference. The Greek plans indicate the modern sewerage system and leave it at that. The Germans, thorough as always where this kind of thing is concerned, have shown the underlying system of drainage tunnels put in by the Turks seven hundred years ago. In some cases they actually used them as main outfalls."

Aleko got up and examined the plans closely. "See, Melos, he is right."

Melos looked over his shoulder. "So, the main outfall is here in this small bay at the foot of Cape Heros and under water, from the look of it."

"Exactly. No problems with those mines on the beaches this way."

"You could be wrong," he said. "Have you considered that? Perhaps the old Turkish workings have simply been missed from the new plan because they have been blocked."

"I don't think so. German plans of this nature are usually extremely thorough and completely reliable. If we accept that, it means that the main tunnels are five and six feet in diameter. To block such a complex would be extremely difficult."

"But you cannot be certain," he persisted.

"You take a chance every day of your life, Captain Melos," I told him. "If it won't go, then we turn back, just like the north face of the Eiger. At any stage of the game if we find the hole has been plugged, we turn back."

"Without Pavlo?"

"If necessary."

"So, the British Marine commandos could not teach you how to make miracles."

"Only sometimes," I said, which seemed to shut him up for the moment.

"What about Phase Two?" Aleko asked impatiently.

"According to the plan there is a storm drain linking up to the garden of that section of the fort which is now being used as a hospital. It also indicates a three foot grid at the entrance which we ought to be able to cope with. At that point, or perhaps earlier if convenient, we change clothes. Once out in the open, I become a prison guard and Ciasim, a prisoner which is how we get into the hospital itself."

"In other words, you become prisoner and escort?"

"Exactly."

"And how do you get to Pavlo?"

Melos again.

"He's on the third floor under guard in the room at

the end of the corridor," I said. "We play it by ear from there. Today's information is that he can walk a little and a little is all we need. Once out of the hospital block, we go back into the sewerage system via the storm drain in the garden."

"And you think he will be able to stand it?" Aleko asked.

I shrugged. "He'll have to stand a damned sight more than that because we come back to the *Seytan* exactly the same way we left. Underwater."

There was a heavy silence. Surprisingly, it was Melos who came in to support me. "With the aquamobile, even with two of you and allowing for the greater load, the trip should take no more than fifteen minutes and it will require no physical effort from Pavlo himself, or very little."

"But what happens afterwards?" Sara said.

Melos frowned. "After what?"

"When they find Pavlo missing. When they start searching the general area of the island. If they know the *Seytan* was in the area, they're bound to start checking, especially when they find she's left during the night."

It was the weak link and I acknowledged the fact. "The *Seytan* is a boat well known in the area. Poor Turkish spongedivers and so on. The excuse for returning to Kyros can be a technical one. A faulty compressor, a leak in the hull. If everything goes according to schedule, we'll be back in Kyros by four a.m. With any luck, Pavlo's absence won't be noticed till six a.m. which is the time things usually start to stir at the prison. Any check on the *Seytan* will be of a routine nature. They'd probably get in touch with police headquarters here and ask them to interview Ciasim."

"Which means Sergeant Loukas," Aleko said and he smiled broadly at Melos.

Melos said briskly, "Nothing to worry about there. An excellent plan. Highly dangerous, but hare-brained enough to work." He added calmly, "Who knows, Captain Savage, you might just make it back alive."

Who knew indeed.

I said, "One last thing. We'll be needing an extra man on the *Seytan*, just in case one of those M.T.B.s decides to make a check. There are supposed to be three in the crew, remember." I turned to Melos. "Come to think of it, you look a lot like a Turk to me."

Ciasim bellowed with laughter and Melos gave him the kind of look any good Greek reserves for a lump of dung on his foot.

Aleko said, "Captain Melos will be happy to help in any way he can."

So, he was back in charge again, or was he? There were many things here I didn't like. Things under the surface. Relationships that were not all they seemed to be.

Later, much later, when I was lying in bed in the darkness of my cabin smoking a cigarette, the door clicked open and she slipped inside, locking it behind her. There was a rustle of something or other and she got in beside me, naked and shivering, her breasts ice-cold.

"Warm me up, Savage," she ordered.

"When I've finished my cigarette." I put an arm around her. "What can you tell me about Melos?"

"Nothing much. He's new, but then they all are. The entire crew. Dimitri had *Firebird* laid up for a year before this cruise. Too busy to have fun, he used to say. Why do you ask?"

"Melos seems to have a lot to say for himself, that's all."

"He's a Greek, just like the rest of them, isn't he? What do you expect?"

I put out my cigarette in the ash tray at the side of the bed and she came on top of me, breasts crushed hard against my chest, her face in the hollow of my neck.

"No, don't move," she said in a muffled voice. "Just let me stay like this for a while. Just hold me."

She started to cry, great sobs racking her body, really letting go for the first time since I'd known her. The desolation, the loneliness in her voice when she at last spoke was like a knife in the heart.

"What happens if I lose you? What happens then?"

And there was nothing I could say. No single thing that would comfort her. Outside, it had started to rain and I held her quiet in my arms.

It was a dull, grey morning and reminiscent of the

English Channel in November with a fair sea running and an easterly wind. It caused chaos for a while in the old harbour, particularly amongst the small boats which were drifting around all over the place for they weren't used to that kind of weather in the Aegean.

I wouldn't have given much for any floatplane's chances of putting down in those conditions, but it wasn't necessary. The firm in Athens who supplied the aquamobiles had half a dozen in stock at their branch on Rhodes and had two of them brought over by fast launch during the night. Anything for the magic name of Aleko.

At least the bad weather and the disturbance it created in the harbour gave us an excellent cover during the period before we left. People were too heavily involved in their own problems to have the time to notice what we were doing.

Melos had boarded the *Seytan* under cover of darkness just before dawn and had kept out of the way ever since. Ciasim and his boys had transferred the diving gear the previous night and the rest of the equipment, including two supply canisters, packed ready to take with us.

The aquamobiles were the only major item remaining and the launch from Rhodes arrived with those just after ten a.m. Ciasim and I took delivery on the north jetty and brought them round on a handcart, still in their packing cases, a couple of fishing nets hiding them from view.

As we turned on to the old jetty, I saw Morgan sitting on a capstan, hunched and miserable in the rain, an old black oilskin over his shoulders. We were almost on top of him before he noticed me and he got to his feet, face cracking into an anxious smile.

"Hell, Jack, I been getting worried. What's been going on?"

I sent Ciasim on ahead with the handcart and pulled Morgan down against the wall out of the rain.

"Listen, Morg," I said, "I'm busy today. I'm giving Ciasim a hand."

"Out there on the wreck?" His eyes brightened. "Maybe I can help. Another diver's always useful, Jack."

He seemed older, more childlike than ever. I put a hand on his shoulder. "Not today, Morg, another time." I took

a one hundred dollar bill from my wallet which was the
smallest change I had. "Here, take this up to Yanni Kytros.
He'll change it for you at a fat discount. You'll be able
to sit in there out of the wet all day. I'll see you in the
morning."

He wanted to argue, but the thirst rose in his throat. I
could see that from his eyes. He took the note and grinned
nervously. "Just as you say, Jack. In the morning."

I patted his shoulder and he shambled away. I stood up
and found Sergeant Loukas leaning against the wall lighting a cigarette. He had an old military raincoat slung from
his shoulders like a cape against the drizzle and his face
carried its usual funereal expression.

"Dreadful weather, Mr. Savage. Just like England, is
it not so?"

"Ireland," I corrected him. "You're forgetting."

"Ah, yes." He nodded sagely. "Still, we are not used to
rain like this down here. Farther north, perhaps, in Macedonia for example. It can be very wet in the Gulf of
Thermai. I had a holiday there once only, on an island
named Pelos. A complete waste of money. We might as
well have stayed at home."

I stood there, frozen into position, waiting for what was
to come next. He sighed, suddenly looking even more
mournful than usual if such a thing was at all possible.

"Nothing is ever what we expect it to be, have you
noticed that, Mr. Savage? On the surface, one thing,
underneath, something else again." He flicked his cigarette
over the wall and glanced up at the sky. "Still raining and
more to come. Take care, my friend, dangerous waters
in the Middle Passage in weather like this."

He walked away and I watched him go, wondering what
the hell he was getting at. A warning, perhaps? Of sorts,
and yet there was more to it than that. And the reference
to Macedonia and Pelos? Too near the mark for comfort.

The speedboat arrived at the slipway below me. Aleko
got out first, turned to help Sara, then they walked towards me together, her hand on his arm.

"Is everything set?" he asked as they arrived.

I nodded towards Loukas who had by now turned on

to the waterfront. "I'm not too happy about him. He seems to know a little bit about everything."

"Loukas?" He smiled in a rather complacent way. "And so he should."

That he had bribed Loukas to get him to act as he had done in the matter of my boat, I had accepted as a fact of life, but this was more. Much more.

"One of yours?" I asked.

"One should always cover every eventuality, Captain Savage. Every possibility. The secret of success in every walk of life, I assure you." And then he stuck out his hand and said briskly, "But I must not detain you. I will expect you just before dawn as arranged. I have the utmost confidence that meeting will take place."

I restrained a mad impulse to salute him and say, "thank you, sir." He glanced briefly at Sara, then walked back towards the slipway leaving us together.

She was wearing a yellow oilskin jacket and sou'wester and looked tired, her eyes hot and far away, too bright and circled by dark smudges.

"So this is it," she said. "The long goodbye."

"Short," I said. "The short goodbye. I'll be back here no later than four a.m. tomorrow. My life on it."

"A hell of a thing to put in pawn," she said acidly.

We had reached the *Seytan*. The packing cases were on board and Yassi was in the wheelhouse waiting the order to go from Ciasim who was on deck with Abu waiting to cast-off.

"Ready, Jack?" he called.

I waved and turned back to her. "Feeling sorry for yourself again?"

"Also good and mad," she said. "Suddenly, it's all a bad dream."

I didn't kiss her, but took her chin firmly in my right hand and said forcefully, "Four a.m. Dead or alive, Sara Hamilton, walking from the sea if I have to, but I'll be here. See that you are."

I went down to the *Seytan* and Abu and Ciasim cast-off immediately. As we moved out towards the harbour entrance, I stood at the rail watching her.

Ciasim said at my shoulder, "There is something special

about her, Jack. It sets her apart from other women and yet it makes me feel sad. You have noticed this?"

"She is going to die, old friend," I said. "She's on borrowed time. It's as simple as that."

That stupid, empty phrase again.

I didn't bother looking at him, but heard his breath go out in a long sigh, heard him turn and walk away, his step heavy. My eyes were only for her standing there at the end of the jetty watching us go.

She was still there twenty minutes later, a faint smudge of yellow against the grey as the island finally faded into the rain.

CHAPTER XV

ASSAULT BY NIGHT

It was a three hour run in the old *Seytan* to the marker buoy Ciasim had left in the Middle Passage to indicate the wreck's position. We arrived just after two in the afternoon, and dropped anchor. Melos and I stayed below out of sight. It was as well that we did for after an hour, one of the M.T.B.s came roaring up to take a look. They didn't even stop. Recognising the *Seytan* they circled once, the young commander waved from the bridge and they raced away again.

Ciasim came down the companionway and leaned in the doorway grinning. "Okay?"

"Will they come back?" Melos asked.

"Probably not. They know who it is, they know we have a licence. Why should they?" He opened a drawer and produced a pack of cards. "A little poker, eh?"

"Better than nothing." Melos sat down at the narrow table and glanced about him with disgust. "What a sty, but what can you expect?"

Ciasim took it very well. "And that, Greek pig, will cost you everything. Every drachma. Your shirt, your pants. I send you naked into the world."

Melos produced a wallet, took out a wad of notes and slapped them on the table. "Put your money where your mouth is, you animal."

Greek and Turk. Seven hundred years of hating and nothing changed. I sighed as I took up my place at the table. It was going to be a long afternoon.

The wind dropped towards evening and took the rain with it and as the horizon darkened, the sea became calmer. The afternoon had been anything but pleasant,

Ciasim baiting Melos at every turn and there wasn't much I could do about it. They didn't actually come to blows, which was a major miracle, but Melos lost a great deal of money and wasn't pleased about it.

From five o'clock on I was able to break the game up by insisting that we had everything ready in advance. There were the aquamobiles to unpack and check along with the rest of the diving equipment. They were simplicity itself to control and it didn't take Ciasim more than a couple of minutes to get the hang of things.

By nine o'clock it was time to go, the sky very dark, stars strung away to the horizon and the moon was on the wane, pale and misty at the edges.

Everything was ready on deck when Ciasim and I finally went up, dark shadows in our black Neoprene wet-suits. Yassi and Abu helped us on with the aqualungs. There was a quick final check and we went over the side.

At that stage, as always on that kind of a job, I wasn't aware of any nervous tension. Too much to think about. The supply canisters came over the side, one for each of us and we clipped them to a trailing harness. Last of all, the aquamobiles.

I positioned the time-elapsed bevel on my watch, adjusted my air supply and gave Ciasim the thumbs up. Then I switched on the aquamobile and went under the surface.

Moonlight filtered down through the water making visibility surprisingly good ten feet down which was the depth I'd selected for the first stage of the run in. The aquamobile had a depth gauge, compass and speedometer which also indicated the distance covered in kilometers. I had my mind fully occupied with that little lot for it was absolutely essential that I stayed exactly on the bearing I had selected from the chart if we were to find the outfall of the main drainage tunnel. And there was the minefield to consider. I couldn't afford any mistake there.

A quarter of a mile—one third. I slowed, gave Ciasim the agreed signal as he came alongside, then I switched on the powerful spot mounted on top of the scooter and went down.

all the time. It was colder here, the air earthy, but not
unpleasant and at least I could breathe again.

I had marked the route carefully on the old German
plan which I carried in one hand, the spot in the other.
We needed the third tunnel on the left and came to it some
ten minutes after starting out. It was no more than four
feet high, but dry as a bone.

"I'll go first from now on, Jack," Ciasim whispered.
"You tell me what to look for. That leaves you free to
concentrate on the plan. The wrong turning in this place
and we're finished."

Which summed the situation up admirably. I told him
we wanted the fourth opening to the right and he led off,
calling each entrance he came to back to me to double-
check so that we knew exactly where we were.

After that it became a curiously timeless experience as
we moved from one tunnel to another. Ciasim counting
off each entrance carefully as I confirmed it on the chart.

The main difficulty in the final stages was the slope of
the last tunnel which was only three feet in diameter
anyway. The stonework was smooth and slippery, making
it difficult to climb. Ciasim jammed himself between the
narrow walls pushing his way upwards foot by foot and
after a while, he called softly that he could smell fresh air
and told me to dowse my light.

It was all I needed. I went on with what's generally
referred to as renewed vigour and a moment later he
reached out a hand and pulled me up to a stone ledge at
one side of the tunnel. Beyond him, I could smell wet
grass and reached across to touch the bars.

"The storm drain you mentioned," he said. "Your navi-
gating is excellent, Jack."

"Don't thank me, thank the German engineer who drew
this plan," I said. "Will it open?"

"Half-buried in soil, but I'll give it a try."

He got his back to it, his feet on the other side of the
tunnel and pushed. Nothing happened. I crouched beside
him, scrabbling through the bars at the loose earth and
found the explanation.

"The damn thing's padlocked," I whispered. "Probably
not been touched since the German Occupation."

Which was no problem because amongst the things we'd had the forethought to bring in the tool bag, was a pair of Solingen two-foot bar cutters. There was the chink of metal in the darkness, a grunt from Ciasim as he applied his considerable strength, then a satisfactory click as the padlock sheared.

Again Ciasim put his back to the grill, his feet on the opposite side of the tunnel and heaved and this time it swung to one side, slowly because of the soil piled against it, the rusty hinges groaning in the night.

He crawled out and I went after him and found myself on my hands and knees in wet grass beneath a bush of some sort beside an old stone wall.

We were in the garden behind the inner walls on the southwest corner of the fort exactly as planned and thirty or forty yards away through the trees was the side entrance to the prison hospital as indicated on the plan supplied to me by Aleko. The only difference was that there was a light over the door.

It was a beautiful night, the air fresh and clean after the foetid atmosphere down there below the ground, the scent of flowers everywhere in the garden except on Ciasim and me. There was no getting away from it. We stank to high heaven and the very freshness of our surroundings seemed to make it worse.

It was Ciasim who, hearing the rattle of a fountain, followed the sound and found a fishpond. We crouched in it together washing the filth from our wet-suits. The result couldn't help but be an improvement; but time was passing. It was almost ten-thirty and there was a lot still to be done.

We unpacked the uniforms and pulled them on over our Neoprene suits. Ciasim's was a faded, pyjama-like affair in vertical stripes with a number stencilled on a white patch on the right breast pocket. Mine was a military looking effort in khaki drill with a forage cap in the same material and a leather belt at the waist. The machine pistol was apparently standard issue to all guards so there was no reason why I should not pass muster.

As a final touch, I bandaged Ciasim's head and left eye,

making him look as convincing a patient as anyone could wish for.

"Let's go," he said. "Straight in, straight out. Nothing to it."

There was no guard on the side door nor had I expected one. Aleko's information was certainly turning out to be accurate so far. The service stairs faced us. I was so familiar with the plan of this place by now that it was strangely like returning to somewhere I'd known well.

We passed a swing door at the end of the corridor on the first floor and went up another flight of steps. Above us, a door banged and someone clattered down the stairs. It was a young man in a white coat—a nurse or a doctor, it was impossible to say which. The only important thing was that he was in a hurry. He brushed past us with a brief apology and kept on going.

Ciasim turned, grinning, a gleam in the single eye that was on view. "See, no trouble—no trouble at all."

It suddenly occurred to me that he was enjoying himself and he actually started to whistle softly as he carried on up the next flight of stairs.

Pavlo's room was at the far end of the corridor on the third floor. We paused, looking through the glass window in the swing door before venturing through. It was quiet and deserted which was what I'd expected and hoped, for according to the information we'd been given, Pavlo's guard stayed in the room with him.

The last guard change had been at ten o'clock, the next was at six in the morning. A long time to go before they discovered he was missing.

We'd discussed how we would do it a score of times. Nothing complicated. Something nice and simple and fast. I knocked on the door and Ciasim took out his knife, holding it ready in his left hand and flattened himself against the wall. There was the sound of a chair moving, a footstep, then the cover of the small eye-level grill was pulled back. I yawned at the crucial moment, a hand to my face. The grill was closed again, there was the sound of a bolt being withdrawn and the door opened. A young guard appeared, minus his belt, collar undone. "What's all this?" he demanded.

A split second later and he was backing into the room, the point of Ciasim's knife nudging him under the chin. I already had a length of twine ready in my hand to tie him as I kicked the door shut behind me. Ciasim withdrew his knife, the young guard's mouth opened as if to cry out and Ciasim hit him in the stomach with his right fist. He went down hard and the big Turk caught the twine I threw, dropped to one knee and tied his hands behind his back.

Andreas Pavlo looked younger than he did in his photo. He was sitting up in the narrow bed, a pillow at his back. His right arm had a plaster cast on it from just below the elbow to the hand. He looked ill, very drawn and pale. Rather like the conventional portrait of a TB victim. Just now, of course, he also looked extremely nervous.

"Nothing to worry about," I said. "We're on your side. We're here to get you out."

"Who sent you?" he demanded.

"A man called Dimitri Aleko."

"The shipping Aleko! The millionaire?" He looked bewildered. "I don't believe it. Why should he bother with me?"

"Apparently he supports this crazy organisation of yours. Freedom for Greece and all that sort of rubbish."

He started to look angry. "Look, I don't understand what you're getting at."

"You'll understand all right when the security police get to work on you. They'll slice pieces off your more important extras or wire you for sound till you tell them what they want to know."

"And what would that be?"

"The exact position where you crashed in the Aztec off Crete. The names on the list in that briefcase chained to Apostolidis's wrist."

He suddenly looked desperate. "Look, I don't know who you are, but I haven't been well. It's my lung. It was badly punctured in the smash. I wouldn't trust myself to hold out for long once they started to pressure me."

"We can get you out," I said. "But it's going to be rough. Are you willing to give it a try?"

He nodded, eagerly. "Anything's better than what those bastards have in store for me."

I said to Ciasim, "Try the guard's boots on him and the greatcoat. He's going to find it cold down there."

He sat on the edge of the bed and allowed Ciasim to lace up the boots for him. They were a size too large, but would do. He got up to put on the heavy military greatcoat and I knew we were in trouble straight away. He swayed from side to side as he stood there and when he walked to the door, I thought each step would be his last.

The boy was sick—very sick. In other circumstances I think I would have urged him to stay where he was and take his chances. But we were very probably the only chance he was going to get—the only hope of living.

"Are you sure you want to go through with this?" I asked.

He nodded impatiently. "Now, while I'm still frightened. Just get me out of here. I'd rather die anyway than fall into the hands of the security police. They killed my brother last year."

He went out into the corridor, leaning heavily on Ciasim. I closed the door, which was self-locking, behind me, and moved ahead of them. As I opened the door to the landing, a guard came up the stairs.

What happened then, happened quickly. He paused several steps down, glanced at me curiously, then at Ciasim and lastly at Pavlo in his military greatcoat whom he obviously recognised at once.

He was already unbuttoning the flap of his holster as I booted him under the chin. He sprawled on his face on the landing below and Ciasim went down quickly and knelt behide him. He glanced up and said calmly, "His neck is broken. I'd better get him out of sight."

There was a storage cupboard for brooms and brushes just off the landing. He dragged the body in there and locked the door, pocketing the key.

I expected the whole place to break into song as we

plunged down those stairs, Pavlo, between us, but there wasn't a sound and we reached the bottom without further incident and hurried through the garden. I went first through the storm drain entrance followed by Pavlo. Ciasim came last, closing the gate behind him. We crouched there in the darkness for a moment till I got my spot lamp on.

Ciasim said, "You concentrate on finding the way back, Jack. I'll see to our friend."

I nodded and turned to Pavlo. "It's downhill all the way so we should be through in half an hour at the most. Not much longer than that anyway."

He looked like a ghost, his face pale in the darkness, but nodded impatiently. "Just get me out of here. Off the island—that's all I ask."

He was right, of course. If it had to be done, it had to be done and there was little sense in standing there talking about it. I got the old German plan out of my breast pocket, examined it quickly and led the way down the steeply sloping tunnel.

Without Ciasim's enormous strength it would have been impossible, for by the time we reached the lower section of the tunnel complex, he was actually carrying Pavlo on his back.

I knew we were close to the outfall by the stench which grew stronger and stronger as we descended. And there was the good sea smell, too, merging with it and I wanted to get into that sea more than I had wanted anything in a long, long time. Wanted to get out of this place.

We reached the platform by the entrance and Ciasim lowered Pavlo gently, resting him against the wall. The boy looked terrible, sweat shining on his face. I opened the brandy bottle and gave him a little.

He managed a smile. "That's better. What happens now?"

"We go underwater," I said. "We've got an aqualung for you. You've nothing to worry about—nothing at all. We'll tie you to one of our underwater scooters and all you have to do is let it pull you along. Fifteen minutes at the most. We'll be back at our boat and we'll have you warm in bed and on your way."

"Don't worry about me." He closed his eyes for a moment, then opened them again. "I'd better tell you about the plane in case anything happens. You know Turk's Head on the northeast coast of Crete?"

"Very well," I said.

"Good. There is a small island called Kapala. It's uninhabited. Not much more than a rock. I crashed about two hundred yards due north in shallow water. Five or six fathoms, that's all. You'll have no trouble finding it."

He was getting too excited. I said, "All right, so you've told me. Now take it easy while we get this suit on you."

He clutched at me desperately. "But I must tell you about Apostolidis and the briefcase. It is very important. Crucial to the whole operation."

He was already feverish so I let him go on for a couple of minutes until he was satisfied he'd covered every eventuality, then we got the wet-suit on him. Ciasim had to cut open the tight-fitting sleeve of the right arm to get it over the plaster cast, but in the end, we had him pretty well covered.

He seemed to rally when we strapped on his aqualung and was surprisingly cheerful when I explained how the regulator worked and pushed the rubber mouthpiece of his breathing tube between his teeth.

He might have been smiling, but I wasn't as I strapped on my own aqualung, for the truth was that I didn't have much faith in his ability to survive the trip. He'd already taken too much for someone in his condition.

We got the aquamobiles into the water first, then eased Pavlo gently in between us. I fastened him to my own scooter by the simple expedient of strapping him to the handles with a couple of webbing belts. I straddled his body and switched on and Ciasim gave us a push out of the mud into the water.

The whole thing worked quite well for the aquamobile was easily capable of pulling the double load and Pavlo floated there beneath me in no apparent discomfort. The main thing now was to get him out of there as fast as

possible. I waited till Ciasim slid out of the gloom to join
us, then switched to full power and moved away silently.

When I surfaced a few yards astern of the *Seytan* it was
twelve-thirty and we were ahead of schedule. But we were
still on dangerous ground. There was an excellent chance
that the guard in Pavlo's room or the body we had left in
the broom cupboard on the staircase, wouldn't be discovered until the morning. Certainly not before six when
Pavlo's guard was changed and we could be in Kyros before four now. On the other hand, nothing was that certain in this life.

I let the aquamobile take us in to the boat and called out
softly. Within a moment or so, there was a movement at
the rail and Melos appeared.

"Is that you, Savage, have you got him?"

"Only just," I said. "Let's have that ladder down here
before he dies on us."

I had already got the straps undone that had bound
him to the handles and now, Ciasim appeared to give me
a hand. Melos leaned over the rail, got the boy by the
shoulders and pulled him over. I followed leaving Ciasim
to pass the rest of the gear up to his two sons who were
already greeting him excitedly.

In the cabin, Melos had Pavlo stretched out on one of
the two bunks and was unzipping the wet-suit. I peeled
off my own hurriedly, pulled on a pair of pants and a
heavy sweater and joined him.

There was no colour in the boy's face at all and his
eyes were closed. Melos said, "He's going to die, I've
seen that look before."

"Not if I can help it," I said. "I killed a man to get him
out of that place tonight."

He didn't seem to understand or perhaps it simply
wasn't important to him. "Did he tell you anything?"

I didn't get a chance to reply because suddenly, there
was a clatter of feet on the stairs and Abu said excitedly,
"My father says come quickly, Mr. Savage. A boat comes."

"You see to him," I told Melos. "And keep out of sight."

My first thought was that the game was up. That the
guards had been discovered up there in the fort and that

one of the M.T.B.s was coming in to make a search. But
as the boat drew nearer, I realised from the sound of the
engine that it was something different.

In fact it proved to be a Johnson power boat with twin
outboard motors, a thirty-five knot job. Morgan Hughes
was at the wheel, Yanni Kytros beside him in the front
passenger seat. The man who sat behind them was a
stranger to me, a seaman from the look of him in knitted
cap and long black oilskin storm coat.

"What in the hell are you doing here?" I demanded as
Morgan threw a line to Yassi.

He grinned as he came up the ladder followed by Kytros
and the other man. "Hell, Jack, Mr. Kytros told me you
was in some kind of trouble. Said he wanted to help, so as
I knew where you was . . ."

He stood there grinning foolishly and the sailor standing behind Kytros produced a machine pistol which he
cocked in a very professional manner.

"Hands behind the neck, Jack. No trouble."

Kytros checked me for arms then tried Ciasim who was
still carrying the .38 automatic I'd given him on the island.
Kytros relieved him of it and stepped back.

"As you're here at this point in time and in one piece,
I presume you succeeded in getting Pavlo out of Sinos."

I said, "What's that to you?"

"I'm taking him off your hands."

I made a move towards him and the barrel of the
machine pistol lifted to meet me.

"I wouldn't, Jack," Ciasim said urgently. "I think he
means it."

"Another of your little business deals, Yanni?" I said
bitterly.

He shook his head. "Not this time, Jack. There are
some things that money can't buy. Andreas Pavlo will be
safer with me and my associates, I assure you, than he will
be with Aleko. At least he will be with friends."

I saw a lot of things then and perhaps Yanni had intended to say more only he didn't get the chance because
Melos stepped quietly out of the companionway and shot
the man with the machine pistol twice in the chest. The
force of the bullets drove him back against the rail and his

finger tightened convulsively on the trigger of the machine pistol, a short burst ploughing up the deck. He dropped it and went over the rail into the power boat.

Yanni was on the deck, clutching his right thigh, blood pumping between his fingers, caught by a stray bullet. And Morgan—poor old Morgan—cracked wide open. He cried out in fear, scrambling for the rail and Melos shot him in the back of the head, driving him down to join the sea-man in the power boat.

I dropped to one knee, reaching for the machine pistol and Melos extended his arm and the Walther didn't even shake. He was a prof if ever I've seen one and certainly no simple ship's captain. I stayed exactly where I was and he picked up the machine pistol, moved to the rail and fired a burst into the power boat which started to sink immediately.

He said calmly to Ciasim, "Now get this style of a boat moving if you know what's good for you. Try anything funny and your sons will be the first to go. Understand?"

He meant it, nothing was more certain so Ciasim did as he was told, touching me briefly on the shoulder before moving away.

As the engine rattled into life and the boys started to haul on the anchor, I went to the rail and looked down at the power boat. It had almost disappeared, but Morgan's face was still clear of the water. Strange, but he looked as if he was trying to tell me something and that wasn't possible because he was dead.

And then the power boat slid beneath the surface taking him with it. Poor old bastard. He was at peace now, but what a way to go. He had not deserved that. I'd owed him more than that. Much more.

Yanni was sitting up, clutching his right thigh with both hands, his face twisted with pain. "I'm sorry Jack," he said.

I ignored him, turned and looked at Melos standing by the wheelhouse, the machine pistol ready in his hands and wondered how I was going to kill him when the time came.

CHAPTER XVI

BAD END FOR A GOOD SHIP

Melos sat in the prow where he could watch Ciasim in the wheelhouse and made Yassi and Abu lie face down on the deck at his feet, the first to die if anyone made any kind of a move against him. Which meant, of course, that for the time being, he was completely safe and he told me to get Yanni below and see to his leg.

"And don't forget, Savage, I want a good job done on him," he warned. "We want him alive, that one."

"You see, Jack," Yanni said as I helped him below. "I have friends everywhere."

He sat on the edge of a bunk, his face twisted with pain and glanced across at Pavlo. "How is he?"

"Not so good. Let's have your trousers down."

He unbuckled his belt. "I didn't believe it could be done, Jack. I didn't think it was possible to get anyone out of that place. A miracle."

"You seem to be pretty well informed," I said.

He smiled faintly. "I have my sources, as they say."

By then, I had Ciasim's medical kit open. Yanni sat there, his trousers around his ankles and I swabbed the blood away from his thigh and had a look. He was lucky. The bullet hadn't gone in. It had simply ploughed a furrow perhaps six inches long before proceeding on its way. Painful, but hardly mortal.

"I thought politics bored you?" I said. "You once told me life was a series of business deals."

"I was raised by my uncle, Jack, who was an Athenian born and bred. He had a small bar near Ommonia Square. You know that section of Athens?"

"What I'd term the livelier end of town."

"Exactly. My aunt married a baker who kept a pastry shop round the corner. They were killed during the war and we took in their only son, Michael."

"Your cousin?" I strapped a gauze dressing across his wound with some surgical tape and stood.

He pulled up his trousers. "My brother, Jack, in all but name. He was a journalist. A good man, not like me at all. He was the kind of person you only meet very occasionally. The kind who can only tell the truth. They closed his newspaper down last year."

"The government?"

"Is that what you call them, the colonels? After that, he started printing and distributing handbills."

"Then what?"

"The usual story." He stubbed out his cigarette carefully on the edge of the old wooden table. "Shot while resisting arrest." His laugh was harsh and ugly. "Resisting arrest. He was the kind of man who couldn't bear to harm any living creature. Ten times, fifty times more worthy to live than me. You understand, Jack?"

Another man, this Kytros. A man with a conscience.

"I'm not so sure," I said. "He probably wouldn't agree with you. Not after tonight."

He seemed both angry and dejected at the same time. "God, what a mess I've made of it. We'd no idea Melos was on board." He hesitated, then said awkwardly, "I'm sorry about Morgan. I used him because he knew exactly where you were and it would have been too late to leave our move till you got to Kyros." He shook his head. "But I never intended that to happen."

He shuddered and I poured some of Ciasim's rot-gut brandy into a mug and gave it to him. "Melos is quite something when he gets going. Who is he exactly? No three-ring yacht captain, that's for sure."

"As far as my information goes, he's a major in the security police."

"And the crew of the *Firebird?* They're all his boys?"

"All that count."

By then I was completely bewildered. I said, "That means Aleko is working for the government which doesn't make any kind of sense at all."

He shook his head. "The present government is bad enough in all conscience, but there are other elements in the country. Powerful men who think they have not gone far enough. Men who would crush any kind of opposition without the slightest hesitation."

"And Aleko represents them?" I said. "Is that what you are saying? It still doesn't explain Melos."

"There are many like him in the army at the moment, in the government itself, who sympathise with the aims of Aleko and his friends. These men are preparing to take over, Jack, which is why it is essential that they lay hands on that list of names. It tells them who are their real opponents. If they can eliminate such individuals, then nothing can stand in their way. Things are bad enough now, but if Aleko and people like him take over, it will be Germany in 1933 and the Nazis all over again."

"Tell me one thing," I said. "And give it to me straight. Are you a Communist?"

He smiled sadly. "If only it were as simple as that, Jack." He shook his head. "I'm nothing. No, let me amend that. I'm a good Greek, if that means anything. I think people have a right to live in peace and to have a say in how things are run, but perhaps that is too much to expect in this day and age."

"You could have warned me," I said. "Why didn't you?"

"I couldn't be sure of you and in this business I am not my own master. Anyway, we wanted you to succeed, we wanted Pavlo out of Sinos as long as we could have him."

"You tried to be too clever, Yanni," I said. "You and whoever gave you your orders. Now you've got nothing."

Pavlo groaned. I examined him quickly. He was still unconscious, sweat on his face. I wiped it away and Yanni said, "Will he live?"

"If he's lucky. It's the lung I'm worried about. This sweating could indicate the start of pneumonia."

"Did he manage to tell you anything?"

I turned, caught slightly off guard by the question. I suppose he saw his answer in my face.

"God help you, Jack, if they even suspect that you have such information. They have their own ways of dealing with that kind of situation and it is anything but pleasant."

"And what makes you think I wouldn't tell them?" I demanded. "Remember me, Yanni? Jack Savage is the name. I used to have a salvage business in Cairo worth better than two hundred thousand quid and I wasn't interested in politics."

He stared at me, shocked, incredulous. "I don't believe you, Jack. You wouldn't. I know you too well."

"A little while ago you were telling me you left me in the dark because you couldn't be sure of me. Make up your mind."

I was suddenly angry, tired of the whole damned business and of men and their silly little games. Schoolboy games that ended in death for too many people when played on the adult level. To hell with them all. What did it have to do with me?

"You try and save Greece if you want to," I said. "I've got more important things on my mind," and I left him there and went up on deck.

Melos still sat in the prow, the boys on the deck in front of him. He was smoking a Dutch cigar and looked remarkably relaxed.

"How about Kytros?" he demanded.

"He'll live."

Inside the wheelhouse, Ciasim's head seemed disembodied in the light from the compass. He was still wearing his wet-suit and it occurred to me that he must be cold.

I said, "I'll take over. You go and change."

Melos cut in sharply, "He's all right where he is. You worry too much, Savage. These Turks are like pigs rooting in a field. They can exist where others die. Animals."

He spat over the side. Ciasim didn't move a muscle. I went below and got the brandy bottle and a mug. Kytros was sitting beside Pavlo, wiping the sweat from his forehead.

"Trouble?" he said.

I shook my head. "The usual thing. Greek and Turk. Do what you can for him. I'll be back in a little while."

I half-filled the mug with brandy and Melos said sharply, "Never mind him. I'll have that."

I gave it to Ciasim anyway. "Go on," I said. "Shoot us all for a cup of brandy."

He glared and then for some reason saw the humour in the situation, however grim, and laughed. "Yes, you are right, Savage. We still have a use for you. So live a little longer."

"As long as I can survive you," I said, "I'll be satisfied."

"Which is unlikely, I assure you," he said and laughed again.

But there was some small comfort in the thought and I held on to that and bided my time.

A couple of miles out of Kyros, Melos gave Ciasim a new course that took us round to the south side of the island, a wild and rugged coast of high cliffs, and scrubland with beaches that were virtually inaccessible from the land side.

There was a bay called Paxos, a place I knew well because of its unusual situation. The entrance was a narrow passage between two jagged peaks known to local fishermen as the Old Women of Paxos. Inside, there was an enormous landlocked lagoon fringed by white beaches and backed by a scattering of stunted pine trees.

There was a heavy coastal mist that morning which didn't help on the way in, for it was a tricky passage at the best of times and doubly so in the dim light of early dawn.

We found the *Firebird* anchored close to the shore, the *Gentle Jane* tied up on the starboard side which was something of a surprise. Ciasim cut the engine of the *trenchadiri* and I got the fenders over the side and stood ready to throw a line.

There was plenty of activity on the deck of the *Firebird* as we got closer. Kapelari and Christou stood waiting by the ladder, Kapelari holding a submachine gun and then Aleko appeared.

"Did you get him?" he called. "Did everything go all right?"

Melos grinned up at him. "What do you think?"

Before Aleko could reply, a door banged, Kapelari was

pulled out of the way and Sara appeared at the rail, a coat thrown over her shoulders.

"Savage?"

She was smiling and then she took in the scene below. Yassi and Abu still flat on their faces, Melos holding the machine pistol jauntily. Her smile faded.

"I know, angel," I called. "We've been had. All of us."

Looking back on it all, the one thing I find difficulty in understanding was the fact that they hadn't bothered to bring a doctor along, although it had been Aleko himself who had pointed out during the planning stage that it would probably be essential. It had been obvious from the beginning that some deterioration in Pavlo's condition must be expected.

I suppose the real truth of the situation was that they had no real interest in his personal survival after he had told them what they wanted to know. The mistake we had all made was in miscalculating so badly what a terrible effect the trip out would have on him.

When Ciasim and I took him up from the cabin, we carried a dying man. We passed him over the rail to Christou and one of the stewards, a man called Lazanis, who took him below at once.

Kapelari waved the submachine gun threateningly and Ciasim and I helped Yanni Kytros up between us. Yassi and Abu followed, watchful and wary like a couple of young tigers waiting to see which way they should jump. Neither of them showed the slightest sign of fear which didn't suprise me in the least as it isn't a characteristic the Turks have much time for.

Yanni Kytros seemed in a bad way, face screwed up in pain and he obviously had difficulty in putting any weight on his right leg. Not that it earned him much sympathy. Melos gave him a shove in the back that sent him staggering across the deck and told Kapelari to take him below with the two Divalni boys, which left Ciasim and me with Sara and Aleko.

She turned on her brother-in-law looking genuinely bewildered. "For heaven's sake, Dimitri, what's all this about?"

"Later." He patted her cheek as if to soothe her. "Later, I will explain everything."

And now she looked angry. "Not good enough, Dimitri, I want to know now."

Melos took her roughly by the arm, for the first time showing his real authority. "You always did have too much to say for yourself. From now on you speak when I tell you to, understand?"

He was hurting her which was obvious from the pain on her face. I took a quick step forward, but Aleko was there before me.

"Take your hands off her," he said sharply, and did a little arm twisting himself on Melos who cried out and staggered back.

A nice touch of melodrama, but Aleko looked angry and for once, genuinely formidable. It struck me then that if he could ever shake off that neurosis of his he would be hell on wheels.

Possibly the same thought came to Melos because he tilted his machine pistol to include Aleko and said viciously, "I am in charge of this operation, Mr. Aleko. You would do well to remember that."

I suppose anything might have happened then if Lazanis hadn't arrived to say that Kytros and the Divalni boys were securely under lock and key in separate cabins.

Melos turned to Aleko. "Take this lot down to the saloon and hold them there. Lazanis will be on the door with orders to shoot anyone who tries to leave before I come. Which means," he added pleasantly to Ciasim, "that those boys of yours will go the same way, so behave yourselves."

But Ciasim was giving nothing away, his face like one of those bronze Byzantine masks with holes for eyes that you can see in the Basilica of Saint Sophia in Istanbul. One thing I knew for certain. Melos was only going to be allowed one slip, one wrong move and he was a dead man.

When the door closed behind us in the saloon, the key clicked in the lock. I said to Aleko cheerfully, "You too, eh? Perhaps they don't need you any more?"

He looked angry and uncertain like a fighting bull in

the plaza with the darts hanging from his shoulders, half-blinded by pain, uncertain who to charge. I went behind the bar, found the Jameson and poured a couple of large ones. Ciasim emptied his glass at a swallow and reached for the bottle.

Sara put a hand on my arm. "Was it bad in there?"

"It could have been worse," I told her brutally. "I only killed one man if that's what you mean. Two if we count Pavlo."

It was Ciasim who attempted to give me some kind of comfort where that one was concerned. "Don't be a fool, Jack. What do you think would have happened if we'd left him in there? These people." Here, he glanced at Aleko, utter contempt on his face. "These pigs differ only in kind. The government in Greece stinks. Aleko and his friends want to make it worse. Lovely people."

"Shut your mouth," Aleko told him savagely.

He had moved towards us, but Sara got in the way. She grabbed him by the jacket with both hands and shook hard, no mean feat. "Tell him he's got it all wrong. Tell him that if you can. I knew there was something funny going on when you left the rest of the crew behind in Kyros."

He shoved her away from him and lurched forward to grab at the edge of the bar as if it stop himself falling like a man with too much drink taken.

"You don't understand, Savage. You don't know what's been happening in Greece. Red scum everywhere and even now, the government isn't doing enough about it."

Strange how it was me he needed to justify himself to. I didn't understand why and don't now, but so it was and he reached out to pluck at my arm across the bar so that I had to pull away from him.

"Reds under the bed again?" I said. "Do you think they'll take your money away, Aleko, is that it?" I shook my head. "It won't wash any more, you poor bloody fool. Greece isn't Communist on one side and Fascist on the other. It's a hell of a lot of ordinary people in between who've been shoved around by both extremes for too damned long. They'll have you both out on your back-sides soon now. Remember I told you that."

Sara's eyes sparkled and she clapped her hands. "Nice going for a man who isn't interested in politics."

"I'm not," I said. "But I like you and I like Ciasim and his boys and conniving, slippery, devious Yanni Kytros. Yes, I even like Yanni, because when it comes right down to it, there are things that even Yanni won't put a price tag on."

Ciasim had a funny look on his face. He poured me another whiskey and shoved it across. "On me, dear friend."

I was an under-age kid in Cohan's Select Bar again, taking it down in one easy swallow so that it exploded like a bomb in your gut, priming you to put your fist into the first face you didn't like.

I said to Sara, "You know what Melos did out there? He killed Morg. Shot him in the back of the head as casually as you would put down an old tired dog that got in your way."

The whiskey had gone straight to my head now. She had a hand to her mouth, horror on her face and things had gone fuzzy at the edges for me. I was a foot off the ground. I was Wolfe Tone and Charles Stewart Parnell and Big Mick Collins and all the others who'd ever spoken straight from the heart, from deep down in the guts where it counts. The only place where it counts.

"Communists—Fascists. The same under the skin. No difference at all when it comes to putting the screws on. No, I'm damned if I will take sides, Aleko, but that still doesn't mean I have to like you. In fact, I don't. I don't like you and I don't like Major-bloody-security-police Melos and his bully boys. Black and Tans, Gestapo, Security Police. They crawl out from under their large flat stones everywhere, in every country if you give them a chance."

I'd hit him, right down there between the legs where it really hurts a man and he reached out in his anguish, forgetting that neurotic fear of his and had me by the arms. I've never known such strength. I went over the bar as easily as a rubber ball bouncing and even Ciasim when he moved in to help me, was sent flying across the saloon with a casual shove.

"You will listen to me now, Savage." Aleko's eyes were
staring and there was froth on his mouth. "They came to
my village—the Reds came to my village during the Civil
War." I tried to struggle and he had me by the throat.
"They slaughtered everyone, Savage, after raping the wom-
en. Even the young girls."

He stared, eyes wide, into an abyss of horror. "My
mother, my two sisters. I lay under a pile of hay in the
yard, Savage. I lay there and did nothing. You understand me? I was so afraid that I lay there and let them do
that to my mother and sisters."

I could smell the burning, hear the screams in the night
and how old would he have been—thirteen? A young boy,
frightened in the darkness and cursed by that fear ever
since. And he wasn't asking for mercy or understanding.
He was seeking no deliverance. What was it Faustus said
in Marlowe's play? *For this is hell and I am in it.*

He released me suddenly, turned and swayed as if he
might fall, his shirt clinging to his back, soaked in sweat.
There was even something close to pity on Ciasim's iron
face, but when Aleko reached out blindly to Sara as if for
support, she turned from him, grasping the edge of the
bar, her eyes closed against the tears.

He stumbled across to a chair and slumped down and a
second later, the key rattled in the lock and Melos entered.
His face was dark and angry and he went behind the bar
and reached for a bottle of gin.

"All for nothing," he said. "The whole bloody affair.
What do you think of that, Savage?"

"He's dead?"

"Never opened his eyes." He drank from the bottle,
wiping his mouth with the back of his hand, then asked
me flatly, "Did he tell you anything back there, Savage?"

"About the plane?" I shrugged. "No time to talk. We'd
all on to get out of there and you saw the state he was
in when we took him below."

He frowned suspiciously, then glanced at Ciasim's im-
passive face. "It's possible, I suppose. We'll see what
Kytros has to say, shall we? He was down there with him
for long enough."

He whistled and Kapelari and Christou brought Yanni

in between them. Lazanis closed the door and stood against it, his submachine gun cocked.

Kytros didn't look too good. He still couldn't take much weight on that leg from the look of it and his mouth was swollen from someone's fist and there was blood on his shirt. His smile was what is known as a gallant try, but it didn't fool anyone for a moment.

Melos took another drink, placed the bottle down carefully on the bar, then walked forward slowly. "Did Pavlo regain consciousness at all when you were alone with him in the cabin on the way here? Did you ask him for the Aztec's position?"

Kytros smiled again. "I'd love to be able to help, Major Melos, if only to help myself, but you can't get blood out of a stone."

Which was an unfortunate simile because Melos struck him heavily in the face and said, "I would not count on that if I were you. I am going to ask you that same question once more, but before I do, let me explain in some detail what happens if you fail to come up with an answer."

"Even when I don't have it in the first place?" Kytros said.

"We take you to the bathroom, strip you and put you into a bath of nice cold water. Then I wire you for sound, Kytros. Your genitals, fingers, toes. Then we turn on the electricity. You will find it extraordinarily painful and it has certain unfortunate after-effects. For example, you will never be able to function as a man again. The Gestapo enjoyed great success with this method."

"What excellent references you must have."

Melos punched him full in the face, so hard that the flesh split on the right side of the mouth, blood spurting.

"Thank you," Kytros said, the most amazing thing of all was that he managed a smile. "I am still proud to be a Greek, even in your company."

"Take him away," Melos said.

Out of the silence, someone said quietly in the tiredest voice I'd ever heard in my life, "A quarter of a mile off Turk's Head on the northeast coast of Crete there's an uninhabited island called Kapala. You'll find the Aztec about two hundred yards due north in shallow water."

He turned to me and smiled gently. "A sentimentalist at heart, I see, Mr. Savage, which is why you are weak and I am strong. Isn't that the story of your life? You've never been able to do the sensible thing. To keep your mouth shut. You always get yourself involved in what is never your business."

"I know," I said, "I'll come to a bad end through that little vice one of these days if I don't watch out."

"Very probably," he said. "And another thing. *We* won't find the Aztec two hundred yards north of that damned island of yours, but you will. You and this Turkish ox here if you know what's good for you."

I had an idea what was coming, but I had to say something. "You'll have to spell that one out for me."

"With pleasure. You don't have any choice. If I allowed you to sail out of here a free man right this minute, what would you do? Go to the authorities and tell them you broke Andreas Pavlo out of Sinos and killed a guard? Have you any idea what they'd do to you? I'm in the security police, remember. I know."

"Let's have the rest of it."

"You go, you and this animal, because this is a job for professional divers. You go to Crete with Kapelari and Christou to keep an eye on you, you find that plane and you bring the briefcase back here. And don't try to open it. There's a detonating device in the lock, remember."

"And if we refuse?"

"How can you? I have the Turk's two sons, haven't I? They've a great sense of family these Turks. Didn't you know that?"

"And what if I told you they are no concern of mine?"

"But I have someone here who is, haven't I, Mr. Savage? Someone who is very much your concern."

Sara stood there at the bar, staring at him for a long moment, at me, then walked to where Aleko sat slumped in the club chair, head in hands.

"Dimitri," she said. "Did you hear that?"

He looked up at her in a kind of supplication. "The

people on that list, Sara. To be really free we must know about vermin like that. We must root them out."

He was incapable of making sense any more, that sick, tortured mind of his finally over the edge. I think she realised that for her hand was gentle when she touched him briefly on the shoulder.

When she loked at Melos, there was real hatred in her eyes as she said, "You tell him to go to hell, Savage."

He turned to me enquiringly, an eyebrow raised. "Well?"

I took a deep breath, fought back a strong impulse to kick him in the groin and won. "No need to involve Divalni any further in this. I'll go myself."

"With me, dear friend." Ciasim smiled. "On salvage work of this nature, two divers, never one. Was it not you who taught me this?"

Sara moved close to me and grabbed for my hand, her voice urgent. "Not for my sake, I won't let you. There must be a lot of good people on that list. Do you think I could live with that?"

I turned and walked out on her, pushing my way past the muscle men with the guns at the door and went up on deck. I stood at the rail and breathed in a little of that cold morning air. It was still pretty misty and visibility in the bay wasn't good at all.

Ciasim spoke from behind me. "She's got a point, Jack."

"Don't you start. I've had about as much as I can take this morning."

The good Irish whiskey was drumming in my brain and I felt mean and angry and there was a dull aching pain at the back of my head that wouldn't go away.

Melos appeared and paused, staring out into the mist. "How deep is it out there in the main channel between the cliffs?"

"Ten or twelve fathoms," I said. "Why?"

"A good place to get rid of your boat, Turk, don't you think so?"

From his point of view it made good sense for if the Seytan went missing, the authorities would be certain to see a link with Pavlo's escape which would set them to scouring the Aegean to no purpose.

But for the first time, Melos succeeded in touching
Ciasim where he lived and breathed, deep down inside,
for to a sailor, a boat is a living thing, part of one's own
being when it is your boat.

Ciasim growled like a mountain bear getting ready to
charge and Melos raised his machine pistol waist-high. "I
could cut you in half very comfortably from here. You
wish me to do this?"

Kapalari and Christou appeared from the main companionway, Yanni between them. He could hardly walk
and looked terrible with his smashed mouth and the blood
soaking his shirt and trouser leg.

Ciasim relaxed, the breath going out of him in a long
sigh and Melos chuckled. "Good, now you are being sensible. First you will transfer the diving equipment and
anything else of value, then you will take her out into the
channel and you will put a hole into her. You understand
me?"

Ciasim nodded. "Perfectly."

Melos turned and seemed to notice Yanni for the first
time. He smiled. "I have just had a rather excellent idea.
A sacrifice to Poseidon, just like the old days. You can
go down with the ship, Kytros."

Yanni managed a ghastly smile and shuffled forward
slowly, "Please Melos, I beg of you . . ."

Melos swung him around and kicked him in the backside, sending him sprawling. Yanni fell flat on his face
with a groan and Kapelari and Christou started to have a
good laugh.

What happened next was not all that funny from their
point of view, for Yanni suddenly sprang to his feet, his
leg apparently no longer a liability, and ran for his life.

Cunning and devious to the end, he had been playing a
part again. He was round the corner of the main deck
house as Christou fired a short burst that chipped the
woodwork.

Melos didn't waste any time on angry shouting, he was
too much the professional for that. He ran along the port
deck towards the stern and was almost there when there
was a splash that told us Yanni had gone into the water.

I caught a glimpse of him swimming into the mist and

then Melos loosed off a burst that lifted a curtain of spray six feet high. I heard Yanni cry out, his arms went up and he disappeared. We waited in the silence that followed, but he did not come up again.

Melos turned, his face grim. "So, now we understand one another, eh? So let's get started. Too much time wasted already."

They left it to Ciasim and me to do all the work. We got the diving gear across, the aquamobiles. Everything that was worth having, or worth having by Melos's standards. He made Ciasim leave his own diving gear on board.

When we were ready, we took the old *trenchardiri* out into the channel and dropped anchor for the current was particularly strong now with a sea running. Melos hadn't bothered sending a guard with us. There was no particular need, so that in the mist, we might as well have been alone.

Ciasim killed the engine and came out of the wheelhouse. He produced a tin of Turkish cigarettes and offered me one. "I had this boat a long time, Jack, and my father before me."

"I know," I said. "It's a bastard, but don't rub it in."

"You know something, Jack? I liked what you said back in the saloon."

"Whiskey talk."

"Always you sell yourself short." He leaned against the wheelhouse. "I want my boys to live. I want Lady Sara to live, you understand me? But this is a bad business. Two hundred men, Jack, two hundred good men will face death or worse, because their names are on that list." He put a hand on my shoulder. "Anything you can think of, anything that might help. You can rely on my support. You know this?"

"I'll give it some thought."

"Good, that is what I had hoped." He picked up a fire axe. "Let us go now. I wish to end this thing."

Trenchadiris didn't have sea cocks so he sank her by the simple expedient of hacking a hole in her hull near the prow with the fire axes, standing up in the dinghy.

I pulled away as she started to go down, resting on my oars when we were perhaps fifty or sixty feet away. Ciasim remained standing, the axe in his hand and watched without the slightest concern as the prow dipped under the surface and the stern lifted.

The old *Seytan* seemed to hang there for a moment, then went all the way down with a sudden smooth rush. As the ripples widened, he tossed the fire axe into the centre of them. When he turned to sit in the stern of the dinghy, tears were running down his cheeks.

CHAPTER XVII

THE RUN TO TURK'S HEAD

Kapelari and Christou, the terrible twins. Melos sent them with us on the run to Turk's Head in the *Gentle Jane* and at the last minute threw in Lazanis as well. Now that was cause for alarm indeed because in the circumstances, it was totally unnecessary.

The plain truth was that Melos had us bound hand and foot for where was there to run to? Not to the authorities. We'd certainly get short shrift there. No, once we had recovered the briefcase, there was only one place to go. To the *Firebird* to exchange it for Sara and the two Divalni boys.

Christou was in the wheelhouse for Melos had made it plain I wasn't to be in physical control of the vessel. Kapelari and Lazanis lounged against the rail, talking to him through the open window.

I suppose they thought they had nothing to worry about. Melos had sewn the whole thing up beautifully and Kapelari gave us only half an eye occasionally as we worked on the stern deck geting the diving gear ready.

Ciasim said, "I have been wondering what guarantee we have that things will turn out as we want when we take this briefcase back to the *Firebird*."

"You mean Melos and his friends are just as likely to finish us all off."

"Exactly. On the other hand, Lady Sara poses them something of a problem. To start with there is Aleko to consider who is hardly likely to stand by while they put a bullet into the back of her head."

"I wouldn't be too sure about that. He's a sick man. He doesn't know what it's all about any more. And nothing as crude as a bullet in the head, please. An unfortunate accident. The *Gentle Jane* might follow the *Seytan*."

"With one subtle difference?"

"That's right. We'd all be locked up nice and tight below."

He took a deep breath. "And why not? These are ruthless men and they play for high stakes, Jack. They play for a whole country. For a great nation."

"Now I've got you worried about that, try this one for size," I told him. "Why has Melos bothered to send Kapelari and his two pals along. We certainly don't need them and he knows we've got to return once we find the briefcase. We have no other choice."

"*If* we find it, you mean?"

"If it's to be found, then we'll find it," I said. "But what happens when we do? When we climb over the rail clutching the thing that's been the object of the whole damned exercise."

His eyes widened and then he sighed gently in that strange way of his. "Ah, I see now. We are no longer needed. We go back over the rail immediately, but full of holes. Is there anything we can do about this?"

"I think so," I said and proceeded to tell him. But it was a long shot. One hell of a long shot. Guts and timing and a great deal of luck. I wondered if the lesser gods were on my side today? It was about time they were.

Finding the plane was one thing, but getting into it might prove to be something else again. You could never be sure when a plane had crash-landed at sea for the impact damage could be formidable, or such had been my experience.

So we made ready for any and every eventuality and got an assortment of tools laid out neatly on the deck beside the diving gear plus the paraphernalia that went with the oxy-hydrogen cutting equipment. It all looked very impressive and Kapelari and Lazanis came and watched us for a while.

"You need all that stuff?" Lazanis demanded.

"That plane could have closed up tight in the crash," I said. "We might have to open it up just like a sardine can."

He grunted and idly kicked a tin biscuit box. "I wouldn't do that if I were you," I added. "Twenty pounds of plastic gelignite in there with a box of chemical fuses. Something nasty might happen."

He turned a very satisfactory shade of grey and took a hurried step back, even going so far as to cross himself, which gave me the first lift I'd had that day. Oh, there was gelignite in the tin all right, but the idea that you could blow yourself up by giving it the odd kick was straight out of the boys' magazines.

Kapelari and Lazanis departed more quickly than they had arrived and Ciasim grinned. "Maybe he messed his pants," he said and spat over the rail. "Greek pigs."

It was better than a three-hour run to Crete and we raised Cape Sidheros first and Turk's Head on the far side, a little way into the Gulf of Merabello. Turk's Head was a good name for it, for that is exactly what the great rocky headland resembled most, a gaunt profile staring blindly out to Kapala a quarter of a mile away.

Kapala itself was little more than an acre or two of barren rock jutting out of the sea, not even a living for goats to be had of it. We finally dropped anchor a couple of hundred yards to the north as Pavlo had indicated, just after noon. The weather had cleared gradually during the morning and the sun was a ball of fire in a sky of brass, the heat was so intense that the ship's metalwork was too hot to touch.

Ciasim and I started to get into our wet-suits and the three of them stood watching us. Kapelari, who seemed to be in charge, said, "It shouldn't take you long this business. Pavlo gave you a pretty accurate position."

"For a man who surfaced, dazed and shocked with multiple injuries after crash-landing at sea in the darkness." I laughed shortly. "It could be right under the boat. On the other hand, it might be anywhere in an arc north from here and several hundred yards out if he miscalculated badly enough."

Not that I believed that myself for a moment. Pavlo hadn't seemed the type to get that sort of information wrong and it is instinctual in any good pilot to note his position accurately on the way down. It can too often make the difference between life and death. But there was no harm and every advantage to be gained by dressing the whole thing up to look as difficult as possible as far as they were concerned.

Ciasim and I helped each other with our aqualung straps, then went over the side together. I adjusted my air supply and signalled to him and we went down together.

We had dropped anchor in five fathoms which was what I had expected for Pavlo had specified shallow water, but I soon found that the sea-bed shelved steeply, a wide expanse of sand stretching into the shadows dotted with clumps of sea grass.

At one point, I came to a jumbled mass of broken pottery, with here and there great double-handled amphora encrusted with marine growth, but otherwise in perfect condition. In ancient times each one had carried seven or eight gallons of wine and they were to be found on the sea-bed all over the Aegean, usually indicating where a ship had foundered in Classical or Roman times. It didn't surprise me for any storm must have made Kapala a bad lee shore to be driven onto in days of sail. At any other time, I'd have been interested enough to make a closer inspection, but not now.

We were ten fathoms and still descending, swimming a parallel course, perhaps thirty or forty feet apart. The sand was behind us and the sea-bed was a great moving carpet of marine grass that undulated constantly, fading into the green mist on either side.

Surely Pavlo couldn't have been so badly out? And then something caught my attention over to the left on the edge of visibility. I signalled to Ciasim and changed direction.

It was the tail section which I had noticed, lifting out of that jungle of marine grass at a sharp angle and the rest of the plane was almost buried in the stuff. It was the Aztec, no mistake about that, and the wings and both engines were still intact. For a moment, my mind skipped back in time to the Mirage III out there beyond the har-

bour bar at Bir el Gafani. A long time ago, or was it?
Certainly a lot of water under the bridge.

Ciasim joined me and we went down together into that
forest of pale green fronds. They seemed to live, those
tendrils. To have a desire to hold on like the tentacles of
an octopus and the sensation was anything but pleasant.

For the first time since my dive to the German wreck
to help Ciasim, I was conscious of a sudden resurgence of
my old neurotic fear. But it was nothing. It no longer had
any power to hurt me. I told myself that, believed in spite
of the fear and it left me as quickly as it had come.

I pressed on, pushing my way through the waving grass,
and reached the main body of the fuselage. The windows
were still intact and I could see the instrument panel inside, the controls, the seat straps moving gently as if suspended in air. The cabin door was partly open and moved
stiffly when I pulled on it. I turned to find Ciasim at my
shoulder, nodded and ventured inside.

It was not so much dark as gloomy in there and a certain amount of light came in through the windows. Something stirred in the shadows and the coldness moved in me
again.

It was Apostolidis, up there against the roof of the
cabin, anchored to a two-foot length of chain from which
was suspended a slim and rather elegant briefcase. I
reached up to touch him and the body spun round and it
was as if the left arm was reaching out to encircle me, to
pull me closer to the swollen, putrid face and bulging eyes.

I closed my own for a moment, opened them again and
found Ciasim at my side. He had his knife in his hand
and there was little doubt about his intentions. Not that he
had a great deal of choice, but when he started to cut off
the dead man's right hand at the wrist, I turned and went
out.

I waited for two or three minutes, hanging on to the
port wing and then he appeared, the briefcase in one hand,
the knife in the other. He fastened the case securely by its
chain to the cabin door handle, raised his thumb and we
made for the surface.

From now on it was going to be strictly improvisation

and hope. And luck, too, of course. One could never have
enough of that.

We surfaced a couple of hundred yards north from the
Gentle Jane. Ciasim stayed to mark the position and I
swam back to the boat.

Christou and Lazanis helped me up the ladder and
Kapelari said eagerly, "You've found it?"

I nodded. "Back there where the Turk is waiting. You'll
have to move the boat."

I started to unbuckle the straps of my aqualung. He
nodded slightly to the other two. "You heard what he
said."

They moved away and I went to the stern and squatted
beside the equipment we'd made ready. Kapelari gave me
a cigarette. "How does it look?"

"Not so good. There's been a hell of a lot of damage,
particularly to the cabin area, but he's in there."

"Apostolidis? You saw him?"

"Through what was left of one of the windows, but
we're going to have to cut our way in to get at him."

He took it, hook and all, his eyes gleaming as he left
me to join his friends who already had the anchor up. The
engines rumbled into life and we moved towards Ciasim
who waited, one arm raised.

I busied myself with the cylinder and lines, making
ready for the great pretence which was to come and my
hands trembled very, very slightly, just like the old days
when you knew you were on the brink of violent action
and death could be waiting to make that last appointment.
It was a sobering thought, but one I couldn't really afford
because there was Sara to think of.

An oxy-hydrogen cutter is ignited from the surface,
gases passing down through a tube to the diver below
where a rather ingenious device allows air to bleed out,
forming an air bubble, an artificial atmosphere inside
which the flames burn.

I went through this useful information step by step with
Kapelari, stressing the considerable personal danger we

would be in if he got the signal wrong and ignited at the wrong time.

It was all good stuff and they swallowed it down and Ciasim and I got our aqualungs on and went over the side for the last time. We went down together, following the lines he had already placed and hovered above the Aztec for a moment. Ciasim descended to the plane itself, checked that the briefcase was where he had left it, looked up towards me and raised a thumb.

Which gave me exactly two minutes. I checked my watch and swam away from him quickly, passing well beneath the Gentle Jane at depth.

I came in towards the boat again from the port side and hovered six feet below the surface to unbuckle the straps of my aqualung. I released it and surfaced close to the hull and amidships so that the wheelhouse was between me and the three Greeks.

I wasn't a moment too soon. A second later, Ciasim sounded with a great splash on the starboard side. Kapelari shouted something to him, I couldn't catch what, although presumably, he wanted to know what was wrong.

I was already hauling myself over the rail as Ciasim cried, "It's Savage. There's been an accident. Stand by the line. I'm going down again."

Which was all supposed to keep the three of them leaning over the starboard rail to await eventualities. And it almost worked. The great difficulty was the fact that the wheelhouse door was on the starboard side, but I calculated I could just reach the chart table through the sliding window to port.

I couldn't see the three Greeks, but I could hear Kapelari cursing freely as I leaned in through the window and reached beneath the chart table. My finger found the secret button and the flap fell down.

But you can never count on anything in this life. I heard one hell of a yell as I yanked the Uzi submachine gun from its holding clips and glanced up to see Christou standing in the stern by the port rail. He was holding a Mauser automatic pistol in his right hand with its wooden holster clipped on at the rear making a stock. And he was good. He fired twice and one of the bullets caught me somewhere in the right leg, knocking me out of the window.

The Uzi is Israel's personal contribution to the submachine gun market and is held in more than average regard by those who know about such things. It has a 25-round detachable magazine which is housed in the right-hand grip and only fires when that grip is squeezed.

I suppose I must have put half the magazine into Christou as I went down because he was lifted off his feet backwards over the rail. I rolled around some more, but not because of the agony in my wounded leg or any of that sort of thing. You feel a punch on the jaw more than you do a bullet when it first hits you because the shock is so great that it numbs the entire nervous system for a while.

In the same moment, I discovered, with some surprise, that I could still use my leg and started to crawl. Kapelari appeared in the prow and loosed off a long burst that ripped up the deck to within a foot or so of me. I squeezed off a few of my own in reply, just to keep his head down, and scrambled round the wheelhouse to find myself no more than six feet away from Lazanis.

The fear on his face was terrible to see, breaking through to the surface like scum on a pond. Such was his panic, that when he fired, which he did as a reflex action the second I appeared, the first burst from his machine pistol was about a yard to my left.

Still on my hands and knees like an animal, I shoved the Uzi straight out in front of me, one-handed, and gave him the rest of the magazine at point-blank range.

Then I scrambled for the entrance to the wheelhouse where the Walther waited in its clip on that secret flap of mine. I almost made it, had got to the door at ground level and was reaching inside with my left hand, when a bullet drilled me neatly through the palm.

I tried to get up and Kapelari stood there by the starboard rail watching me, a dramatic enough figure to represent death, a submachine gun in one hand, a .38 revolver, the one which had done the damage, extended in the other.

"I told Melos you were trouble," he said bitterly, "but he wouldn't listen. At least we'll have it my way now."

But he had lost his chance by talking too much. A black wraith came up out of the sea behind him, knife gleaming wickedly in the sunlight. They went back into the water together and only Ciasim came up again.

He picked up Lazanis, heaved him over the rail into the water and crouched beside me. I put a hand against his chest. "The briefcase, Ciasim, get that first."

He tried to argue and I managed to get my good leg up and shoved him away. "My way," I said. "We'll do it my way. I've earned it, haven't I?"

I suppose I wasn't in my right mind for a time which was hardly surprising but I think he realised that fact and acted upon it.

"Five minutes, Jack, no longer, I swear. Then I fix up good. Better than new."

I lay there, back against the side of the wheelhouse, while he went down to the stern for another aqualung. I heard the splash when he went in and looked up at the sun. The sky was very blue and bright, so bright that it was all I could do to keep my eyes open.

I closed them for what seemed no more than a second. When I opened them again, he was crouched in front of me holding the briefcase. *I noticed the fine quality of the moroccan leather, the beautiful workmanship of the brass clasp and lock and then remembered that the damned thing was booby-trapped.*

In a curiously detached way I wondered whether it might explode as Ciasim passed it to me and I clutched it against my chest, but as I lost consciousness round about then, it didn't really seem to matter.

CHAPTER XVIII

POINT-BLANK

I surfaced to find myself on my back on the table in the saloon minus my wet-suit. Ciasim sat in a chair beside me, a look of intense concentration on his face as he worked on the hole in my right leg. He'd found my medical kit which was navy surplus, twin to the one I'd used with Guyon that night a thousand years ago when Sara and I had discovered him on the floor of my hotel room at Bir el Gafani.

"How are we doing?" I said.

"So there you are." He grinned. "It is nothing. A flea-bite. When the Chinese took me prisoner in fifty-one, they made me walk two hundred miles with worse than this. Two months before they got around to taking the bullet out. See, I show you."

He helped me to sit up and I raised my right knee and had a look at the damage. There was the usual ragged hole on the outside of the thigh just above the knee where the bullet had entered, a larger one on the inside where it had exited, which explained why I had been able to scramble around so energetically during the fight on the deck.

"Lucky it didn't go through the other while it was at it," I said.

"You said we needed luck today and luck you got," was his only comment.

He took out a couple of field dressings, positioned them on each side of the thigh and bandaged me with surprising dexterity. *Korea again, I suppose.*

My left hand was another matter entirely. I could move the fingers, but only just and it felt swollen and useless.

By the time he'd finished taping it up, it was beginning to hurt like hell and he broke out the ampoules of pain killer the kit contained, and gave me a couple. One in the thigh, the other in the hand.

After that, he went into the galley and made coffee, something the Turks do better than anyone else on earth. When he returned, I told him where the whiskey was hidden. Two cups of coffee, well-laced, and I felt almost human again. By that time, the pain killer had got to work and I found that I could actually walk as far as the door without falling down.

"Too much, too soon, Jack," he protested. "You lie down for a while now. Try a little sleep."

"And go out like a light for twenty-four hours? No thanks," I said. "I haven't the time. Anyway, if you could march two hundred miles over rough country with a bullet in your leg, I can make it to the bloody door."

But I was glad to sit down, all the same, and accepted the cigarette he offered. "What happens now?" he asked.

"God knows. I'll have to think about it. We ought to be able to come up with something. There's only the two of them to deal with. Aleko and Melos. He left the rest of his crew in Kyros."

"It still stinks," he said. "Melos is a special breed of man, Jack. He'll kill them—my two boys, Lady Sara—as casually as he would snap his fingers, if we give him even a hint of trouble."

"He'll kill them anyway, old friend," I told him. "One way or another and us with them. It's the only ending there can be to this business from his point of view."

"And Aleko?"

"He can't even help himself any more."

"Then what do we do?"

His face was grave as he waited for my answer. *Jack Savage, miracle worker.* I was getting tired of that role and my head was beginning to ache again. The whiskey had been a poor idea. Alcohol and drugs didn't sit well together or perhaps I was going into shock? It was possible.

"I need some air," I said and got to my feet.

The truth was that I didn't have an answer for him.

Any kind of an answer. I was simply stalling for time and I suppose he knew that as well as I did.

I not only made it to the door. I even managed to negotiate the companionway on my own, mainly because my right leg had lost all feeling by now and my left hand might as well have been chopped off at the wrist.

He was right behind me and put a hand to my elbow as I ventured into the sunlight. It was very quiet up there in the pale afternoon light. Had it happened? Had any of it happened? But the line of bullet holes in the deck on the port side where Kapelari had fired his first burst at me, the blood, already dry in the heat, where Lazanis had fallen, told me it had not all been part of some mad, impossible nightmare.

The briefcase was on the floor of the wheelhouse, presumably put there by Ciasim when he had carried me below. I picked it up and sat down.

"You know about these things," he said. "Just how dangerous is that?"

"Ever seen a hand grenade land amongst a group of infantry?"

"This could be as bad?"

"It would finish whoever was tinkering with it and kill or maim anyone else standing close. Perhaps not the same killing radius as a grenade, but good enough."

"And this would happen the moment you tried to open it?"

"Unless you have the special key that goes with it." There was a screwdriver on the chart table. I picked it up and inserted the end under the brass clasp. "All I need to do is start levering and up we go."

And that, he didn't like and I saw with something close to wonder, that even he could be touched by fear, if only a little.

He shivered, distaste on his face. "A nasty way to go."

"And it could be worse," I told him. "You could survive hopelessly maimed. No hands. Perhaps blinded."

"I would not wish such a fate on my worst enemy."

I think it was about then, helped by that final comment, that I suddenly saw exactly what had to be done. The only thing which could be done.

So I told him.

When I had finished his face was grim. "You go to your own death, you know this?"

"Not if I'm lucky, but in any case, it gives Sara and your boys a chance—a real chance, which is better than what they've got now."

"And you really think Melos will fall for this thing?"

"Nobody wants to die," I told him. "Not even Melos wants that. He wants to live to be the new chief of the security police when he and his friends take over the country if they ever do. Power, women, money. Whatever it is he really wants, he can only have alive and kicking."

He crouched there on the deck at my feet beside the wheelhouse door, a cigarette burning between his lips, his eyes dark and far away. Finally he sighed, that strange, inimitable sigh of his that was like a dying fall.

"Right, dear friend, I will not stand in your way. If you must do this thing, you must, but I insist on making my own small contribution."

He got up and went down to the stern where the diving gear and equipment was still spread out and I limped after him. When I got there, he had the tin of plastic gelignite open and was examining the collection of chemical fuses.

"The short ones," he said. "Five seconds. Am I right?"

"You'd have to swim like hell to get away from the main concussion area."

"But a small diversion. Say five pounds of gelignite exploding at the appropriate moment? This would be helpful?"

I couldn't think of anything to say and he smiled gently as if well pleased. "We will survive, dear friend, for you and I are great survivors. It is our special talent. Now go down to your cabin and sleep for sleep is what you need now. I will wake you when the time comes."

"Your promise on that," I said. "No one-man shows."

"My word on it."

Which was enough for he was, indeed, a man of finest honour. And I was tired—so damned tired. I made it down to the saloon and got on my bunk and stared up at the ceiling and nothing seemed to make much sense any

more. The last thing I recall was hearing the rattle of the
chain as he raised the anchor and then I went down deep.

It was evening when we raised Kyros, the sun hovering
just above the horizon, and the slight, small wind that
lifted off the sea touched me coldly as I went out on deck.

The *Gentle Jane* was on automatic pilot and Ciasim was
down at the stern making his preparations. He had his
wet-suit on again and was checking an aqualung.

He glanced up as I limped into view. "I was going to
wake you. Half an hour yet. How do you feel?"

"Fine," I said, which was a direct lie. "The sleep did
me a power of good."

He didn't believe me, I could tell, but let it pass. "Well,
here we are, Jack, the final run, eh?"

He opened his tin of Turkish cigarettes. There was only
one left and he broke it in two and offered me half. It
tasted terrible, but gave me something to hold on to.

I said, "I'm sorry about your boat. I know what that
must have meant."

"It is in the past, dear friend. All things come to the
same end, sooner or later."

There was a sadness in him then, or was it simply
that he was tired, and small wonder. Whatever it was, it
touched us both. Resignation, perhaps, or a kind of
fatalistic acceptance of what was to come. Certainly it was
a mad venture, but then the whole affair had been touched
with madness from the beginning.

But sometimes violent ends brought a new beginning. I
wasn't too sure about that, wasn't even certain of the
rights and wrongs of it all any longer. Could any kind
of good come out of so much killing?

There were only two things of which I was certain, two
worthwhile items in the whole sorry business. This man's
true friendship and a dying girl's love. And there's the
Irishman for you, the soft underbelly beneath the hard
shell. In the final analysis, I was exactly as Melos had
described me—a sentimentalist at heart.

I was aware of a hand on my arm, came back to the
present with a start and found him buckling on his aqua-

lung. The plastic gelignite was already pouched in a canvas belt that he had strapped to his waist.

We were close inshore, the cliffs dark in the late evening light and the Old Women of Paxos, standing sentinel at the entrance to the bay, were black against gold. I went into the wheelhouse and took over, reducing the engine speed as we approached the passage until we seemed to barely move through the water.

He stood in the entrance, a formidable figure in his black wet-suit and aqualung. And then he did a strange thing. He reached in and patted my face gently as he might have done to one of his own sons, a gesture of affection I had seen him use with them many times.

"Go with God, my dear friend," he said.

I watched him move to the rail. He paused for a moment to pull down his mask and adjust his mouthpiece and then he was gone.

I don't think I've ever felt so lonely in my life as I did when I turned the *Gentle Jane* into that narrow passage. The Old Women of Paxos towered above me, black as night, and half a dozen gulls cried a warning, swooping down across my deck and up again as if despairing of me.

The water, reflecting the evening sun, was burnished gold, and I was suspended in it, gliding forward at the same slow rate as if reluctant to venture out into the lagoon.

Strange, but I thought of my father then as I had not thought of him in years and remembered the way of his going. There must have been a moment, one final moment like this for him also. The last second before he had opened the cottage door and stepped out to meet his death.

A waste? So I had told Sara Hamilton, but who was I to judge him. A man had to do what he had to do according to his own judgement of the situation. Nothing less would do. I knew that now, so let it end there.

I coasted into the lagoon and found the *Firebird* anchored fifty yards from the shore exactly as I had left her. There was no sign of life, so I sounded my Klaxon. Birds

lifted out of the pine trees that fringed the shore, calling
harshly, and then Melos appeared, Aleko at his heels.

The edge of the sun was just touching the horizon now,
but there was still plenty of light, certainly enough for
them to see that something was very much wrong. Melos
was holding a machine pistol and raised it as I cut in
close, no more than twenty feet between the two boats.

I shouted and my panic was not all simulated. "For
God's sake, no shooting, Melos. I've got the briefcase.
Let me come on board and explain."

I was already past as he lowered the gun. What else
could he do?

"I warned you what would happen, Savage," he called.

I cut the engines and felt the prow of the *Gentle Jane*
slide into soft sand as we ran aground. I took the briefcase and went to the stern and lowered the dinghy into
the water, which took a little time as my left hand wasn't
much use.

So now I was ready—ready for the final throw of the
dice. Beyond *Firebird,* I seemed to see a dark shadow
against the burnished gold of the water. *Ciasim?* I could
only hope so. I got down into the dinghy, awkwardly
because of my bad leg, and sculled towards *Firebird*
using a single oar over the stern.

There had been signs of activity on deck and as I approached, Melos appeared by the rail, the two Divalni
boys and Sara in front of him.

"Point-blank, Savage. One squeeze of the trigger and I
cut them in half. Where are the others? Quick, now."

"Dead," I told him.

It took the wind out of him for a moment and he lowered the muzzle of the machine pistol. "All of them? It
isn't possible."

"You should know, you bastard," I said bitterly. "Kapelari and his friends—they tried to finish us off after we'd
brought up the briefcase. Are you trying to tell me you
had nothing to do with that?"

"What happened?" he said flatly.

"Divalni put his knife into Kapelari and got his hands

on his submachine gun, then he turned it on the other two. They shot him to pieces, but he took them with him."

Abu started to weep and Melos cuffed him roughly. "You don't look so good yourself."

"You might say I got in the way of the action. I had a hell of a job getting here, but I've got the briefcase."

"You'd better come up."

I hooked the handle of the briefcase over my bandaged hand and pulled myself up the ladder. Abu was still sobbing and Yassi had an arm around his shoulders.

Sara's expression was remote, yet watchful and there was about her an extraordinary quality of stillness as if she was waiting for something, sensing that all was not as it seemed.

She made the slightest of movements towards me and Melos put the barrel of the machine pistol to her head, holding it one-handed. "Stay where you are, Savage."

Aleko said nothing, simply stood there as if carved from stone. I knew then exactly how much hope there was of any intervention by him on her behalf.

Melos held out his left hand. "The briefcase."

"Aren't you forgetting something? You're supposed to release Sara and the boys."

He laughed coldly. "Is that what I said? You poor simple peasant, Savage, like all the Irish. No wonder it took you seven hundred years to get rid of the English. Now give me the briefcase."

I moved close and held it up suspended from my left wrist. "You know about the detonator? Marvellous things. Safe as houses until you start messing about with the lock. The slightest interference, that's all it takes, and up you go. Like this, for instance."

I'd had the screwdriver ready in my right sleeve and now I jammed the end of it under the briefcase clasp. Abu stopped crying abruptly and there was one hell of a silence.

Melos said in a whisper, "You wouldn't dare. We'd all be killed, yourself included."

"You were going to kill us anyway, isn't that the truth of it?" I glanced at Aleko. "Isn't that right, Aleko?"

But he didn't appear to be listening. He looked up as

three or four gulls cried harshly overhead, then turned and walked towards the prow whistling tunelessly.

"He's lost his reason," Sara said quietly.

Dear God, was there no end to it?

"When these three are safely on shore, then you can have your briefcase, Melos," I said.

He was caught and knew it and sought desperately for a way out. "And you? You will stay here?"

"I have no choice," I said. "And neither have you. What the Americans would call a stand-off."

He nodded. "All right, they can go."

He gave the two boys a push towards the ladder. Sara hesitated, then moved to my side. She opened her mouth to speak and I said brutally, "Get out of it! You're in the way!"

I could not afford to take my eyes off him for a moment, that was the trouble, so I didn't see the look on her face, that last look before she went down the ladder into the dinghy to join the boys.

"And now?" Melos said.

"When they reach the beach and not before."

I could hear the sounds of their progress on the calm evening air, but didn't dare turn my head away for a moment. "Safely home," he told me at last and extended his hand. "The briefcase."

Aleko stood in the prow and gazed through the passage out to sea, silhouetted against the burnished water. *Ciasim, where in the hell are you?* The thought circled my brain and I managed a wry grin.

"And afterwards? What then? A bullet in the head? Not good enough, Melos."

The prow of the *Firebird* was blown wide open in that moment, dissolved in a fury of smashed planking and debris of every description and Dimitri Aleko simply vanished from sight so that he might never have existed.

The whole boat tilted, started to slide under at once. Melos lost his balance and his machine pistol together and slid down the sloping deck into the maelstrom below. I was in no better case and grabbed for the rail with my good hand, missed and went sliding down to join him.

We fetched up together against a stanchion, half in the

water, half out and he was in better shape than I. He
lashed out, his fist catching me under the eye, and grabbed
for the chain of the briefcase.

It hurt like hell as the handle was yanked over my
injured hand and I yelled in agony, but there was no one
to hear for he was already over the rail and swimming
for it.

There was only four fathoms of water at that point,
but it was still enough to drown you in a sinking ship
and I couldn't get over the rail fast enough myself. I was
barely in time and as I started to swim, and damned awkwardly because of my arm and leg, the *Firebird* went
down.

I wasn't doing too well. All of a sudden I felt very
tired and then Ciasim broke through to the surface beside
me like some great black seal.

He pushed up his mask and spat out his mouthpiece.
"Did I not tell you that we were great survivors, dear
friend? Hold tight, now, and I will take you in."

Melos was about ten or fifteen yards in front of us and
swimming strongly using both arms, the chain of the briefcase clenched between his teeth. He stopped swimming
when he was waist-deep and started to wade forward,
holding the briefcase in his left hand.

And then an astounding thing happened. There was a
movement up there in the shadows amongst the pine trees
and Sergeant Loukas stepped into view. He unbuttoned
the flap of his leather holster as he crossed the narrow
strip of beach, and took out his automatic pistol, looking
even more mournful than ever.

"Good evening, Captain Melos," he said.

Melos paused, thigh-deep in water, staring at him
stupidly, then suddenly seemed to recover his senses. "Not
captain—major. Major Andrew Melos of the security
police, Loukas. You will arrest these people for crimes
against the state. All of them. Do you understand?"

"Perfectly," Loukas said and he raised his pistol, took
deliberate aim and shot him between the eyes.

I could have believed in any possibility after that and
had to, for Yanni Kytros appeared next from the shadows

up there in the pines and limped towards us, leaning heavily on a walking stick. Sara and the two boys were running along the water's edge as Ciasim and I grounded. I coughed up a little water and managed some semblance of a grin for Yanni.

"Nine lives, eh, Yanni?"

He was positively beaming, obviously enormously pleased with himself. "You once complimented me on the excellence of my lungs considering my way of life, Jack, but I must confess I swam rather farther underwater this morning than I ever have before."

"I'm sure you did." I nodded at Loukas. "So this is the man you take orders from?"

"We work together, Mr. Savage," Loukas said. "And with a great many other people who have the same ideas about freedom and Greece that we do."

"You certainly took Aleko for a ride," I said. "He seemed to think he had you firmly in his pocket."

Melos was face-down in the water a couple of yards away still clutching the chain, the briefcase floating beside him.

"I will have that now, please," Loukas said.

Ciasim pulled it out of the dead man's grip and looked questioningly at me. I nodded and he waded forward and gave it to Loukas.

"Watch it, for God's sake," I said as I joined them. "Your people put a little item in the lock, remember?"

He held up a long key that seemed to be double-edged from what I could see. "Easy when you know how, Mr. Savage."

He inserted it in the lock, there was a very distinct double click as we all held our breath and then he smiled, for the first time since I'd known him. Sara and the boys had arrived and stood there uncertainly for a moment, then young Abu ran forward and flung himself into his father's arms.

Loukas produced a long sealed envelope from inside the briefcase and tore it open. "Amazing," he said as he took out the sheets of paper it contained. "Still bone dry. These really are most excellent briefcases."

Yanni produced a cigarette lighter and flicked it into

life. Loukas touched the sheets of paper to its flame, held them there until they were well alight.

"A lot of trouble, Mr. Savage, a hell of a lot of trouble and all because a few well-meaning idiots committed names to paper."

"An unfortunate habit most revolutionaries seem to share," I said.

His fingers were getting warm, he dropped the sheets to the sand and we watched the flames eat up the final trace of white paper. He ground the ashes into the sand with his heel.

"What happens now?" I asked.

"To you and your friends?" He shrugged. "That is no concern of mine. A fine night and a calm sea. In that boat of yours, you could be in Turkish waters within a couple of hours."

"And what about you two?"

"We left a Land-Rover back there beyond the hill. An hour to the harbour. Kytros has a boat ready. No need to worry about us."

"Then what?"

It was Yanni who answered me. "Moral indignation is a shocking thing, Jack. It simply won't go away and leave a man in peace, you see. There's work waiting for us elsewhere in Greece."

"Then all I can do is wish you both luck."

Loukas saluted Sara gravely, turned and walked away. Yanni took my hand, held it briefly. Even then, there at the very end of things, he had to make a joke out of it all.

"The terrible thing about getting mixed up in this sort of thing is that I'm just not the stuff heroes are made out of." He gave me a helpless smile, turned and limped after Loukas.

"Yanni!" He paused, glancing back over his shoulder. "I think Michael would have been proud of you."

He raised his stick in a half-salute and disappeared into the trees.

I'll always be glad I said that to him.

Ciasim was at the wheel as we slipped through the dark passage and turned out to sea. He started to sing and I heard his sons' laughter, happy to be together again as is the way with families. I owed him more than I had thought to owe any man. How was it possible to repay that kind of friendship?

He leaned from the window on the port side of the wheelhouse. "You are all right, dear friend? Leave everything to me. In a boat like this I could take you round the world. For a boat like this, I would give up women." His laughter boomed out across the water. "On alternate days, of course."

The Gentle Jane. Would he take her? It was a thought and she couldn't go into better hands.

I stood at the rail, fumbled for a cigarette and found none. There was a movement in the shadows, a match flared, pulling her face out of the darkness as she lit a cigarette and passed it to me.

"They made one hell of a mess of you, didn't they?" she said.

"They didn't damage anything important."

I put an arm around her shoulders and she leaned against me. "We'll be a long time dead, Savage."

"True," I said. "But we've got each other for a while yet."

"And hope?"

I nodded slowly. "Oh, yes, there's always that."

We moved forward into the great, mysterious, purple evening and out there in the gathering darkness, the sea was touched with fire as the sun died and night fell.

Dell Bestsellers

- [ ] **NOBLE HOUSE** by James Clavell..............$5.95 (16483-4)
- [ ] **PAPER MONEY** by Adam Smith................$3.95 (16891-0)
- [ ] **CATHEDRAL** by Nelson De Mille..............$3.95 (11620-1)
- [ ] **YANKEE** by Dana Fuller Ross....................$3.50 (19841-0)
- [ ] **LOVE, DAD** by Evan Hunter.......................$3.95 (14998-3)
- [ ] **WILD WIND WESTWARD**
  by Vanessa Royal....................................$3.50 (19363-X)
- [ ] **A PERFECT STRANGER**
  by Danielle Steel $3.50 (17221-7)
- [ ] **FEED YOUR KIDS RIGHT**
  by Lendon Smith, M.D. $3.50 (12706-8)
- [ ] **THE FOUNDING**
  by Cynthia Harrod-Eagles........................$3.50 (12677-0)
- [ ] **GOODBYE, DARKNESS**
  by William Manchester.............................$3.95 (13110-3)
- [ ] **GENESIS** by W.A. Harbinson.....................$3.50 (12832-3)
- [ ] **FAULT LINES** by James Carroll $3.50 (12436-0)
- [ ] **MORTAL FRIENDS** by James Carroll $3.95 (15790-0)
- [ ] **THE SOLID GOLD CIRCLE**
  by Sheila Schwartz $3.50 (18156-9)
- [ ] **AMERICAN CAESAR**
  by William Manchester.................................$4.50 (10424-6)

At your local bookstore or use this handy coupon for ordering:

Dell **DELL BOOKS**
P.O. BOX 1000, PINE BROOK, N.J. 07058-1000

Please send me the books I have checked above. I am enclosing $_____ (please add 75c per copy to cover postage and handling). Send check or money order—no cash or C.O.D.'s. Please allow up to 8 weeks for shipment.

Mr./Mrs./Miss_____

Address_____

City_____ State/Zip_____